"As long as you swear not to tell my secret, I won't tell yours."

Mia couldn't stop the blooming smile. "We have made these messes, haven't we? We'll have to muddle through on our own, but it's nice to have company on the journey."

Grant stared down at her hand, tracing one finger back and forth. "When you're building a brand as a bad boy, heartwarming stories of the amazing couple who adopted you from the foster care system and the impressive brothers who round out the rest of the family don't fit the tale."

Mia wasn't sure why, but she believed this was a piece of the puzzle she was trying to assemble. She needed more pieces to fill out the border. "Who decided being the bad boy was the right way to go?"

Grant tipped his head back. "Which time?" His wry grin landed somewhere in her chest with a warm thump. He was nearly irresistible like this.

Dear Reader,

Life has a way of reordering our plans, doesn't it? Some people have everything mapped out, even when detours and dead ends mean plenty of recalculating. In *The Right Cowboy*, Grant Armstrong has had one goal his whole life: winning rodeo championships. Now that life has bucked him from that saddle, he's having a hard time dusting himself off. Coming home to Prospect is his only choice, until he finds his new direction.

On the other hand, some people go where the wind takes them, trusting that they'll end up in the right place at the right time. That's Mia Romero. And she's never been wrong. Prospect is definitely where she needs to be to track down the story that can redirect her plans—and Grant's—forever.

I'm so happy we're returning to Prospect, Colorado, together. I hope you enjoy visiting! To find out more about my books and what's coming next, visit me at cherylharperbooks.com.

Cheryl

HEARTWARMING

The Right Cowboy

—

Cheryl Harper

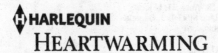

HARLEQUIN®
HEARTWARMING™

Recycling programs
for this product may
not exist in your area.

ISBN-13: 978-1-335-47579-4

The Right Cowboy

Copyright © 2024 by Cheryl Harper

For questions and comments about the quality of this book,
please contact us at CustomerService@Harlequin.com.

TM and ® are trademarks of Harlequin Enterprises ULC.

Harlequin Enterprises ULC
22 Adelaide St. West, 41st Floor
Toronto, Ontario M5H 4E3, Canada
www.Harlequin.com

Printed in U.S.A.

Cheryl Harper discovered her love for books and words as a little girl, thanks to a mother who made countless library trips and an introduction to Laura Ingalls Wilder's Little House books. Whether the stories she reads are set in the prairie, the American West, Regency England or earth a hundred years in the future, Cheryl enjoys strong characters who make her laugh. Now Cheryl spends her days searching for the right words while she stares out the window and her dog, Jack, snoozes beside her. And she considers herself very lucky to do so.

For more information about Cheryl's books, visit her online at cherylharperbooks.com or follow her on Twitter @cherylharperbks.

Books by Cheryl Harper

Harlequin Heartwarming

The Fortunes of Prospect

The Cowboy's Second Chance
Her Cowboy's Promise
The Cowboy Next Door

Veterans' Road

Winning the Veteran's Heart
Second Chance Love
Her Holiday Reunion
The Doctor and the Matchmaker
The Dalmatian Dilemma
A Soldier Saved

Visit the Author Profile page at Harlequin.com for more titles.

Cheryl Harper discovered her love for books and writing as a young reader, ...

...

Books by Cheryl Harper

Harlequin Heartwarming

The Fortunes of Texas
The Cowboy's Secret...
...
The Cowboy...

Veterans' Road
...

CHAPTER ONE

GRANT ARMSTRONG GRABBED the handle over the window and swallowed an embarrassing yelp as he watched the highway's narrow shoulder disappear beneath the tires of his brother's speeding pickup. Matt always drove as if he could outrun consequences, unless there was a trailer attached to the hitch. His brother, the veterinarian, didn't take any chances with livestock, but humans had to brace themselves and hope.

"I thought saddle bronc riders were supposed to be brave," Matt said with a teasing grin. "Mama makes less noise when she rides shotgun. Betty doesn't even twitch an ear. You should be more like Betty."

Grant checked the hound dog that went almost everywhere with Matt. Betty had somehow stretched her forty-pound length to cover the entire backseat. Her floppy ears draped over her face. The only sign she was still alive was the whiffle of breath that flapped her loose lips. Betty had a clean conscience, and all was right with her world.

Matt was right. Grant would love to be more like Betty.

"Guess I'm a cat who's already eight lives in and holding on to number nine for all I'm worth," Grant muttered and forced his fingers to un-clench. "What's the rush?"

"No rush." Matt waved one hand as if he was as relaxed as could be. "But we both know we need to be back to the Rocking A before dinner's on the table. These roads after dark are a real adventure."

Instead of ordering his brother to put both hands on the steering wheel or to slow down on the twisting two-lane highway through the Rocky Mountains, Grant stared straight ahead through the bug-spattered windshield. If he didn't look to his right, the specter of shooting over the edge like they were stuntmen in an action movie would recede.

And if he didn't look left at his brother, he would stop fantasizing about evicting Matt from the driver's seat and leaving him on the side of the road.

His mother would make him return to pick up her baby boy anyway.

"Thank you for going with me today." Matt finally took his foot off the gas to make a turn. "I wanted to see the course Macon had set up. The big splashy commercial I saw caught my attention, gave me ideas for something smaller in town. I'm determined to show your mother that I have a few exciting ideas up my sleeve for Western Days."

"*Our* mother would expect nothing less from her favorite," Grant replied.

Matt batted his eyelashes at Grant. "Aw, don't be jealous. It's a four-way tie for second place."

Grant grunted but it was difficult to blame Prue if Matt was her favorite. He was the easiest of the five of them to get along with.

"We couldn't waste a warm snap in February," Matt said. "Perfect weather to go for a ride."

The beautiful sunny day had presented a rare opportunity for a quick road trip, so when Matt had asked him to ride along to tour Horace Macon's Cowboy Games in Leadville, Grant had jumped at the chance. One quick look at the flashy website convinced Grant it was a bunch of activities for tourists who had seen some of Hollywood's glitziest Western movies and wanted the full experience from their Rocky Mountain vacation. That wouldn't work in Prospect, but it was an interesting setup. Chaps-wearing employees had taught visitors how to lasso a cute little cow statue and then taken their souvenir pictures with it. There was target practice with a mock six-shooter, ax throwing and a train ride that featured a staged robbery, where the white-hatted town sheriff rode in to save the day.

Grant and his brothers had reenacted several different versions of that same show, only with a bank since they'd had no train. The old ghost town in the hills above the ranch had been irresistible for such scenes when they were kids, and they might have done it better. Grant had definitely enjoyed his role as the bad guy.

Matt had always preferred to "rest," so he was usually the banker, who could snooze in the shade, while the rest of the brothers were the good guys, with Wes in the white hat leading the charge to save the day.

If someone had convinced Grant to instead try on the white hat as a teenager, would he have made different choices as an adult? Instead of playing up a reckless side, he might have become the hero. Grant squeezed his eyes shut. No use in asking questions that had no answers.

Today's tour of Cowboy Games had confirmed his suspicions that the place was less cowboy and heavy on the games, but if he survived the ride home in one piece, it would be a pretty good day overall.

"We can do better, right?" Matt asked. "In my head, I was picturing something less glitzy and more real for Prospect, although I can't deny that the kids did seem to love tossing the lasso. Make a note that we need to include that somewhere in town."

Grant rolled his eyes. Matt had been trying the make-a-note thing all day as if he was employing a top-notch assistant or something.

"We definitely want one of a kind," Matt added, "but I'm not sure I see how to get there yet."

"Yeah, what we saw was an amusement park, not a real competition. Pretty sure everything there was presented as a backdrop for the most impressive vacation photos instead of a test of skill." Grant glanced over at him. "If you stage a real competition, with riding and shooting and all of that, Prospect's Western Days weekend will have to draw the cream of the cowboy crop or you'll never hear the end of it."

"*We'll* never hear the end of it." Matt smiled slowly. "You're going to help me. Mama said so."

Grant sighed. At some point, he and his brothers would learn to tell Prue Armstrong no, but Grant hadn't reached that blessed moment yet. Lately, he'd been ducking his mother every chance he got, because all the Armstrong men knew that once the calendar flipped over to a new year, planning the town's festival, known far and wide as Western Days, took over her life.

And she made sure to drag everyone she knew along for the ride.

They still had two whole months of increasing pressure to see out.

Matt had been late to a meeting months ago

and been named the head person in charge this year. Grant was bored and available today. That was it. He didn't want any tasks or folks relying on him for this year's centennial anniversary weekend.

But frankly, none of the Armstrongs would escape the work ahead. Grant's only hope to avoid responsibility would be to lay low when Prue was on the hunt for volunteers. Since he was fully unemployed and also underemployed helping on the Rocking A, he would be at the top of his mother's list.

Ranching meant plenty of work, and all five Armstrong brothers loved the place, even when they were away from home. Prue and Walt had fostered them here before adopting them all, so the Rocking A was special.

For years, their father, Walt, and Wes had managed all of it. Then Travis had retired from the military to take up fostering another generation here. His brother jumped on every job around the place. Renovations on the ranch house had taken up the first couple of months after Grant's sudden return, but now having too much time on his hands was becoming noticeable. Luckily, many people wanted to give him unpaid jobs.

Being busy was good, but nothing excited him like rodeo. He missed the excitement of facing off against a wild bronco and the camaraderie of the rodeo circuit. He was supposed to be competing, not event planning.

"Problem is that we don't have a permanent setup for a riding course and marksmanship booth, like Macon does. The festival will take over all of the old town center, and whatever we build for shooting or riding competition will need to go up a week or two before and tear down quickly after the festival is over. We can put up tents, but we'll need a lot of open space." Grant tugged his hat lower on his head. He sounded confident even if he'd never done anything like this. Fortunately, he'd never met a horse he didn't like, and Macon had offered some names who might help design and judge shooting competition. His mother wanted something big and new for this special anniversary. Matt was on the right track.

She was also counting on Grant being a "celebrity" draw for competitors and visitors alike. Good thing he hadn't tossed all his gear in the trash when he had retired from the circuit and come home. He hadn't confessed how that came about in the first place to his family, and he wasn't certain he had any star power left.

For years, Western Days had featured a large quilt show, other judged categories for crafts and baked goods, vendors lined up along the street through town, a parade, and plenty of opportunity to attract visitors to the town's businesses. Adding a cowboy games competition with riding and shooting would help Prospect's Western Days stand out from all the other festivals. Matt's idea was good, if they could pull it off.

That was the question that was nagging at him. Could he pull it off?

When Matt swooped through a dip in the road at high speed, Grant clutched his stomach with one hand and realized that if they bucked right over the side of the mountain ledge, neither one of them had to worry much about the future anymore.

Even so, he said, "If you don't slow down, I'm going to tell Mama that you were being reckless, Matty. You don't want that. That's my job, not yours."

His brother's lips curled but he eased off the gas. "Imagine how much shine a riding competition will bring when we say it's being run by Grant Armstrong, saddle bronc champion for four years straight. Could it have been five? Yes, but he decided to come home and sleep in his old bunk bed instead."

Grant tightened his lips, determined to ignore Matt's prodding.

The sound of the road under the pickup's tires was too quiet to keep Matt under control for long.

"Why did he do that? Leave his successful career, the one he'd been dreaming of his whole life, to return to Prospect when he was rising straight to the top? When he was being approached for magazine cover stories and small parts in made-for-TV movies?" Matt shrugged. "No one knows."

Grant returned to gripping the grab handle. The anger that boiled in his chest every time that he considered giving up the career he loved burned, but it was better for everyone if he kept the lid tightly shut. He was afraid of the fallout if all that emotion spilled over.

Matt sighed. "Well, technically one person knows, but he ain't talking. Why is that?"

Grant cut his brother a mean glare. "Do you really care? You got somebody to run your big idea. That should make you happy."

Matt's slow grin was irritating. "Oh, it does, believe me. Doesn't change the fact that fixing whatever is wrong with you during a one-day trip would convince the whole family I'm a hero. I'm used to being the best-looking brother, but I'd like to try for more. Give Travis a run for his money. Becoming a foster dad may have given him an unbeatable advantage there."

"Mama already thinks you hung the moon," Grant grumbled. To be fair, Prue Armstrong would have gone to war for any one of her boys… unless they were picking on Matt.

"Being the baby of the family has some perks."

Matt took both hands off the wheel to shrug. Grant had to bite his lip not to snap about that.

Instead, he closed his eyes. That was his last defense.

The five Armstrong sons had been adopted through the foster system. Wes claimed the spot of "oldest" because he'd arrived first, but Wes, Clay, Travis and Grant were only months apart in age, and had all been in the same grade in school. Matt was a little younger, so he was the baby. He'd learned to accept the pestering older brothers and take full advantage of his mother's protective instincts.

"What about if I promise not to discuss whatever you tell me with anyone else? Not Wes, Clay or Travis. Not Mom or Dad. Not even if dessert is hanging in the balance and it happens to be banana pudding," Matt said. "You can trust me."

The concern in Matt's voice matched the expressions Grant had seen on his family's faces since he'd shown up at the Rocking A with a duffel, a box and a flimsy explanation that he'd grown tired of life on the circuit. For a few months, he'd faced pressure on all sides to spill the truth, but life and the ranch's beautiful neighbors on either side had taken some of the pressure off. His brothers were so busy falling in love that they'd had less time to poke at his bruises.

He and Matt were the last unattached ones left

standing. Even his parents, who had divorced years ago and argued like grumpy badgers, had been struck by Cupid's arrow. Their bickering had turned to teasing with forays into flirting. Love seemed to be well on its way to conquering all of the Armstrong family.

But even if another interesting someone new did show up, if she happened to meet Matt first, she'd be hypnotized by his looks, so Grant wasn't too worried about getting tangled up with love. He needed a minute to get his life straightened out before he was ready for another knot.

Grant tried to loosen the tension in his shoulders. "I do. I trust all of you. I just…" He didn't want to tell them his whole career had been a lie. Not yet. The grift his best friends on the rodeo circuit were running wouldn't stay secret forever, but Grant wanted to be far away from that world when the news broke. He'd worked to build his bad-boy persona, taking risks others might not. Finding anyone to believe his side of the story seemed impossible.

Lying low in Prospect was his obvious choice. Eventually he'd figure out his next career and what happened to the last one would matter less.

Nothing bad could touch an Armstrong in Prospect. His family was here and he had known every person in town for most of his life. The rest of the rodeo world would deal with the shock of a cheating scandal when it came out, the people he trusted most could try pointing fingers at him and even succeed in turning Grant's fans against him, but it might as well be happening on another planet as long as he was in Prospect.

Since he'd come home, he'd convinced himself that he'd ended that chapter. This after-rodeo life still fit him like new chaps, pinched in the spots that hadn't been broken in yet, but every day was easier. He'd stopped looking over his shoulder and waiting for the mess to detonate.

If being betrayed by old friends still stung, Grant could look around to see Matt, Clay, Travis and Wes and know they were exactly who they said they were. Walt and Prue Armstrong were salt-of-the-earth types who had taught them all to live that way. Every single one of them would choose to be a white hat in any scenario.

Days back at the Rocking A weren't a dream come true, not like winning rodeo prizes and celebrating on the road, but there were no surprises, either.

All he had to do now was find a way to be content with life in a place where nothing ever changed much.

CHAPTER TWO

Mia Romero had always trusted the universe to put her in the right place at the right time, but she'd learned that sometimes the universe's sense of humor could be extremely inconvenient. On the one hand, being on the phone with her mother when her left front tire blew out along the deserted highway leading into Prospect, Colorado, could be considered good timing. Having someone on the line listening as she pulled over on the narrow shoulder meant that Mia wasn't alone in the growing shadows before sunset.

On the other hand, this was Mia's mother.

"What was that? Is someone shooting at you? If you'd stayed in Billings like I asked, this wouldn't happen," her mother squawked. "I'm calling 9-1-1 right now." It was easy to picture her mother snapping her fingers and pointing at an assistant to start punching numbers on the phone. Mia wasn't sure where her mother was calling from, but it was easiest to picture her behind the ornate desk in her office.

After Mia was safely off the road, she said, "It was a tire. That's all, Mother. I'm fine."

Was she fine? Not really. Changing a flat tire before dark would be a challenge for a person who had managed to change their own tire before. Mia assumed that to be true. She'd never even watched someone fix a flat on the side of the road, so she expected it to be difficult, but there was no way she was admitting that to her mother. Not now.

Mia had learned when to tell her mother the truth. This was not one of those times.

Besides that, this would work out. Things always worked out in the end.

"I'll change it and get back on the road. No need to worry." Mia dug through her glove compartment to pull out the owner's manual. Quickly perusing the instructions on how to remove the tire seemed a logical first step.

"No, I'm calling roadside assistance. I knew this would happen. Have you been doing the proper maintenance, Mia?" her mother asked before answering, "Of course not, what am I thinking?"

Asking her mother exactly what that maintenance would entail would be satisfying, but it wouldn't do anything to end this conversation. Carla Romero let her driver handle all the automotive details.

"I can take care of this myself. You don't have to call anyone." Was she sometimes hit-and-miss about things like routine appointments? Yes, but there was no need to confirm her mother's suspicions now. The tire was flat. There was no way to go back in time to have these tires rotated and inspected now.

As her grandfather would have said, "That horse has left the barn, Mia mine." He'd been the one to teach her to drive. It was too bad she'd skipped the lesson on how to use a jack.

"I should never have let you talk me into this fluff story. Taking a trip up into the mountains in the winter, Mia? You should be at home. When I tell you it's time to finish your degree or learn the business side of the magazine or think about the future instead of 'living in the present,' this is what I'm trying to avoid—you stranded on the side of the road." Her mother's tone was sharp, but that wasn't unusual. The magazine's advertising dollars were falling. All magazine advertising was falling, thanks to fewer subscribers, and her mother's glossy monthly dedicated to the American West was no exception to the rule. She'd sacrificed a lot to keep the magazine going, and she'd been telling Mia she needed a break. Repeatedly. "*The Way West* needs something big. Your little travel articles on local festivals are fine, but this one's still a month away."

Those "little travel articles" had been all her mother would allow Mia to contribute. Treating her education "like a hobby" by never actually graduating meant she was only ready for writing "like a hobby." A journalism degree might please her mother, but it wasn't necessary. Experience had been the teacher she needed most. Her small travel section had given that to Mia.

When her mother let go of the magazine's reins, Mia wanted to take off in a whole new direction, but they'd never agree about that, either. Her grandfather had built *The Way West*. Her mother wouldn't let anyone change it.

And when she'd told her mother that she'd "forgotten" to enroll for the spring semester, a semester that might have been her last if she'd managed to pass all the classes she needed, her mother had gotten angry and loud. Explaining that the classes were a boring math, science, and "health and wellness" hadn't improved her mother's understanding, but they had nothing to do with Mia's plans for her career.

Why waste that time in a classroom when she could be out working? For a piece of paper that said she could do what she was already doing?

If she could have taken only writing courses and walked out with a degree, Mia would have finished college on her first attempt right after high school. She had plenty of those class credits from the early years when her mother was paying no attention to her grades or her plans. The first time around, only a business degree would satisfy her mother. Dropping out had been Mia's answer.

Going back to finish something had been her mother's price for continued employment with the magazine.

That employment paid Mia's bills, so keeping it had seemed prudent. They had negotiated a truce with an agreement that journalism would satisfy neither of them but equally, so it was a fair compromise.

If her mother had had a deadline for graduation, she should have been more specific.

And adult children over thirty should be exempt from most of this interference.

Mia swallowed a sigh. She had more immediate problems than convincing her mother that she was good at finding the stories the magazine needed. They'd spent years having that argument. Nothing would change in the time that it took to fix the tire and get back on the road.

"I'll call you as soon as I make it into Prospect. My weekend stay has probably stretched into a longer visit now, but I'll get good background for Western Days and be back home soon." Mia noticed headlights in her rearview mirror and felt the leap of hope that she might not be changing this tire herself. That was followed almost instantly by the worry that she might not be meeting a Good Samaritan here in this deserted spot. Snippets of countless dark stories featuring innocent stranded women filtered through her brain before she got a handle on her wayward thoughts. There was no use in jumping straight to catastrophe. That was her mother's move, not Mia's.

"Actually, can you stay on the phone with me? Someone's driving up." Mia watched the truck pull up behind her vehicle.

"So I can identify your kidnapper by the sound of his voice, I guess?" her mother snapped. "When you're home, it's time to discuss closing the magazine again. The worry is exhausting. Instead of going with the flow, you're going to need a plan for a real career."

Mia shook her head as she dug around in the backseat of her car. This wasn't the first time her mother had floated the idea of shutting down the magazine she'd inherited. Rodeo news once had a huge fan base of subscribers, but now the internet provided more results faster. *The Way West* had tried to pivot to lifestyle, but her mother's insistence that it was an extra instead of the feature meant they weren't ever all-in.

But back to the potential threat Mia was facing. She needed something… Any sort of defense she could scrounge up would be weak, but she wasn't naive. Even a flimsy weapon would be better than none if she needed one.

Unfortunately, the only thing at hand was a black golf umbrella branded with the magazine's distinct logo, a silver bucking bronc. Mia said, "Be quiet, okay? Just listen."

Her mother didn't answer, but the car's display showed the call was still connected, so Mia decided to take that as confirmation that her mother was following directions. It was also a sign that miracles still happened.

When two long, tall cowboys slid out of the truck on either side and ambled toward her slowly, Mia tightened her hold on the umbrella and rolled down the window. The cowboy on the driver's side tipped his hat back, and she immediately crossed her fingers, hoping that he was good with a jack. No one with a face like that should be a villain. He held his hands up as if he was trying to calm a skittish colt. "Car trouble, ma'am? I'm Matt. Prospect's vet." Everything about his posture and tone seemed intended to say "harmless."

Mia wrinkled her nose. "Flat tire. Could you help me change it? I was heading into Prospect for the night. If there's a garage, I'll see if they can repair it tomorrow."

His smile was nice. Open. Easy. Mia relaxed her posture. Then she opened the car door and slid out, noticing the second man had a hand braced against the back of the car. He was looking down.

"Pop the trunk." When he glanced up as if to make sure she'd heard him, Mia managed to maintain her composure, but it took every bit of brain power she had.

Her ability to follow his instruction froze when she realized she was meeting Grant Armstrong for the first time. Rodeo bad boy. Brooding, handsome and strangely absent from the biggest rodeo event of the year held every December.

Mia had a flat tire.

Grant Armstrong had pulled over to fix it.

Because lightning bolts like this coincidental meeting on the side of the road convinced her that the universe would work things out in Mia Romero's favor.

And so the secret idea popped into her mind. Mia had pitched several story ideas every issue for months and watched her mother take some of them and give them to more experienced writers. She'd heard the discussions of pursuing this loose thread of where Grant Armstrong had disappeared to, but no one was certain there was any kind of payoff to the story.

If this story was good, how many magazines could it sell? Enough to buy time to attract new advertisers?

And here he was. Right in front of her, one impatient eyebrow raised while he waited for her to raise the trunk so that he could get to the spare and the jack.

"Sorry," Mia blurted before she turned around to pull the trunk release. "I guess relief caused my brain to short circuit." She waved the manual in her hand. "I was cramming for the test when you pulled up, but I'm not certain I'd pass."

Matt moved to the truck and opened the back door to let a rangy brown hound dog flow out onto the pavement. "This is Betty. She's a rotten guard dog, but she is an excellent character witness. Bring your pointy umbrella over to talk to her while you wait and we'll get you fixed up in no time."

This time, it was much simpler to follow instructions. Betty was still stretching when Mia bent to scratch behind her ears. "Hi, Betty, it's very nice to meet you." She dropped the umbrella on the pavement to free up both hands for important ear coverage.

The cowboys worked quickly to raise the car, remove the tire and put on the spare. After they had everything back in the trunk, Matt pointed. "We'll follow you the rest of the way. You'll see the Garage right inside the town limits, a big clearing over on your left. Not sure whether Lucky or Dante will still be there at this hour, so we'll make sure you get to where you're going."

The urge to reassure them that it wouldn't be necessary burned on the tip of her tongue, but she needed a minute to figure out how best to continue her acquaintance with Grant Armstrong without tipping her hand too soon.

The universe had presented her with an amazing opportunity. No way was she going to waste it.

Maybe he wanted his story to be splashed across the magazine's front cover, but the way he'd vanished from sight suggested he would be less than excited to meet a reporter from *The Way West*.

"That would be great, Matt. I appreciate it." Then she tossed the umbrella in the backseat, slipped into the driver's seat, and drove slowly into Prospect. "You still on the line, Mother?"

"Yes, nervous as a cat, but I'm still here." Her mother huffed out a breath. "Can't see how this research is going to be worth such trouble, Mia."

The urge to tell her who had been her roadside hero burned, but Mia wasn't about to hype this might-be news story until she had something solid.

"I'll call you when I'm leaving town to let you know I'm headed home," Mia said and waited for her mother to end the call. She was relieved to see the town sign and the houses signaling civilization on the horizon. Traveling wide-open spaces was fun and the scenery was grand, but nearby food and restrooms were always a welcome change.

Matt's description was perfect. She pulled into the Garcia Auto Repair parking lot in minutes, but the dark windows and Closed sign answered the question about whether they were still open. She rolled down her window. "Is the garage open tomorrow?"

Matt nodded. "Yeah, they're open half days on Saturdays. If you're here first thing, they should be able to make a repair. If you need a new tire…" He tilted his head to the side as if he had bad news.

"I guess I'll be waiting until Monday for a delivery if they don't have the tire in stock." Mia shrugged. This could work out in her favor. She could use the extra time in Prospect to further her acquaintance with Grant Armstrong, somehow.

"Might even be Tuesday." Matt's beautiful smile softened the blow. "But this isn't a bad place to spend time. I didn't catch your name." He propped an elbow on the truck door as if shooting the breeze with a stranger was the easiest thing in the world.

"Mia. Mia Romero. I should have introduced myself." She got out and offered him her hand to shake. "I'll be happy to buy you both a cup of coffee in thanks if you'll point me to a restaurant somewhere between here and Bell House."

She crossed in front of the truck. Shaking Grant's hand would be a step in the right direction. Since she couldn't figure out the next one, she better make the moment count. Mia was pretty comfortable with this part of the plan. She had a whole lifetime of experience watching and waiting for her next direction to appear.

Grant watched her closely. The fear that he had recognized her name made her pause, but she didn't let it stop her. It was doubtful a rodeo star like Grant was reading travel articles in his spare time. Besides that, she had a very valid reason to be here, and that made an excellent cover story for the scoop she wanted most.

"Hi, I'm Mia." She held out her hand. When he shook it, the shot of warmth caught her by surprise. His hand was strong, calloused, tan. And the power of his dark eyes convinced her he didn't miss anything. Mia had met people from all walks of life and shaken countless hands, but the instant connection between the two of them was brand new.

"Grant. Armstrong." He tilted his head back. Was he waiting for her reaction?

She smiled and stepped back.

"Good thing you have a reservation at the B-and-B, Mia. February is not a big tourism month around here, but the craft store is running a popular retreat. You are going to be surrounded by sewing machines humming and usually a lot of laughter." Matt nodded. "That's a good Friday night, right there."

Mia bit her lip. If she'd learned the universe provided, she'd also come to understand that she could do a better job of looking out for herself occasionally. "Think all the rooms are booked up?"

"No reservation," Grant muttered, but she couldn't detect much judgment there. He pulled out his cell phone and hit a button. When the call was answered, he said, "Could you ask Rose if her place is full up this weekend?"

They all waited. "Yes, ma'am, I know better than to start a conversation like that. I do, Mama. I'll make chitchat first next time, but we've got a visitor to town who needs a place to stay tonight, so I was in a hurry." He closed his eyes as if he already had regrets about his choices. Meanwhile, Mia's grin matched Matt's. "Thank you. I love you, too." He hung up the phone before shaking his head.

Mia sighed. "No. So…can you give me directions to the nearest place that will have rooms tonight? What else is close by?"

Grant made another call before Matt could answer.

This time when the call was answered, Grant said, "Hey, Jordan, how are you?"

He waited patiently for her to answer. "Those curtains sound really pretty." He shot a look at Matt before saying, "I was calling because we've got a visitor to town who needs a hotel room. Do you have one available?"

Grant yanked the phone away from his ear. Mia smiled at the squawking that even she could hear from where he was standing. "Yeah, we'll show her the way out there. Best room, yeah, I'll tell her. No restaurant yet but you're working on it. I'll make sure she knows that." Grant nodded. "Okay." Then he nodded again and repeated himself. "Okay." Finally he said, "Tell me the rest when we get there, Jordan." Then he hung up the phone and slapped it back in his pocket. "There's room out at the Majestic. It's a completely different atmosphere than Bell House, but it's close and comfortable."

And Grant was a friend of whoever ran the place, which suggested Mia could get some good background there.

"The Majestic is light on amenities like food, but we'll make sure you've got something to eat." Grant pointed at her car. "You okay to follow us?"

Mia nodded and hurried back to her car. She wasn't sure what might be coming next, thanks to the universe's always-on-time delivery, but all signs were pointing to Grant. This was the story that would change everything.

CHAPTER THREE

WHEN MATT PARKED the truck next to Mia's expensive luxury sedan in front of the Majestic Prospect Lodge, Grant was still trying to decide how to handle their visitor. There was no mistaking the logo on the umbrella she'd hoped would be an effective weapon in the worst-case scenario there on the side of the road. *The Way West* was one of the magazines that covered rodeo events. Maybe she was a fan who had won free swag in some kind of giveaway.

That didn't explain her lack of reaction on meeting Grant Armstrong in the middle of nowhere.

Was she here to dig up dirt on him?

"Okay, so the broody silence on the drive out from the Garage was broodier than usual." Matt pulled the key out of the ignition. "Why do I think it has to do with our rescued visitor and how do I know you aren't going to tell me why?"

Grant grunted. "Right on both accounts."

Matt was still shaking his head when they met Mia at the bridge that connected the Majestic's parking lot to the lodge on the opposite side of the stream that fed into Key Lake. Her doubts about the place were politely reflected on her face. The growing shadows hadn't done much to improve the curb appeal of the rundown exterior. Dry, weathered siding made a dull backdrop for empty landscaping around the lodge. When spring arrived, things would improve, but for now, the Majestic's outsides didn't match her insides.

Mia was the one who hadn't made a reservation ahead of time, so she was going to have to trust them.

"They're renovating. Inside to out." Grant bent and picked up her small suitcase, relieved to see that whatever her purpose was for coming to Prospect, she hadn't intended to stay long. He was ahead of them when Matt added, "And the rooms are ready for guests, I promise."

The pain in his jaw alerted Grant to the way he was gritting his teeth at Matt's charming tone.

Jordan Hearst stepped out of the lodge, with a brilliant smile on her face. "Welcome to the Majestic Prospect Lodge." Whatever perks the lodge might lack, the Hearst sisters did their best to make up for with warm welcomes.

While the women introduced themselves to each other and Matt flirted to keep all eyes on him, Grant stepped inside the lodge and set Mia's luggage down in front of the check-in desk. The place looked good. The Hearst sisters and every single one of the Armstrong clan, including Damon and Micah, the two boys fostering at the ranch, had been working hard to make sure of that.

Warm hardwood floors gleamed in the light from the rustic iron chandelier he'd nearly broken his neck installing in the center of the lobby's high ceiling. Wes didn't do heights, Travis didn't do electrical and Matt was absent as always, so Grant had been the one up the ladder. Pretending to be confident was second nature to him, but he was proud to see his work added a homeyness to the lobby. Jordan had insisted painting some of the wooden walls was the correct answer, and Sarah had finally given in once the third sister had voted yes over a video call from New York. All of the remaining wood beams and the panels flanking the large fireplace had been refinished. Instead of a rugged, old fishing lodge fit for crusty anglers, this lobby had been transformed into a modern, comfortable space anyone would be comfortable in.

If Mia wasn't impressed, Grant would take her bag right back out to her car and give her directions to the highway.

"It's a work in progress, of course. We haven't done several of the big-ticket items yet. New furniture for the lobby, and we're still holding off on bathroom renovations, but I've got my best room ready for you." Jordan smiled at Mia as she moved behind the check-in desk. "We've had a computer system installed, so let me see if I know how to use it."

Grant leaned against the counter, his arms crossed over his chest as he listened to Mia give her address and phone number. Billings was home, and if he remembered correctly, that was where the magazine was based. Before he could spring the "ah-ha," like a detective solving a mystery in an old black-and-white movie, Mia sighed. Her eyes were locked on the large landscape of the Rocky Mountains hanging behind the desk. "This painting is amazing, Jordan. I know you've said this lodge has been a lot of work, but this space is a dream. I'm a travel writer, so I should know."

Grant pursed his lips as he considered that. "Travel writer for *The Way West*, I guess."

Mia's eyebrows shot up, and he shrugged. "The umbrella had a logo."

She smoothed a long piece of dark brown hair behind one ear. Was she nervous? Because he knew she was connected to the publication?

"Yeah, for the magazine. I wanted to do research on Prospect's Western Days festival. This year is a big anniversary. One hundred years of history should make for a pretty good story." Mia waved a hand around the lobby's great room. "And that was before I knew what was happening here at the lodge. It seems like the Majestic Prospect Lodge will need to be featured, too."

Jordan immediately clasped her hands to her chest and jumped up and down. Muffled squeals escaped before she closed her eyes and forced herself to breathe in through her nose and out through her mouth. "Oh, Mia, you don't know how thrilled I am."

Mia grinned. "I had planned to dig through the archives of *The Prospect Post*, pull up interesting information for background, and then return for photos and the finishing touches in April when the festival's happening, but I'm thinking I may need to stay a bit longer. I don't want to miss anything noteworthy now, do I?"

Her innocent expression as she met Grant's stare did not reassure him at all.

"Oh yes, you have come to the right place. Matt and Grant live next door at the Rocking A. Their parents, Prue and Walt, are the heartbeat of Prospect. If you ask them something and they don't know the answer, it's not worth knowing. They also have the five sons." Jordan leaned across the desk as if she was about to share confidential information. "Wes Armstrong and my sister and Travis and the new doctor in town are over-the-top in love. Clay is mine. But Matt and Grant are the single Armstrongs, so…"

Mia frowned at him, as if she couldn't make the connection as to why she needed that information, but he had no intention of acknowledging Jordan's boldness. If he argued with Jordan every time she tweaked him, he'd need to start taking vitamins to boost his stamina. The two of them were a lot alike, in that they enjoyed keeping people on their toes. He'd never wished for a sister, but getting one like Jordan seemed to be a very clever form of karma. When Wes, Clay and Travis managed to pop the impending question, his collection of sisters would be nearly complete.

Matt's open grin as Grant picked up Mia's bag convinced him he needed to spill at least part of the cheating story and fast.

What Jordan said was true. His family knew everything there was to know about Prospect, and his mother would make sure every door was thrown open for Mia to get the best story she could. Publicizing the town was his mother's pet project.

The fact that Jordan was laying a matchmaking trail was further proof that his family should be warned about Mia's potential danger.

"Bring Mia's suitcase down the hall, Grant." Jordan was already on the move. She never hesitated when it came to the lodge, and they'd all learned to follow orders when they were issued inside the Majestic. He ambled behind them to the last room in the hallway. This had been the first room tackled at each stage of the renovation, so it was the furthest along and the best the lodge had to offer.

"I love the artwork, Jordan." Mia had moved to stand in front of a landscape that showed Key Lake in fall colors. Right now, the lake was frozen in spots, even on a sunny day like today, but it was still a beautiful scene outside the window. The lake didn't have a bad season.

"Thank you. My father painted everything you'll see here. The big piece in the lobby, the mountains and this landscape. He teaches classes in town if you're interested in learning more about painting or him." Jordan clasped her hands together and fluttered her eyelashes. She was a hard-nosed businessperson with an eye out for capitalizing on all the opportunities a magazine feature could mean for Prospect. It was no wonder his mother loved Jordan as much as his brother, Clay, did.

Maybe more.

"I will make a note of that." Mia pointed at her bag. "Do you have Wi-Fi that I can connect to in the room?"

Jordan hissed as if someone had let out all of her air. "No internet connection yet, but I'll take you to the library in town, which has a good setup. We've got an installation scheduled, but it's a couple of weeks away."

Mia waved her hand. "No problem. I need to get to the library tomorrow anyway." Then she winced. "I forgot about the car repair and… Is the library open on Saturday? I could have planned this trip better."

Grant propped his hands on his hips as he considered that. It was true. If she wanted to see newspaper archives and spend time in the library, a weekday would have been smarter.

But if she was here to snoop around town to find out information on him, a busy Saturday in Prospect was a good bet.

"Yes, the library is open all day on Saturday. I'll take you myself after we drop your car off at the Garage in the morning. Tonight I'll leave you to get settled in. We don't have a restaurant yet, but sandwiches are free and available at all hours in the restaurant's refrigerator. I'll make us both some breakfast in the morning, and you can visit the Ace High for lunch or dinner. That's in town, and you'll need to make sure you rave over Faye's desserts. They're all based on Sadie Hearst recipes." Jordan waited patiently for some recognition.

The first sign that Mia might not be warmly received in Prospect was the fact that dropping

Sadie's name brought about no reaction. Grant knew that would be a problem for the Hearst sisters, for sure.

"The Colorado Cookie Queen?" Jordan added. "She was my great-aunt. Left me the lodge." The change in Jordan's voice, as enthusiasm for Mia faded, was impossible to miss.

Mia grimaced. "I don't cook much, Mia. I'm sorry, but I am definitely looking forward to tasting these desserts. I love cookies."

Jordan's smile was professional as she agreed. "Of course. We'll make sure you know who Sadie was before you leave Prospect." Then she stepped out in the hallway. "Please let me know if you need anything."

When Jordan was gone, Mia turned to face him. "I messed up. Seems like everyone should know who Sadie Hearst is, I guess."

Grant shrugged. "Don't worry too much. Plenty of people around to help bring you up to speed."

"What a relief." She huffed out a laugh. "Thank you for carrying in my suitcase. Actually, thank you for making sure I'm not still sitting on the side of the road trying to figure out how to put the jack under the car."

He nodded. "Instead of a cup of coffee, you could tell me the real reason you're in Prospect. Seems an odd time to be doing research on the festival when it's still two months away."

When she smoothed her hair behind her ears, he knew it was one of her tells. Mia was nervous, most likely because she was hiding something. He'd learned early on that people could bluff, try to tell him lies, but their body language usually dealt the truth.

"Believe it or not, I came to Prospect because I'm a dedicated travel writer for *The Way West* magazine. Meet me in the library and I'll pull up the website and show you the pieces I've written." Then she mirrored his stance, arms crossed over her chest, feet planted solidly. "But imagine my surprise at running into Grant Armstrong here. No one on the rodeo circuit knows where he went for sure or why he disappeared."

Surprised by her honesty and impressed that she put her cards on the table without hesitation, Grant nodded. "Right. Exactly. My real question is what are you going to do about that?"

Mia bit her lip. "I'm going to write a story about Prospect, the festival and all the attractions."

Grant waited. There was more coming. He could see it in her eyes.

"And if I hear any other stories that need to be told, I'll find a place to tell them." Mia shrugged, as if she understood how the stark words might land, but she'd had no other choice but to say them. "I'll be happy to listen if there's something you want the world to know."

Since that was the furthest thing from what he wanted, revealing to the world the truth about his retirement, Grant dipped his head. "I'll keep all of that in mind, Mia. If nothing else, thank you for being so frank. Good or bad, that makes everything much easier."

She wrinkled her nose. "Does it? Even if it's something you don't like? You might be the only person I've ever met who would say that. I would have lied about my favorite Sadie Hearst recipes if I'd known how to. I want Jordan to like me, you understand?"

The urge to chuckle at the cute expression surprised him. Mia Romero could expose his story when he wanted it to stay buried. He shouldn't like her. Laughing with her could be a slippery slope, and a slide to the bottom would have serious consequences for a lot of people. Keeping his guard up was the right thing to do.

Why did repeating that over and over as he followed Matt to the truck feel like wasted effort?

CHAPTER FOUR

Mᴵᴬ's ꜰɪʀꜱᴛ ɴɪɢʜᴛ at the Majestic Prospect Lodge was more relaxing than she'd expected. Every one of Matt Armstrong's and Jordan Hearst's promises about the experience had been fulfilled. Mia stretched between the crisp, clean sheets, and noticed the early morning sunshine glowing along the edges of the curtains covering her room's window and realized she'd slept soundly through the night. There had been none of the usual turning and settling and adjusting that always accompanied her first night in a new bed.

Being the only guest at the lodge contributed to that peace, no doubt, but there was also something comfortable about the bare-bones room. Mia slipped out of bed and crossed the floor to tug the curtains open. The lake outside was surrounded by pines and shady banks with patches of snow. In the brilliant sunlight glittering across the surface, Mia could see ice crystals, but it was easy to imagine how the water would call to her on a summer day.

The Hearsts couldn't have chosen prettier scenery for their inherited lodge.

After a quick shower, Mia dried her hair and dressed quickly in jeans and an oversize purple sweatshirt. She slipped on the sneakers that her mother said made her look like a 1950s junior varsity basketball player and briefly considered whether she should have brought different clothes. She'd packed for doing research in the newspaper archives about the history of the Western Days festival and Prospect in general, which meant comfort above all else. If she'd known the high probability of meeting a handsome cowboy like Grant Armstrong, she might have chosen differently.

But breakfast was underway somewhere in the lodge, and she didn't want to miss it. The scent of something sweet filtered through and her stomach growled in response.

Mia heard a quiet tap on the door and opened it.

Jordan was standing in the hallway, her head cocked as if she was listening for movement inside. "Good morning. I hope I didn't wake you. I thought I heard the shower."

Mia nodded. "You did and this is excellent timing. Whatever you're cooking smells delicious. Is it pancakes? Waffles?" She loved both. Anything that could work as a maple syrup delivery mechanism was high on her list of preferred breakfast foods.

Jordan sniffed dramatically. "Hmm, sorry. I don't smell anything." Then she grimaced. "I obviously should have set lower expectations for the quality of the breakfast available here. I have toast. Scrambled eggs?" Her hopeful expression made Mia laugh.

"Also very good choices." Mia followed Jordan around the corner and stepped inside an apartment nestled at the back of the lodge. It was small but comfortable, with a large open kitchen area that joined with a cozy living room. Another woman was attempting to fry bacon on the stovetop when Jordan pointed Mia to one of the seats at the island.

"This is my sister, Sarah. As you can probably tell, neither one of us is a proper chef. Sadie did her best but we managed to forget everything she taught us." Jordan pointed to the oven mitt Sarah was wearing as she flipped the bacon. "It's a miracle we haven't burned the place down. We don't make bacon under normal circumstances. Too much potential for disaster."

Sarah waved her oven-mitted hand. "Protective measures are required, but we wanted to step up our usual morning meal in your honor. I was at the Homestead Market last night when Jordan called to tell me we had a guest. I might have overestimated our abilities in this area, I was so excited to have a real-live visitor. But we do have coffee and orange juice to go with your toast, eggs and uh, burned bacon."

"Don't forget the company," Jordan said as she gestured at Mia. "That's one of a kind. You won't find better company anywhere."

Mia poured a large glass of pulpy orange juice and sipped before she nodded broadly. "And the finest juice I have tasted in… I can't even remember how long it's been since I've had orange juice this perfect."

Sarah's lips were twitching as she slid a plate of dark, shriveled bacon onto the island. "I believe she's humoring us."

"It's like she's known us forever," Jordan agreed.

Mia relaxed into the easy back and forth the sisters used as they dished up their plates and settled at the island. She had taken her second bite of toast when Jordan asked, "How is your room? Did you sleep well?"

Before she could answer, Sarah's phone rang. "Oh, it's Brooke. She's getting an early start." She answered the call and set the phone up against the juice carafe so they could see the screen. "The youngest Hearst sister. Lives in New York."

Mia nodded and spread strawberry jelly on her toast as Sarah said, "Brooke, meet our current guest. This is Mia. She's a travel writer." Her hushed tones suggested Mia was important. Since that didn't happen very often, Mia appreciated it.

"Hi, Mia," Brooke said with a wave. "How has your stay been?"

"Very nice," Mia said, "and everything is so comfortable. Not fancy, but like…home?" She shrugged. "It's hard to put into a few words, but I travel enough to recognize that there's something special about how I can stretch out in the bed and, instead of immediately cataloging all the differences, my mind settles in to rest. That's unique."

Jordan immediately hopped up out of her chair and did a victory lap around the island while Sarah shook her head. "If you wanted a new best friend for life, you just got one, Mia. The shortest way to Jordan's heart is to recognize how special the Majestic is." Sarah sipped her coffee while Jordan settled herself at the bar. "Better now?"

"I was anxious to hear Mia's verdict. I am not surprised the feedback is good, but I am gratified." Jordan picked up her fork. "We've had a few people stay with us, Mia, but we're getting close to reopening officially, so it's nice to hear that all this hard work is paying off."

"Jordan has cleaned and cleaned and cleaned, painted, sanded floors, stained floors, repaired furniture and dug through years of storage to get right here to this place. If she does victory laps now and then, I can't blame her." Sarah bumped her sister's shoulder. "We've got a few hurdles still to clear, but I see success on the horizon."

Jordan sighed. "I need warmer weather to work on the exterior. And money." She grimaced.

"I'll call Howard again next week to find out about the dispersion of the funds." Sarah hugged Jordan tightly. "Sadie's LA house finally sold, so it should be anytime now that we'll get our share of the funds." She turned to Mia to explain. "Sadie left the three of us the lodge, but most of her other assets were to be sold and distributed among the whole family, seventeen of us in total. Howard Fine is her lawyer and the executor of her estate. Sadie didn't leave us any hints on what to do with this place, sell or reopen it, so we've been moving slowly. Actually, Jordan has been moving quickly, but most of this she's managed to repair on her own...or with help from the neighbors." She raised her eyebrows. "Big improvements we can make are on hold until that money happens."

Brooke leaned closer to the screen "And they have this sister in New York who is struggling, so any extra funds have gone to her, and since her ex-husband is being a real—"

"We're trying to be smart about how we proceed, so it's wonderful to hear your feedback," Sarah said.

Mia picked up a piece of lightly charred bacon. "Well, I imagine you're anxious to get the renovations finished, but what you've got here will absolutely work."

Jordan propped her elbow on the counter. "Think the burned bacon will keep the guests coming back?"

Sarah frowned at her sister. "First of all, I will get better at making bacon, but secondly, no way am I cooking up breakfast for a lodge filled with guests. We'll have to find a solution for that quickly."

"No leads on a chef for the restaurant?" Brooke asked. "The sous chef I talked to at the diner next door heard the words *mountain* and *lodge* and evaporated into a mist like a vampire at sunrise. I don't believe he'll be leaving the city."

Jordan said, "I can do juice and pastries for a while, but we need to find a chef to run our kitchen. Mia was probably brokenhearted to expect pancakes or waffles and to get black bacon instead."

Mia laughed. "I happen to like my bacon cooked exactly like this. It's perfect. But I do also love pancakes. I wouldn't have mentioned that except I smelled something sweet in the air, like you were making them for breakfast."

The furtive glance the sisters exchanged caught Mia's attention, but she wasn't sure how to ask about what they were communicating.

"Since you had a good night's sleep, I wonder…" Jordan bit her lip. "With all your traveling, do you have any experience in haunted hotels, Mia?"

Mia leaned back in her chair as she considered the question. Brooke's resigned expression convinced her that the topic wasn't as unexpected for the three sisters as it was for her. "Staying in them? No. I have mentioned them in passing, using other traveler's descriptions of the places, but I generally do my best to avoid the supernatural."

Jordan nodded slowly. "Yeah."

Sarah blinked and they shared more silent conversation.

"We don't know that we have a ghost." Sarah pursed her lips. "But we wouldn't be all that surprised if we did."

Mia crossed her arms, determined to wait for more explanation.

"Our Aunt Sadie…" Jordan stood and paced slowly back and forth in front of the island. "This was her apartment while she managed the lodge. She started a public-access cooking show from the restaurant here and places in Prospect before she moved to LA and her career exploded into the Cookie Queen Corporation." She tapped a stack of books on the counter. "These are all her cookbooks. All best sellers. All 100 percent Sadie through and through. Her own line of appliances and kitchenware. Ladies' Western wear. Television. Stars loved her. Audiences loved her more. She was a great cook but she was a huge personality, Mia."

Mia realized this was when a better understanding of Sadie Hearst, the Colorado Cookie Queen, would have helped her. Jordan seemed to have forgiven her for not knowing Sadie the night before, but it was clear that the icon was a part of the fabric of this lodge.

Perhaps literally, if she was haunting the place.

"I don't believe in ghosts." Sarah pressed her hands to her chest. "We don't believe in ghosts."

Brooke interjected, "They didn't believe in ghosts before they met the Majestic."

"But…" Mia was certain that ghosts would not have been discussed unless their belief was being tested.

"Vanilla. Was it vanilla that you smelled this morning?" Jordan braced her arm on the island as if she was preparing herself for the answer.

Mia considered. "Wouldn't vanilla have been a pretty common ingredient for a cookie queen? Maybe it's part of the…walls?" Why didn't that almost reasonable explanation feel better than having a friendly ghost?

"Yes. Of course." Sarah agreed firmly. "The only issue is that we can't smell it all the time. It comes and goes. Some people and some places get vanilla and some don't."

All four of them were silent as they considered the implications of that.

"And she was the friendliest person you'd ever meet in real life. We wouldn't mind if she decided to hang around, but we also realize guests might not be as comfortable with that." Sarah sighed. "At least they have another choice for a place to stay in Prospect."

Mia realized Sarah and Jordan were both anxiously awaiting her verdict. If she didn't immediately pack up her suitcase and head for town, they could relax.

"Have you ever considered that Sadie's ghost could be a selling point? Fans might visit to have the chance to meet her, so to speak." Mia finished her juice. "I don't know how you work that into the advertising, but I'll be sure to pass along any encounters of the spooky kind I experience while I'm here."

Jordan, clearly relieved, exhaled loudly. "If you'd seen the reaction we got when the bats flew out of the attic, my concern about Sadie's presence would make perfect sense. But I am happy to hear that we aren't looking at disaster of the ghostly variety."

Before Mia could ask for more information related to the bats and where exactly they'd left the building and when or if they might return, Sarah asked, "Brooke, did you call to catch up or did you need something?"

Brooke seemed unsettled. Mia would have called it forlorn and a little dramatic, but she only said, "I was missing you and I wanted to complain about my ex-husband, who refuses to pay his settlement, so I refuse to leave the apartment and he's being a real—"

Sarah smiled brightly. "Okay, you and I can talk about that. Mia, I guess you're ready to get to town."

"Oh, I already volunteered to show Mia the way to the library after we stop at the Garage. If you don't mind washing the dishes, Sarah, I'll take care of Mia's room when I get back. Love you, Brooke. Let us know if it's time for us to come get you." Jordan didn't give Sarah time to argue. She urged Mia out into the hallway. "You have to be fast to escape kitchen duty around here, Mia. Outmaneuvering my older sister isn't easy, but it is sweet every time it happens. I'll meet you around front." She pointed at a door and nodded.

Mia was grinning as she picked up her purse

and laptop and headed for the lodge's parking lot. Breakfast was normally a solitary event in her life, whether she was on the road or home in her luxury apartment in Billings. Traveling regularly meant she'd gotten comfortable with her own company, but it had been nice to spend the time with Jordan and Sarah. Mia was an only child. She had no experience with the kind of bickering the two sisters did as naturally as they breathed, but it was funny and sweet at the same time. They might argue now and then, but Mia could see that Sarah and Jordan were close.

She was still thinking about the mystery vanilla scent and the briefly mentioned bats when she slid behind the wheel of her car and waved as Jordan passed in front of her in a red SUV. On the way to town, Mia craned her neck to see the scenery. It looked different in the daylight. The night before, the growing shadows had made it difficult to spot the details, but the lodge's closest neighbor was the Rocking A and it looked like a cattle ranch. Then she realized it was Rocking A for Armstrong. Grant was nearby, once she figured out an angle on how to corner him for information.

There was a small house close to the road that might or might not be a part of the ranch, and then in the distance, there was a barn and another house, but beautiful scenery surrounded her on all sides. Winter still had a firm grip on the grass and trees, but every now and then, Mia could see the promise that spring wasn't so very far away.

Coming into Prospect again, this time from the opposite direction, inspired several different ideas on what she might feature in an article about the town...or the town's most famous bronc-riding champion. Prospect was idyllic, the postcard image of small-town life. How did the Bad Boy of Bronc Busting come from such a place?

Jordan led Mia back to Garcia Auto Repair and hopped out to escort Mia into the shop attached to the garage. "I'll introduce you to Lucky and Dante."

Before Jordan reached for the door, a handsome man stepped through it, his hand outstretched. "You must be Mia. Heard you have a flat."

"This is Dante." Jordan shook her head. "I haven't been here long, Mia, but I have learned that this is life in a small town. Everyone knows everything about you before you open your mouth."

Mia dropped the keys in Dante's hand. "I won't ask why or how. I'll say thank you and the tire's in the trunk."

He nodded and headed for her car.

"I'm guessing Matt called ahead to let you know we were coming," Jordan said to the beautiful woman behind the counter. Two little girls were playing in a toy-strewn corner of the office, penned in by a low mesh...fence?

Mia wasn't sure the right word was *fence*. She didn't know much about toddler security systems, but it was clear that the Garcias were interested in any help they could get corralling their daughters. The happy shouts that accompanied the clatter of a stack of blocks being demolished as one of the girls drove a large fire truck through the structure made the woman wince.

"Hi, Mia, we don't know if they have a brighter future in demolition or screaming, but they practice both regularly. I'm Lucky. Those two are Eliana and Selena."

Mia laughed and nodded. "Yes, they show a lot of promise in both."

Lucky smiled. "You have no idea."

"They're adorable." Mia knew it was the right thing to say, but it was also true. Both little girls had happy, confident grins...even as they were obviously plotting mayhem of some sort.

"It won't take Dante long to see if the tire can be patched. If we have to order tires for you, I'm afraid it will be Monday afternoon before we can get you fixed up." Lucky stood on her tiptoes to peer into the window that lined the wall between the office and the garage. She was wincing as she turned back.

"Bad news?" Jordan asked.

"He was shaking his head," Lucky said as Dante walked back in...still shaking his head.

"I can try patching it, but I wouldn't advise that, Mia. The placement of the puncture is bad. If it fails, it would be dangerous, especially on these roads. You have tread left on those tires, but the smart thing to do is replace this one. For safety and better handling, I'd recommend buying two. Otherwise, you'll have a noticeable difference in tread from one side to the other." Dante motioned over his shoulder. "Follow me and I'll show you what I'm talking about."

Mia held up her hands. "You could show me, but I wouldn't know much more than I know now, never having replaced a tire in my life. Can you recommend a good choice to replace two tires?" Mia followed Dante around the counter to the computer, where he pulled up a list of possible tires and launched into the pros and cons of each option. When his lecture wound down, he tapped the screen over the mid-priced option. "All in all, this is what I would put on Lucky's car if I were making the choice for my beloved wife and mother of my children."

His smile was contagious. Mia realized he was teasing her.

"That's the highest endorsement he can give anything," Lucky said from the seat she'd taken near the door. "Everyone around here knows that, according to Dante, Lucky deserves nothing but the best." She winked at her husband.

"Gross." Jordan rolled her eyes. "So much love and respect in the room." She pulled the neck of her sweater as if it was choking her. "It's a real epidemic of couples in love around this town."

"Says the woman who freaked out the Ace High when Clay Armstrong made an unexpected early arrival last week." Lucky's eyebrows rose as she motioned toward Mia. "Shrieked louder than either of these two, ran to meet him at the door of the restaurant and jumped into his arms right there in front of his mama and everybody."

Mia knew her jaw had dropped as she turned to Jordan.

Her blush was confirmation that the whole story was nothing but the truth.

"He'd been gone for three weeks." Jordan held out her hands.

Dante cleared his throat. "Should I get these tires ordered, Mia? Driving on the spare should be okay if you're staying close, but I wouldn't go too far or too fast. We can give you a call when they come in."

Mia nodded. "Yes, I have some work to do in Prospect, so I'll stay until the car is ready for travel."

"What kind of work?" Lucky asked as she held

open the door after Jordan slunk out in embarrassment.

"I'm writing a magazine article about Prospect's Western Days weekend, so I'm doing background. We're headed to the library next." Mia pointed at Jordan who was fanning her hot cheeks.

"Oh, what magazine?" Lucky asked.

"*The Way West.* If I can talk my mother into it, I might try for more than one story." And if she got any good details about Grant Armstrong and what he was doing here, laying low out of the spotlight, her mother would never say no.

Lucky crossed her arms over her chest. "Okay, we'll get you back on the road as quick as we can. Can't wait to see Prospect featured in a glossy magazine. I've missed having a newspaper in town. I do my best keeping up with events and posting them all over social media, but having a weekly roundup was special, you know?"

"I bet. It's tough to be in the newspaper business now." Or magazine or print, Mia added but didn't say aloud.

"Yeah, I think about setting up an online version, with the articles written by anyone who wants to submit a story. We'd do some advertising to pay the bills, but..." Lucky's daughters screamed, this time in a different, less happy tone. "But then that happens, and I remember I also like to sleep sometimes and I'd have to completely give that up to do anything else." Lucky motioned her outside and inhaled slowly in the silence of the parking lot. She was waving as Mia slid behind the wheel of her car.

Jordan pointed toward the road and Mia nodded. She'd lead the way to the library.

Once Jordan was occupied elsewhere, Mia would need to return to Garcia Auto Repair to see if she could get insider information on Grant Armstrong's sudden departure from the rodeo.

Why did that fill her with dread? Lucky and Dante had been welcoming.

Would they be as friendly with her when she started hunting for answers?

And what about Sarah and Jordan? If Jordan was wrapped up with one of Grant's brothers, how would they react to a juicy story about Grant?

She was enjoying the life Prospect offered.

Perhaps it would be smart to maintain her distance. Mia wasn't here to meet new friends; she was looking for threads to pull to build her story. A smart reporter would keep that in mind.

CHAPTER FIVE

GRANT RODE ON Jet behind his mother, who was on her dappled quarter horse, Lady. They ambled down through the pasture toward the barn. It was a quiet Saturday morning and Grant thought the perfect window to reveal what he'd been trying to hide ever since he came back to Prospect. Time was closing in on him rapidly. Mia seemed sharp as a tack, and as a journalist by trade, surely her instincts would ramp up anytime. As he'd walked out of the Majestic the night before, he'd promised himself that whatever happened after his confession, he would tell his family the truth. All of it.

Unfortunately, worrying over it all night hadn't led him to find the proper delivery.

That was his first problem.

Grant and his brothers had all been adopted by Walt and Prue Armstrong after fostering with them. The boys' beginnings were pretty similar, as far as the families and the situations they'd left behind, but Grant had still always been out of step with the others.

For a while, he'd measured up. His career had been solid. He'd been as successful in rodeo as everyone had always told him he would be.

Wes, the "oldest" because he'd arrived at the ranch first and because he couldn't keep himself from stepping up to lead, was the good brother who had come home to take over the ranch. He was also the town's only lawyer and juggled a lot of responsibility. He could be counted on to do the right thing and know the correct answer. It was annoying, sure, but if Grant explained the tricky situation to Wes, his brother would immediately take over.

Having a lawyer on his side was good. It was. Wes would refuse to leave his brother to face any fallout all on his own.

So would Clay, the smartest of them all, the architect and builder who dropped everything if the family needed his expertise. Creating his own development company from the ground up had been a gamble, but Clay had made it pay off.

Travis, who was settling into foster parenthood as if the role was made for him, wanted to believe in the good in everyone, even after life had made that faith hard to hold onto. He'd served his country in the army, and now he was adding on to Walt and Prue's legacy with a new generation of fostered boys.

And Matt would love him, no matter what. His freakishly handsome face and ridiculous charm protected a soft heart that drew animals and people to him. The "baby" managed to skirt broken hearts by never letting that guard drop for long.

On paper, the Armstrongs were impressive.

In real life? Some people might call them intimidating.

Then, there was Grant, who'd never met a dare or a bit of trouble he could say no to.

And now all his "success" was about to disappear.

But right or wrong, Armstrongs stuck together, he told himself.

In the grand scheme of things, he was the one who usually brought the "wrong" to the table. The problem. The one in the family who kept things interesting. That was his role. Needling to get answers, pushing to make progress, pranks to keep his brothers humble... He'd taken his job seriously.

Even after a lifetime of trouble and with zero explanation offered, his family had accepted him when he'd returned home.

Grant wouldn't say they'd rejoiced, since the space had been pretty cramped when he'd landed at the ranch again. For months, he'd fielded questions about why he'd come back, with only vague answers about retirement. The fact that none of them had given up on digging to the heart of the matter was proof that the Armstrongs were steadfast.

Or cussed stubborn.

Grant wasn't convinced they'd believe his story. His whole life had been about testing the rules, but cheating to win had never crossed his mind. The Armstrongs would rally around him and come to his defense, sure, but would they trust that he was innocent here?

Did it matter? Grant knew the truth behind that scheme.

He'd never doubted his ability to ride horses better than anyone...until now. That big question mark had shaken him. If he wasn't that guy, the one who competed fairly and won time and again, what did he have left?

Where did he go from here?

Spilling the whole story over the dinner table would have been easier, now that a reporter had popped up in Prospect. If any one of them had poked at him, pushing for information on why he'd come home the way Matt had on their drive back to town, Grant could have seized the opening.

But his parents had eaten in town with Wes and Sarah, Clay was in Denver overnight, so

Jordan had been absent, and Travis and Keena had eyes only for each other. He and Matt had outlined some ideas for Cowboy Games at Western Days to present at the next planning meeting, and everyone had scattered. Breakfast had been noisy and filled with lots of interrogation about the "double date" his divorced parents had been on. That would have been satisfying, but his parents' cagey answers had left Grant and his brothers with very few solid details.

"Whole lot of huffing going on back there," his mother called over her shoulder as she and Lady led the way down the cleared path turning back to the barn. "If I'd wanted a grumbly bear for company this morning, I would have made you wash the dishes instead of your daddy. I'm used to all his grumbles by now. I do love cooking in the farmhouse kitchen, now that he finally agreed to renovations, but heading back to my cozy, clean apartment and leaving the cleanup to you boys sure is sweet."

Grant tipped his head back to study the wide blue sky. He'd forgotten how startlingly clear the sky could get on cold winter days at the ranch. The blue was intense.

Just like his mother's stare as she waited for him to draw alongside. "Me and Lady not moving fast enough for your liking, son?"

"No, ma'am, just thinking too hard." Grant

tugged his hat down to give his hand something to do. "Nice day to get Lady some exercise."

When his mother didn't move, Grant forced himself to meet her stare directly. "This dating thing you and Dad are up to… Is the divorce over? Can we expect an announcement soon?"

The corner of her mouth curled. "That's for us to know. I expect we'll be fighting again in no time, so don't go getting measured for a ring bearer's suit yet."

Grant smiled because that conjured up an image of him and Matt walking down the aisle, one tossing flower petals and the other carrying the wedding bands. He had no doubt his mother would rope all of them in to any second wedding ceremony if she could find a way to do it.

"Speaking of brides, Matt mentioned your neighborly assistance yesterday, stopping to help a stranded visitor with a flat tire." She ran her hand down Lady's neck and watched him. "Does all this heavy sighing have anything to do with this beautiful woman or is this a general return to the black cloud you were under when you first came home? Really thought Damon and Micah had jollied you out of those doldrums, the way the three of you trash talk over your video games."

They had. She was right. Having the kids around

was the perfect distraction. Fun uncle was the job he'd been training for his whole life.

"Was anyone talking about brides? I don't remember that." Grant urged his horse forward, hoping his mother would follow. If he was going to get into the whole mess, he needed more family present. Not for support, but because he didn't want to have to tell the story again. "I guess Matt said she was beautiful."

When his mother rode up beside him, her lips were curled smugly. "No, I added that part. Figured she had to be something to catch your attention like this."

Grant grunted. If he agreed that Mia Romero was beautiful, his mother's matchmaking would intensify. If he said she wasn't beautiful, his mother might shove him off the horse for being ungentlemanly. There was no way to win.

But starting off his confession with lying about Mia's attraction didn't appeal to him. "She was cute. That's what I'll say." Like the kind of woman who would match him step for step and still keep him on his toes.

His mother's grin grew. "*Cute* might be even better. *Beautiful* you can admire from afar, but cute will slip right through your defenses time and time again."

Grant huffed again. She was right. He didn't have to say that because she knew how correctly she'd summed up one of the issues with Mia. Even in the brief period they'd been together and knowing how dangerous she could be to his peace in Prospect, Grant's defenses had faltered. He couldn't let his mother catch a hint of that, though.

"It's time to talk about why I decided to retire, Mama." Grant watched her amusement transform into concern. "If we're gonna discuss Mia, we need the whole story out in the open."

She nodded as they passed the paddock. The barn door opened wide and Grant could see his father seated on the stack of feed that lined the interior wall. As if he was waiting patiently for their ride to end.

And he wasn't alone. Wes and Travis were cleaning stalls while Matt was checking the strained tendon on Travis's horse, Sonny. On his last trek to break ice on the pond for the cattle, Sonny had slipped, so he was getting some extra TLC.

He and his mother slid out of their saddles and moved their horses into their stalls. "You boys have been busy," his mother called. "Now, Lady, it looks like you have a full bucket of feed and all the water a pretty girl needs." Grant relaxed a bit as he removed Jet's saddle and listened to her murmur to Lady like a precious loved one. He and Jet locked eyes. The horse whiffled out a breath, and Grant nodded in agreement before running his hand down the horse's neck. His best friend understood him better than even his family. No words were necessary between them.

"Did I miss it? Am I too late?"

When Grant heard Clay hurry into the barn, his suspicion that this was an ambush, carefully planned and cleverly carried out, was confirmed.

"Just in time," his father said before sliding the door closed. "We're gettin' to the nitty-gritty part."

Grant stepped out of the stall and braced his shoulder against it. "Is this an intervention? Who's watching the boys?"

"Last I saw, Keena was playing that video game of yours. She was driving an ambulance through a car wash while Damon tried to coach her how to outrun the police and Micah was busting a gut, laughing." Matt climbed to sit on one of the stall slats. "Just as Keena intended, I'm guessing."

Wes, Clay and Travis found folding chairs and braced their elbows on their knees. After Lady was settled and curiously watching his family assemble in the aisle of the barn, his mother moved to sit on his father's lap.

When every head in the barn, even Lady's, swiveled to absorb that new development, Grant's hopes that this could be an easy conversation rose. He'd hit the highlights, smooth over as much as he could and warn all of them to be very careful around Mia Romero. They didn't need any exposés disrupting life in town.

"Do you think I'm beautiful or cute, Walt?" Prue asked as she settled his hat back on his head.

Walt was a man who understood the precarious nature of the question. After their divorce, Walt and Prue had argued and flirted in equal measure, confusing their sons and neighbors as to the will-they-or-won't-they nature of the relationship.

Walt was also a man who didn't want to lose any of the ground he'd recovered. "Yes," he nodded firmly. "Both on different days and depending on the weather."

Prue pursed her lips as she considered that answer, but she didn't show her cards. Whether or not the answer was successful remained a mystery as she turned back to Grant and said, "Tell us about your retirement."

Grant was disappointed but not surprised when all of his brothers turned back toward him instead of following what was happening between their parents farther down the rabbit trail.

Wes clamped his shoulder. "All of it, Grant. You've been nursing this long enough."

"So…" Grant clasped his hands together and

rubbed them as he considered where to start. No obvious answer came to mind and he wasn't good with words, like Wes, anyway. "Turns out, my whole career is a fabrication, a scheme run by the guy I thought was my best friend and the man I looked up to on the circuit. They've been pulling strings and conspiring with other riders to cheat, throw rides, to push me to the top."

Silence filled the barn. Even Lady had quietly stepped back into her stall. She didn't want any of the family drama. Smart horse.

"For what purpose?" his mother asked, confusion wrinkling her brow. It didn't surprise him that she couldn't see the upside of the grift immediately. None of the Armstrongs would lie to earn a dollar.

Grant rubbed a hand over his mouth. "Believe it was twofold. Betting on the outcome when you already know who will win is easy, sure profit, right?" That was bad enough, but it was the second piece that bothered him more. "And in Red's case, he could sell access to me, the price going up every time I won. He set me up against competition, controlled the standings. Since he also earned a piece of every prize pot, endorsement and boot commercial I taped, as my 'manager,' he was doing very well indeed. All he had to do was convince me to trust him."

When they were all silent, Grant crossed his

arms over his chest. Waiting for them to ask the question he dreaded wasn't easy.

"How did you find out about this? Why didn't you burn the whole operation to the ground before you left?" Travis asked before he yanked his hat off and smacked it against his thigh. "Of all the disgusting maneuvers, to take a man's trust and use it against him. I'll help you embarrass Red Williams so bad his mama won't claim him."

Clay leaned back and rested his head against the wall. "Can we ride out in the morning? I need a nap first."

Grant chuckled when no one else did. He appreciated the effort to dispel some of the tension. Hearing Travis, the quiet one, ready to exact payback had surprised him.

"So...you walked away?" Walt asked slowly. "From this career that you built, put all your heart into. You just quit and came home."

"I didn't know what else to do." Grant scuffed his boot in the scraps of hay on the floor. "If the story comes out, the fallout could be devastating."

"But you're not involved," his mother said. "How can that affect you?"

Grant shoved his hands in his pockets. He'd spent too many sleepless nights considering this. "Afraid proof of my innocence is going to be hard to come by, my word against Red's. But even if I can convince the Association I'm not involved, what if they strip me of my wins? Try to recoup prize money?" The whispers about a cheating Armstrong, the blow to his pride would be awful, and financially…any savings he'd managed to build had been rolled into the Rocking A and the purchase of land from the Hearsts. His whole family could pay consequences even if he was somehow cleared of any cheating himself.

"All of that and you didn't tell *us*, either." Wes frowned. "To me, that's the most puzzling part. Your family. All around you. People ready to step up to settle this thing beside you got not a word about any of it until months later. Why?"

Wes was the lawyer in the family. He was good with words. Winning arguments against him was next to impossible. The tone in his voice suggested he was determined to get to the bottom of the issue immediately.

The last thing Grant wanted to admit was his shame. He should have known better, but Red had known his weakness: his own pride.

"Mia Romero works for *The Way West*. The magazine. It covers the rodeo circuit." Grant shoved his hands in his pockets. "I haven't heard any whispers about the cheating yet, but when they leak, wherever I am will turn into a circus for a bit. I can't tell if she knows something already or if she's a danger because she will probably start asking questions about me, but I'd rather not appear in any coverage about Western Days at all. And somehow I need help warning our neighbors about how much to tell her."

Everyone was silent as they absorbed the problem of Mia's arrival.

"So he doesn't tell us anything until he needs our help?" Matt said. "Is anyone surprised?"

He wanted to explain about protecting them and the Armstrong name, but Grant knew he deserved that arrow.

Wes pushed on. "What's the piece you aren't saying, Grant? Why didn't you talk to any of us about this before now?"

"I didn't…" Grant studied the faces of his family and realized this was the moment he'd been so afraid of all along. There was no way out of this except through it. "I've built this reputation of being the bad boy. Here at home. There on the circuit. The Bad Boy of Bronc Busting, right? That was Red's idea, too. A brand. It's a new age of rodeo, and everyone needs a brand." Grant shook his head. He could remember the way Red had talked up the "brand" as if it was yesterday. Grant had eaten up every word, believing that his "personality" was exactly what rodeo needed. "I overheard Red and Trey discussing their next steps. Trey asked what would happen if they got caught. That answer was simple. Blame it all on me. Red explained that no one would bat an eyelash to find out this whole scheme was my idea all along. They might get some bruises, but I'd be the one to suffer the fall."

His father snorted. "And you believed that steaming pile of—"

"He expected all of us to believe it," his mother interrupted. "That's why he didn't tell us. He was afraid we'd believe Grant Armstrong was capable of such a thing. This boy we've known since he was fifteen and tame as a bobcat when he arrived here..." His mother stood and pointed her finger at him. "You better give me a minute here, son, because I am angry that you'd even entertain that thought for a second." Then she marched out of the barn.

They all watched her go. Walt's grimace when he turned back would be funny except it transitioned to pity immediately. "I believe the hole you dug for yourself is going to take some major work to climb out of, son."

"I expected you to wonder if I was telling the truth. What would stop me from agreeing to such a plan? I wanted to be at the top of the pile, and it was guaranteed to put me there. My best friend. My mentor. It makes so much sense." Grant propped his hands on his hips. "No one experienced a second of doubt that I would walk away because I wanted to do the right thing the right way?" How could that be true?

"My son doesn't trust his family." Walt shook his head slowly. "Now I believe that I'm almost as angry as your mama." He left the barn at a mosey instead of a march, but it was easy enough to tell by the slump of his shoulders that his father was disappointed, too.

Grant flopped down on the hay bale and dropped his head in his hands. "Anybody else want to heap shame on?" The misery he'd experienced in the early days was nothing like this. The center of his chest burned and he had no idea how to put the fire out.

Clay clapped a hand on his shoulder. "Nah. I get it. It's still silly, to think the people who know you best would believe anything like that, but I'd wager the five of us understand where you're coming from."

Grant watched Travis open his mouth to say something and then snap it closed, twice. Of the five of them, he and Travis were the most alike. But while Travis had retreated when he'd first got to the ranch as a kid, Grant had planted his boots squarely and fought until all the rough edges had been filed down. They often butted heads, but he and Travis understood each other, too. In their own minds, neither one of them measured up to the other guys.

"Go on. Hit me with it." Grant waved him over. "I told you not to listen to your doubts when you were getting ready to start fostering. Lecture me. Yell at me. You were right not to put me in line to take over when you wanted to back out. I'm the problem. Always have been. Got us grounded for most of our junior year in high school by convincing you to come with me to the rodeo at the fairgrounds in Eagle after Dad told me I couldn't go. Then, there was the time I wrecked Dad's truck because I was trying to drive backwards down Main Street before school." He shook his head. "My birth mother's drinking, landing in foster care... I made sure more than one foster family washed their hands of me before I met Prue and Walt. The Armstrongs outlasted even my own anger, and I thought I was coming to terms with that wildness, but I make bad choices. Always have. This time, I trusted the wrong people. That's all on me."

Travis tossed his hat down in disgust. "All this time, and all this emotional angst because you didn't even know us. It's a problem, Grant. You can try to pretend that it's a joke that you expected us to believe the worst of you, but it ain't." Instead of storming off, Travis inhaled and exhaled slowly. "You're lucky we know where that comes from, that fear that people will only believe the worst, me better than any of them."

Grant nodded. He was right. Travis had held so much of his past close to his chest until the doubts about his ability to be a good foster parent forced them out. None of them wanted him to carry all that old baggage around. How silly was it that he'd been doing his version of the same?

"I am lucky. I needed a reminder of how lucky, I guess." Grant cursed under his breath. "Now I gotta figure out how to make that right with Mom and Dad."

Matt whistled. "We are going to need more help with all of this, especially that part. Anyone know where Sarah, Jordan and Keena are?" Keena, Travis's girlfriend and the town doc, had proved herself to be an expert strategist when he'd accidentally messed everything up between them. "If we let them in on the planning, we improve our odds of smoothing things over here and containing Mia Romero's access around town to stories and gossip about Grant."

Wes stepped forward. He was their leader, so they all waited for him to study the problem from all angles and propose the best course of action. "Absolutely, we tell them. Let's get them some good information to work with first. They're Armstrongs in all but name…" He shot Matt a look to shut him down. The question about how soon he, Clay and Travis would fix the name part hung in the air between them. "Not now, Matt.

Let's work on the immediate problem first. Do you know how long Mia will be in Prospect?"

Grant shook his head.

"Okay, do you know where she is right now or should I call the lodge?" He pulled out his phone, prepared to call Sarah for intel.

"In town. She has to stop in at the Garage to check on repairing the tire, for sure." Grant ran his damp hands down his jeans, nervous at the thought of tracking Mia down. "We could send Matt to charm some information from her. She was as bedazzled by his face as every other woman he meets."

Wes looked as if he was taking this suggestion seriously. "Having an eye on her is important. We can rope in Faye at the diner. Until we know whether Mia has been tipped off about the cheating or not, it's hard to determine the proper plan." Then he smiled at Grant. "But not one of us will be as good at testing the waters as you." Grant wanted to object, but the idea had him speechless. "You have all the facts, you've been on the rodeo circuit, know all the players and even the magazine Mia works for. None of us have that. Haven't you heard the saying that offense is the best defense? Find out what she knows first. Then we'll move on to the next step."

CHAPTER SIX

S<small>AM</small>, <small>THE RETIRED</small> postal carrier who staffed the Prospect Library on Saturdays, put a cold bottle of water down on the table in front of Mia, and she realized she'd been poring over newspaper archives for so long that her shoulders had stiffened into an awkward hunch. The pop of her neck as she straightened up and stretched out her arms made Sam wince. "Shoulda forced you to take a break sooner, I reckon."

Mia removed the cap from the bottle of water. "I do that. I get so caught up in research that the time escapes me. When I resurface, everything hurts, but I can't believe how much time has passed." After a long sip, she added, "And that's my favorite kind of day, Sam. Can you believe it? Give me a library and a laptop over a hot sandy beach, please."

He straightened the pile of books on her table. "Well, now, they say variety is the spice of life, so I'll accept it even if I don't understand."

Delighted by his dry response, Mia laughed.

She was exaggerating about her love of research but only a little.

She'd been traveling backward in time for hours, getting a clear picture of the way Prospect had changed in the past decade. In the beginning, she'd been disappointed by the lack of information about Grant Armstrong, but she'd started to identify different people in town, following their threads as if they were characters in a soap opera. When she stumbled across a photo that allowed her to put a face to the character, the whole story grew more solid in her mind.

"You finding everything you need?" Sam asked. "If you come back on Monday, the librarian can give you better instruction on where to find what you're looking for. Lillian's got a whole card catalog stored in her brain."

Since most of Sam's suggestions had been to vaguely point her to the filing cabinets containing microfilm of the defunct Prospect newspaper, *The Prospect Post*, Mia was certain he was correct and she would definitely need more time in the library. "You've done a fine job, Sam. I appreciate your help." Mia braced her hands at the small of her back as she stood to walk around the square table in the center of the library. The bones of the church that had been built here made far more beautiful architecture than many of the blocky municipal buildings she'd visited. "This place is amazing. So pretty and so calming. How long have you worked here?"

Sam cleared his throat awkwardly. Was she making him uncomfortable? "I started volunteering a few months ago. Strictly part-time. The doc… Dr. Singh thought it might do me some good to get out of the house. Interact more with folks. Take my mind off of some of the worries that cropped up after my wife died." He turned in a slow circle as he surveyed the room. "Never was a big reader myself, but my wife made regular stops in here. Nice to be reminded of her. Retirement has not been everything I'd expected. I guess that's down to doing it alone when I'd assumed I'd have my best friend keeping me busy. My wife never ran out of activities for us."

Mia worried that she'd stumbled on to a difficult subject. "I sure am thankful you decided to add volunteering here, Sam. I bet your wife would love it that you're making your own activities now."

"Hadn't quite thought of it like that. Could be you're right." Sam motioned with his finger toward the door. "Closing up in about half an hour, miss. Might be a good idea to get to a stopping point for the day."

Ah, he was ready for quitting time. Mia had been there often enough, watching the clock, to understand the urge. She removed the film she'd finished scanning from the machine and replaced it in the box. "Do you know anything about the building's history?" When Jordan had led her to what appeared to be a church instead of a library, Mia had been confused. Then Jordan explained how all the historical structures in Prospect had been carefully maintained and many of them had taken on new lives, even while they kept the original facades, and Mia had been instantly charmed. A library inside of a church.

As a woman who loved the written word, she found the arrangement fitting. Simple stained glass windows lined both long walls and a larger window formed a beautiful frame for any preacher lucky enough to stand in front of a congregation here. More modern glass windows let in light along the sides of the church closest to the entrance, but mellow red-and-gold light floated down from above.

Spending time researching here could never be a hardship.

"Believe this building replaced one that burned around 1900, but the church itself was founded not too long after the town sprung up during the silver rush days. Had a couple of renovations to make the building safe. Library was moved out of the town hall annex in the seventies, if I recall correctly." He frowned as he considered that. "There's a plaque outside near the flagpole with the dates and information on the congregation if you'd like more specific facts for your story."

"I'll check that out." She wondered if he would recognize the pun. Check out. In the library. But decided not to get distracted. "Are there any books about the town and its history?" If she had any extra time, Mia needed research into the background of the Colorado Cookie Queen, if only to make her conversations with Sarah and Jordan easier.

Sam tapped his chin and moved to his computer to type what she figured were a few keyword searches. "Well, I'll be. Nothing comes up. You'd think a place like this would inspire a history for sure. Some of the tall tales I've heard about the original silver miners who began all this sound like action movies." His confusion cleared. "Better check with the librarian on Monday, too, Mia. Can't say I believe there's not a single book dedicated to Prospect. Closest we'd have is Sadie Hearst's cookbooks. She does some storytellin' in them, about Prospect. We do have a complete collection of those. Would you like to apply for a library card? I can send you home with a few of those volumes."

The memory of books lining the counter in Sadie's old apartment at the Majestic flashed through her mind. She had a hunch that might make for a nice start on the Sadie Hearst cookbook library. She was surprised Jordan hadn't pressed the stack in her hands and told her not to skip a page of background.

"Not necessary this afternoon. Thanks, Sam, you've been a big help. I hope I'll have a chance to say goodbye before I leave town." Mia closed her laptop as it occurred to her that the retired mail carrier himself might be an excellent source of town news. Sam could have good information about Grant Armstrong if she knew how to access it. The clock was ticking on her time in Prospect, so Mia decided she had to take a shot. "I was surprised at how often the Armstrongs landed on the front page of the newspaper. Seems like their family is front and center in Prospect."

Sam sniffed as he considered that. "Guess Walt and Prue and their boys do a lot for the town. The Mercantile's the unofficial community center, with lots of coming and going. Walt's family has been out at the Rocking A for generations. His dad and mine were fishing partners. Prue moved in after they got married, can't imagine her anywhere else, despite that silly divorce."

"How many sons do they have? Is it four or five?" she asked, even though she'd carefully jotted down the names and occupations of all five Armstrongs. She'd started scrolling through the newspaper archives hunting for stories about Western Days, but somewhere along the way, she'd gotten offtrack and widened her scope to any mention of Grant or his family.

Mia didn't have to think too hard to figure out where she'd gone wrong.

The front page color photo of Grant Armstrong leading the parade down Main Street as the grand marshal, tall and handsome on a shiny black horse, would be hard to forget. He'd been younger, in his twenties, and clearly hailed as a hometown hero.

"Five boys. All adopted after ending up in foster care."

Surprised, Mia spun to face Sam. That was a new detail. It seemed important to the story. "They were part of the foster care system?"

"Walt and Prue opened up the ranch to boys who needed a different kind of place. None of them were cowboys before they got here, but they sure found their way once they did. First met them all through Prospect's high school rodeo club. Used to meet out at my place, long time ago. The ranch made them feel safe, gave them confidence, Walt always said. These five became Armstrongs, too. Now they're doing the same for another generation. Travis has two boys on the ranch now who he's fostering. News around town is that the oldest is smart as a whip and the youngest is…a real humdinger." Sam took the box of microfilm and returned it to the filing cabinet.

"A real humdinger?" Mia repeated slowly, amused and charmed at the description. It could mean anything from devil to angel, but either way, it seemed sweet. Old-fashioned, maybe, but also supportive somehow?

Sam held out his hands. "Librarian asked for backup for when the boy's class visits, based on the teacher's recommendation. Apparently he asks enough questions for a battalion of fifth graders."

Mia laughed. "That reminds me of the comment on my fifth-grade report card. 'Could learn more if she talked less.'"

Sam's rusty chuckle pleased her. She wanted to push for more details, but she was enjoying their conversation.

"As I recall, a couple of the original Armstrong boys were live wires, too. All good-hearted and smart, but Grant? That boy came into town wild. When our rodeo club met, he'd be first in the saddle and the first bucked off into the dirt. Never stopped him. It was like, once he found the horses and the barn and the thrill of rodeo, he had to make up for lost time. He was exciting to watch as a kid, but when he hit the circuit, every eye was locked on Grant Armstrong." Sam's eyes twinkled. "He eventually learned to stay in the saddle and win."

Mia could easily think of several photos of

Grant holding prizes that had been featured in the magazine.

"Not sure how much time has knocked down the rough edges, but he'd help any neighbor in need. Wes came home after law school, helped run the ranch, while the rest of 'em went here and there. All them boys came home to help get the ranch ready for the fosters. Now they're pairing off with the Hearst sisters and the new doctor in town. 'Spect if we had a newspaper these days, the Armstrongs would be newsworthy still." Sam tugged the chain on the desk lamp to turn off the light. "Wouldn't be surprised if there weren't wedding announcements in the near future, either."

Mia stored her laptop, tablet and pen in the bag she carried everywhere, before slipping the strap over her head to hang across her torso. Her time with Sam was drawing to a close, so she decided to press her luck. "Surely Grant Armstrong will be leaving town soon, though. He's still a big rodeo star, right?"

She was pleased at how innocent her query sounded. It flowed perfectly in with the conversation. Only someone who was suspicious of her in the first place would guess she was digging for information.

"Heard he retired." Sam shrugged as he pointed toward the front door. "I hope he don't come to regret that like I did in the early days. People don't know how much they need important work to do until they've got entirely too much time on their hands."

Disappointed that she'd hit a dead end, Mia bit her lip as she tried to find another angle. "Maybe he has a plan, a new business idea, or..." She let the thought trail off, hoping that Sam would take up the invitation to spread any tidbit of gossip.

"Guess we'll see. That boy knows horses better'n anybody around, so I imagine he'll land on his feet if staying in Prospect is his plan." Sam dipped his head. "And if a pretty lady catches his eye in the meantime, this place makes a good home."

Mia froze with her hand on the library's door handle. Was he implying that she might be such a pretty lady? As in she was pretty and also a lady or as in the pretty lady for Grant Armstrong?

Then she realized Sam believed she was fishing for information on Grant for a completely different reason than her real impetus. He saw a woman hunting for information on a romantic interest.

Would he spread that news around town?

If so, it could help her. Most people loved love and wouldn't mind assisting her if that was her goal.

But if Grant Armstrong heard she had a crush on him, would he know it was her journalistic

instinct prompting the questions or would he believe they were trapped in a movie-like rom-com?

"Let me get that door for you, ma'am," Sam
said and carefully brushed her hand aside. "Time
to lock up now and head for dinner."

Mia followed his very polite urging and stepped
out on the landing where steps led down to the neat
sidewalk, bemused at how easily library-volunteer
Sam had ended her line of questioning. Had it been
deliberate? Hard to say, but he was whistling as he
locked the door behind them.

She hadn't realized she was still watching him
when Sam straightened and pointed at a parked
truck. "Well, now, speak of the devil."

Mia turned to see Grant leaning one arm out
the driver's side window of a pickup. "You talking about me, Sam? You know how the rest of
that saying goes. 'Speak of the devil and he shall
appear.'" He patted the truck door. "At your service."

"Some things do not change, Grant Armstrong."
Sam's rusty chuckle was a little less adorable this
time, mainly because he was walking away.

Leaving her to face Grant all alone.

Grant's lips curled slowly. "Let me buy you
dinner at the Ace High, Mia, and I'll answer any
question you ask."

Mia's mouth was dry, but she tipped her chin
up and nodded.

When his amusement spread into a full-blown grin, Mia gulped and headed for her car. She'd follow him to the restaurant and use the time to lecture herself not to be taken in by a handsome man's smile. Grant Armstrong was no devil, but if she wasn't careful, he would become a temptation she couldn't refuse.

CHAPTER SEVEN

CHAPTER SEVEN

As GRANT SLID into the booth across from Mia at the Ace High, he regretted leaving the barn before he picked Wes's brain for a strategy. His orders had seemed straightforward: find out what Mia knew.

But as he'd driven into town, he'd realized that discovering the real reason Mia had arrived in Prospect without tipping her off that there was a story he was hoping to keep hidden would require careful moves.

Grant Armstrong didn't do caution all that well.

Never had.

He could do blunt.

Sometimes he might try for charming. It worked often enough that he always had plenty of company out on the rodeo circuit.

Diplomacy wasn't in his saddlebag.

It might be too late to learn at this point.

Mia smiled up at Faye as she put napkins and silverware on the table.

"Well, now, I wondered if I was going to have

an Armstrong-less dinner service, but here comes Grant to keep my streak alive." Faye squeezed his shoulder and met his wince with a smile. "I'm Faye. How'd you get stuck with this rascal tonight?"

Faye had been as close as family, growing up as she had next door, so she was on the list of people he wanted keeping an eye on Mia as she moved through Prospect. Running the Ace High meant that Faye always knew what was happening in town before everyone else. He wasn't sure anyone had had the chance to brief her yet.

"This is Mia Romero. She's writing a profile of Prospect and Western Days for *The Way West*." Grant watched Mia closely as she shook hands with Faye. It was impossible to find any warning signs in her open, friendly grin. He had no doubt she'd made an admirer of Sam, and Faye would be next.

His mother was right. Cute was dangerous. People didn't see her coming until it was too late. Mia was dressed casually, and her bright eyes gleamed with humor. He wouldn't mind sitting down to dinner across from her, but it would be better not to have this story he wanted to stay far away from standing between them.

"A profile! Well, now, I'm surprised Grant's mama isn't personally escorting you around town and rolling out our version of the red carpet. Prue will want to make sure you don't miss a single, solitary highlight. She loves this place." Faye thumped her pen on her notepad. "Tonight we've got roast beef or roasted chicken, honey-glazed carrots, scalloped potatoes, parmesan-crusted broccoli." She sighed. "That broccoli is a new recipe, so I'll be curious to get some feedback. Gran insists she's an artist and she needs freedom to explore ingredients. Whereas I believe we're business people and if it ain't broke, we don't fix the steamed broccoli and cheese sauce that even the Garcia twins will eat." Faye closed her eyes before shaking her head. "Never mind all that. Choice is simple tonight—beef or chicken. Which will it be?"

"You know me. Beef. Always beef." Grant tugged his hat off and set it down, interested in the way Mia studied his movements as he ruffled out the hat hair. Women had complimented his hair often enough, but he enjoyed the boost of Mia's attention.

"I'll have the chicken. I like to buck a trend." Mia licked her lips before turning to face Faye. "And if you have a minute or two, I'd love to get some thoughts from you about Western Days and what it means to the town, to your family and business, a personal story. I want to cover the centennial for the magazine, so I'm working on the background now."

Faye slipped her pen behind her ear. "Oh, Western Days? Do I have stories. This one here—" Grant grunted as she thumped his shoulder hard "—when he was a reckless youth, managed to dump a full carafe of lemonade on my new dress, the one Gran made especially for me to wear on the float all the high school senior girls got to ride on that year. And it was before the parade, so yours truly looked like a drenched raccoon, just waving to beat the band. Once in a lifetime, and Grant had to splash me as he clip-clopped by on his fancy horse." Grant winced. "Don't know if it was because he was the only one of those Armstrong boys I never dated for two or three weeks before coming to my senses. Or if that helped me make my decision to avoid him. Most likely a chicken-and-egg situation, I'm guessing. What can I get you to drink, Grant?"

He coughed and eased out of her reach. "Iced tea, please."

"No lemonade? Hmm. His manners have improved over the years, Mia," Faye said sweetly. "Can I get you the same?"

When Mia nodded, Faye hurried away.

It left the two of them alone again and him with no good opening gambit.

"Does Faye hold a grudge? Beyond breaking your high school heart by never being your girlfriend? Are you worried about your food when you come in here?" Mia asked as she fiddled with her cutlery. Before he could answer, Faye slid a basket of rolls and cornbread onto the table, deposited their drinks and whizzed away.

"Good question. Obviously, yes, she holds a grudge. I'll never live that accident down. I was riding a new horse at the time, one that wasn't quite ready to be out in a crowd. He shied and by the time I got him back under control, I had scattered the crowd and bumped the carafe she was serving from. She brings it up at least once every time I come home to Prospect." Grant shook his head. "But no, I'm not worried about the food. Her grandmother runs the kitchen. Poisoning me would cause too much trouble."

"If you ruined Faye's dress, the one that Gran made special, she might not be a fan of you, either." Mia shrugged as she sipped her tea.

Grant pursed his lips. "Now that you mention it…" He waited for her to smile. "At this point, if it's poison, I'm probably immune. This is the only sit-down restaurant in town, so I've eaten here so often that they've been spoiled for choice in ways to get their revenge by now."

Mia nodded. "Sure. Unless they're biding their time, waiting for the right opportunity."

"You hoping for a murder while you're sitting in the front row?" he asked.

She shrugged. "I am a lucky woman, Grant.

The universe drops unexpected gifts in my lap all the time. I've learned that if I'm open to fate, there's no limit to what might happen." She leaned forward. "Even revenge served cold at long last. My career needs a big story, one that will land me on the cover. Gran, Faye and I possibly converged at this point in time for that very reason." The teasing glint in her eyes was tempting, but Faye brought their dinners before he could choose between flirting, or... What was the other option? Why couldn't he name one?

"Whoa, this is a plate of food," Mia said softly.

Grant watched her consider her options before he took a bite of his roast beef. It was perfection, as always. If Faye was playing the long game, waiting to bring him down, he was ready to take his chances.

"So, no repair. New tire." Grant eased back against the booth, determined to pretend he was making casual conversation. "No easy solution from the universe for your flat."

"Not beyond the timely arrival of two strong, helpful, handsome cowboys in my moment of need." Mia popped a bit of broccoli in her mouth, chewed and nodded her approval. "New tires will be here Monday afternoon at the earliest. Dante and Lucky and their twins are great, though. I was happy to have the introduction. And then there's you, turning up like a lucky penny every time I turn around. All things considered, my faith in the universe is unshaken." She closed her eyes as she sampled the scalloped potatoes. "Oh my."

Grant's attempt at amusement came out as a choked grunt. Her face as she learned why no one complained too much about the missing menu options at the Ace High was unforgettable. The chef's way with potatoes was miraculous. Mia blinked slowly and laughed. "I wasn't expecting heaven on a plate."

Grant had to force himself to return his attention to his own dinner when she grinned at him. The warm glow that grew his chest by her happiness surprised him. It was too much.

"Everyone in town has been lovely. The Hearsts. The Garcias. And Sam? Over at the library? He was a big help with the newspaper archives. It's sad that the newspaper closed." Mia sipped her drink.

"Yeah, small towns can't support them, I guess." Grant turned his fork in his hand absentmindedly. Here was another opening but he wasn't sure how to capitalize on it. He needed Wes's lawyer brain right about now.

"Print is expensive. Distribution costs. Writers and photographers. If there's not enough advertising, these newspaper owners have to make hard decisions." She sighed. "Magazine owners, too, for that matter. My mother harps on falling advertising revenue and the need for bigger and bigger stories often enough that even the travel writer has it memorized."

Grant put his fork down. "Your mother? Does she work for the magazine, too?"

Mia huffed out a breath. "Interesting question. She…owns it and runs it, but her work is less hands on and more…making phone calls to tell other people to get their hands-on or else. My grandfather knew how to do every single job, even down to answering the front desk phone. My mother prefers a less direct approach." Her lop-sided grimace was adorable. "I used to think she was only holding on long enough to drop every-thing in my lap and head for a resort somewhere, but she has proven resistant to that solution."

Her grimace was almost adorable enough to distract him from the fact that she was more than a reporter. Mia was not just an employee, but had a family stake in getting important sto-ries for *The Way West*.

"I needed to get some space from Billings, so this little weekend visit was my solution."

He wished he'd spent more time preparing for this dinner conversation, because the next re-mark…

"So you see why, if I could write a story about the real reason Grant Armstrong left the rodeo circuit behind, I'd get all kinds of coverage for Prospect, Western Days and anything else I wanted. Scooping every reporter that follows the sport would be huge." Mia pinched a chunk off the cornbread muffin, applied a dab of butter and popped it in her mouth. She sighed happily, and Grant realized she wasn't acting out her pleasure for effect. The food at the Ace demanded a pause for enjoyment every now and then.

"Instead of listening to my mother's threats about closing down the magazine," Mia said as she buttered another bite, "I could make my own decisions." Her serious expression convinced him that, whatever she did or didn't know about his situation, this was the truth. Mia wanted a story that would prove her capability to her mother.

Since he'd been tormenting himself with worries about how his own family viewed him and his traits, Grant understood where she was coming from.

"My family needed me here. That's the truth. We were all involved in this renovation so that we could take in fosters. The Rocking A ranch house was too small, cramped and out-of-date. Since all five of us needed the ranch when we were kids, we all wanted to help Travis. And it was a good time to leave. Smart people go out when they're on top. Sliding back to the middle or worse is a sad way to be remembered." Not as gut-punching as being remembered as a cheater who never deserved the prizes he'd won, but that was the part of the story he wanted to knock down or at least keep away from.

Grant rested his elbow on the table and waited to see where she took the conversation next. This was the story he'd given his family in the beginning, when he'd been desperate to deflect their anxious concern. They hadn't believed it, but they knew him too well.

Mia's eyes were warm as she mirrored his pose, one elbow on the table as if they were having an easy discussion. "Sure. What else could chase you out of the limelight? You seem to be lying pretty low here in the shadows. That surprises me. Sam mentioned how hard filling his time in retirement has been. Are you finding the same issue? No other projects on the horizon?"

Grant tipped his chin up. "Lying low? This whole town knows my every movement, and if anyone from that old life wanted to track me down, seems like it would be easy enough to guess home might be a good place to look." He held his arms out to show he had nothing to hide.

"Okay. Your friends could track you down, but I guess they know the whole story about why you left anyway. I'm trying to remember if I've seen any heartwarming background pieces about the rodeo star who was adopted or even any background on where you grew up." Mia took a bite of her chicken as she seemed to be considering her next question, and Grant wished he had a good distraction. Telling her that it didn't fit with his "image" would make him feel twice as foolish as admitting it to his family.

Mia didn't let the topic go. "I'm not sure anyone started asking questions until you failed to show up for Nationals in December. That was weird. Before you disappeared, the odds were good that you might even take the lead this year as one of the league's richest overall purse winners. You've been on such an amazing ride. Even I heard about it from the travel desk."

That was true, even if the "ride" had been carefully orchestrated by Red Williams. He'd never been in it for money, but he'd eaten up all the attention.

"Well, you know how it is, one cowboy leaves, another one takes his place." Grant pinched the brim of his hat resting on the table. Should he drop names? But if she were the one to mention Red Williams or Trey McClintock here, Grant could take that as solid proof that Mia knew more than she was admitting. Trey was the most likely candidate to step up to keep the scheme alive.

They were quiet as he considered conversational tactics and discarded each one and Mia methodically finished every morsel on her plate.

Instead, she flopped back against the booth and covered her stomach with both hands. "I can see how you would be drawn back to Prospect if the appeal of your family is half as powerful as Faye's food. In fact, I'm surprised you ever left. I'd love to know more about that, how you hit the circuit in the first place, but you haven't answered my question about your plans or any projects. What comes next for Grant Armstrong?"

Her question was valid. He needed the answer himself. "I'm organizing a new competition for Western Days. That's been keeping me busy." If she bothered to really consider that, she'd quickly determine that last part was false. A change in subject would be good. Why couldn't he find one?

If this had been a normal conversation, like a date, where getting to know him was an important step, Grant would have been happy to tell her wild tales of life on the road. Fans loved those stories. Most of the women he met were fans in one way or another.

He couldn't tell if this was a simple change in topic or a subtle probe for another way into his story.

"Are we talking on the record or off?" he asked, reminding himself as much as her that any conversation between them was dangerous.

She propped her chin on her hand. "Well, now, what an interesting way to pose that question. You have something you'd like to share that would need to be off-the-record, Grant? I am a very good listener."

He realized that he'd stumbled badly. He should have kept to his original story about the renovations and leaving on top. Mia was smart enough to realize that he'd let on more than he should have.

Grant didn't have time to attempt a recovery, because his mother stepped into the dining room, her eyes scanning the crowd. There was no doubt in his mind that she was a heat-seeking missile aimed right for them.

Relief settled over him. She would have been the first call his brothers made to rally the troops.

Prue Armstrong might be disappointed that he didn't share everything that was happening because he'd been afraid his family would believe the stories were true, but there was no way she'd abandon him in the midst of battle. She was their chief strategist, and she was going to save the day here.

"There's my boy," she trilled theatrically as she crossed the dining room, waving here and there as if she were a star acknowledging her fans. "I heard you came into town for a good meal."

When she wrapped her arms around his neck in a warm hug, Grant patted her back awkwardly, very aware that his mother had captured every bit of attention in the room and it was all now centered on their table.

His mother stepped back and turned toward to Mia. "And who is this? Introduce me to your friend, Grant."

The way her voice carried through the Ace convinced Grant that this was part of an escape plan. Retellings of this meeting would sweep through town overnight, with extra color commentary added that would influence how his neighbors welcomed Mia after.

So he cleared his throat and announced, "This is Mia Romero. She's working on a story for *The Way West* all about Western Days." He didn't glance around to make sure everyone heard him. He'd have to rely on the power of the story to carry it where it needed to go.

"Oh my goodness." His mother clapped her hands together. "Publicity for our little festival! How wonderful. I know everyone will have a good story to tell you about our famous weekend. You know, we all take part in it. The whole thing depends on volunteers."

Grant would have laughed at her obvious campaign to recruit helping hands, if he wasn't aware of the accompanying message she was sending: tell the nice reporter visiting town only the glowing stories about Western Days.

To solidify her pitch, his mother turned to

survey the room. "We'll be holding an informal meeting about the festival tomorrow afternoon at the Mercantile to discuss committees and next steps. Everyone's invited. I'll be serving Sadie Hearst's famous Palomino Peanut Butter Cookies to everyone who drops by…just to hear the plans." She held her hands up as if to show she had no ulterior motives and there was nothing up her sleeves. He was pretty certain everyone listening was already wise to her ways.

Except Mia Romero.

"You should join us, Mia." His mother tapped the table. "Get a solid start on your article that way."

Mia nodded. "What an excellent idea and such great timing." How she held his stare made Grant wonder if Mia was an expert at reading between the lines. Did it matter if she knew exactly what they were hoping to accomplish with this scene? "Grant tells me he's been working hard on this year's festival. Sounds like there must be big things brewing."

His mother glanced down at him. He could see the calculations in her eyes. What could she volunteer him to do right now that he wouldn't be able to escape, thanks to Mia's presence?

"Can I get you a plate?" Faye asked when it became clear that his mother hadn't written an exit line into her script.

"Oh no, Faye, I've got a fridge full of leftovers I need to run out to the ranch before they go bad as it is," his mother said. "It's been too long since I saw this rascal." She nodded at him, and neither one of them acknowledged that it had been less than three hours since she'd swept out of the barn with an epic cold shoulder.

"Well, the timing is excellent." Mia pointed at Faye. "If you'll give me the bill for this meal, I will be able to repay at least one of the Armstrongs for helping me with a flat tire." She craned her neck to make sure the rest of the diners were listening. The resemblance to his mother's delivery was uncanny.

Faye ripped off the top page from her order pad and passed it over. "Holly can ring you up at the front there. If I somehow miss this planning meeting tomorrow," Faye said without looking at his mother, "I hope you'll come back in for another meal or two before you go, Mia. I have many stories to pass along of Grant Armstrong's misbegotten youth. Not for the article. Just because."

Mia grinned at Grant before nodding. "Definitely. I wouldn't miss my chance to try more from the Ace High's kitchen."

After she slid out of the booth, Mia touched his hand briefly. "I will definitely see you again, Grant." Then she offered his mother her hand. "And Prue, I spent the afternoon reading front-page stories about you and your family. It's nice to meet you in person. Can't wait to find out what you have in store for me…and the town's big celebration."

His mother took Mia's vacated seat, but Grant watched Mia slide through the tables toward the cashier and the exit. Before she left, she glanced over her shoulder at him, one corner of her mouth curled in amusement. They might have successfully spread the word throughout town about what the official story should be if Mia showed up on any doorstep, but he wasn't convinced she didn't see right through their tactics.

"No one told me she was adorable." His mother tangled her fingers together on the table.

"Does it matter?" Grant asked, fidgeting as he was caught dead center in her sights. He had the urge to defend himself and remind her that he'd definitely called Mia "cute," but he had a feeling that was his mother's ultimate goal: to get Grant to admit he was attracted to Mia Romero. Why? Grant had no idea. His mother always had an end goal for her sons: happy marriages and settling back down in Prospect. If Mia was the one to tempt Grant into staying, his mother would change sides in the middle of battle.

If one of his brothers had been here, Grant could have created a diversion by starting an argument.

"It might matter, Grant." The gleam in his mother's eyes wasn't reassuring.

It commonly accompanied her matchmaking efforts.

He needed a distraction pretty darn quick. "My gut says she knows something is up, but I'm not getting any hints that she has a line on the story yet. I do think she saw straight through your acting."

His mother waved a hand. "I wasn't acting. We'll have a preplanning meeting. I want to make sure Matt has all the help he needs. I also believe it's important that we make Prospect look good in this story. If that's what she saw, mission accomplished."

Grant rolled up the straw wrapper as he considered that. She was right. "You gonna be mad at me forever?" He had tried to prepare himself for that, to be on the outside of the circle because he was the one who couldn't avoid trouble. That's where the guilt had come from. Prue and Walt had done their best, but there was something in him that let them down.

Losing his career hurt.

He would never recover if he couldn't get everything between him and his parents straightened out.

The way she rolled her eyes immediately reassured him. "The only thing I'm gonna do forever is love you, Grant Armstrong, and you know it."

He gripped her hands to hold her attention. "I'm sorry. This time I messed up and had no idea it was even happening."

Prue frowned. "You didn't do a thing wrong except carry too much of this yourself, son. Consider how you'd explain such foolishness if it was one of your brothers acting so silly." Her lips curled. "Pretty sure you get that from your dad."

She touched his cheek.

Overcome with her easy acceptance and the love that was clear in her eyes, Grant said, "Thank you."

She patted his hands and slid out of the booth before he could apologize again. "Don't you miss this meeting at the Mercantile, you hear me? I love you, but I will volunteer you for more work if you aren't there to defend yourself."

She marched away to make small talk with one of the teachers from the high school before he could agree or disagree.

"Seems like Prue has rallied the troops. Not much to worry about, right?" Faye asked as she cleared the dishes from the table in front of him.

"Hope so. Nothing to do but hold on for the ride." Grant shook his head. He wasn't a worrier like Travis or Clay. His whole life, he did the best he could. Put him on a bucking horse and he'd hold on until he couldn't anymore. Transplant him from the home he knew to a ranch in the mountains, and he'd strap in until the ride smoothed out. Even putting an end to the career he'd built had been a simple decision. All it had taken was pointing his truck toward home and never looking back.

Mia's arrival had given him that nervous knot in his stomach, which made him think that even if the story that would change everything never came out, something big was still about to happen and he wasn't prepared.

CHAPTER EIGHT

MIA'S HUNCH THAT something changed on Saturday, after the theatrical encounter with Prue Armstrong in the Ace High, was confirmed by the second breakfast at the Majestic Prospect Lodge. Instead of a family occasion where the Hearsts bantered and bickered while they all ate toast, Sarah tapped on the door as soon as Mia stepped out of the shower. She was holding a tray with a covered plate and a small carafe.

"Good morning. Jordan discovered these trays and plate covers when she was rummaging through Sadie's storage closet. Apparently your stay here is a 'golden opportunity' to test our room service items." Sarah's smile was warm but it didn't make it all the way to her eyes.

Mia hated the sinking feeling that came from being shut out of the Hearsts' easy company, but she took the tray with a smile. Whatever happened between her and Grant, Sarah and Jordan had been excellent hosts. "I'm happy to be the test subject. It looks like another beautiful day outside." The curtains were open because she'd wanted more of the bright sunshine.

"Better get out and explore while we have it. I have my fingers crossed we've seen the last of the messy winter storms, but the forecast does include flurries and cold for the rest of the week. The lake is pretty all four seasons, and if you want to walk, there's a marina down the hill. It's still closed but we've got it on the list of things to work on, too." Sarah awkwardly glanced over her shoulder. "We're getting an early start today, headed over to the Rocking A for a family… meal. I hope you won't mind having some time to yourself." She wrinkled her nose. Mia wasn't certain she was reading it correctly but she would label it regret. "Prue mentioned that you're planning to come to the meeting at the Mercantile. It's in the center of Prospect, across from the Ace High. Do you remember seeing it?" She rocked from one foot to the other. Was she nervous around Mia now?

"I do. What time should I be there?" Mia asked.

"Three. Prue said it will be a short check-in." Sarah licked her lips. "But don't miss the cookies."

"A famous Sadie recipe, I heard." Mia picked up the covering to see scrambled eggs and toast.

"I skipped burning the bacon this morning."

There was an apology in Sarah's voice, so Mia laughed.

"Hey, before you go, I asked if there were any books about Prospect at the library. Sam said no, but he suggested I check out Sadie's cookbooks to find out more about the town through her stories." Mia shoved her hands in her pockets, aware that nerves had kicked in while she was talking with Sarah. She hated the awkwardness between them. "It seems like Sadie might have been one of the best sources to understand this place."

Sarah tilted her head to the side. "Hmm."

Mia waited. It was a strange answer, not confused but…considering.

"A book about Prospect." Sarah huffed out a breath. "I can't believe Sadie didn't think of that herself. You would not believe some of the photos we found in Sadie's old files." She marched away without explaining.

"Okay." Mia turned toward the table where her breakfast waited but instead headed out into the hallway and walked to Sadie's apartment. If Jordan was still there, she'd make a direct request to borrow the cookbooks. When she stuck her head around the corner, Jordan was seated at the island, scrolling through something on her phone. Mia tapped lightly on the doorjamb, interested to see Jordan jerk guiltily in her chair.

"Hey, Mia," Jordan said brightly and loudly. "Finished breakfast already?"

Mia fought to keep her face pleasantly bland. She was desperate to know what the conversation was about her presence in town, and what Grant Armstrong was working to keep her from discovering, but she understood that the family had chosen his side.

She liked them better for it.

"Could I borrow some of Sadie's cookbooks?" She pointed to the stack on the counter. "I'm still building a background on the town, and I hear she was a good storyteller. Without Wi-Fi, I'd be stuck squinting at my phone for internet searches." The way Jordan had just been squinting.

Jordan seemed ready to try some excuse, but Sarah breezed into the apartment, a cardboard box in her hands. "A book, Jordan. That's another project we can add to our list. We have so much material, this box, all the others we moved into the kitchen to sort through. Sadie loved this place. Can you imagine how awesome it would be to have a book for sale in the museum?"

Jordan's eyebrows shot up. "Who is writing a book? I am not writing any book. I will learn to retile all the bathrooms, but there is no way you are going to chain me to a laptop to write a book, Sarah." She scooped up the stack of cookbooks and handed them to Mia. "Where did this idea come from?"

Sarah wrapped her arm around Mia's shoulders. "Neither of us will write it, but we can hire someone to do that. This is so much easier than renovating this lodge, Jordan." Sarah bit her lip. "I wonder if Brooke could write it…"

Jordan was wildly shaking her head when Sarah disappeared down a hall that must lead to the bedrooms.

"I was thinking about *reading* a book, not suggesting anyone write one." Mia shifted the books in her arms. "So I'll go do that. With my breakfast. See you later."

"Okay, when you're finished you can set the tray in the hallway or return it to the restaurant's kitchen. We've been going through all the serving dishes, pots and pans that were in storage." Jordan rubbed a hand on her forehead. "One million things still to do around here before the Majestic is ready for guests and Sarah also wants us to do a book."

Jordan seemed exhausted as she stood there, so Mia froze in place, worried that she wasn't well.

Sarah breezed back in. "When my sister has inspiration, it's a grand thing. When I do it, Jordan shuts down. With the deadline to reopen the lodge looming and the museum in town, we're both overwhelmed with the items on the to-do list." She patted her sister on the back. "No worries, little sister, this can be done later. Okay? No panicking today. I believe Michael might even be able to handle this through the corporation." She turned to Mia. "Michael's the cousin who was named CEO of Sadie's company. He's been pretty supportive of all these projects we're rolling out in Prospect. I came up with a way to get him to pay for the siding refresh last night, so when Jordan returns to the land of the living, I will share it with her. That will give her a shot of energy like nothing else." Sarah tapped her temple. "Jordan's the brawn. I'm the brains."

"I can hear you. I'm standing right here," Jordan mumbled.

"Go put on your shoes. We're going to be late for…" Sarah turned back to Mia with a fake, polite smile. "Our family breakfast."

Ignoring the urge to comfort Sarah by explaining that she understood their "family breakfast" was intended to discuss "family business" that might be centered on what to say around her, Mia nodded. "Enjoy. Tell all the Armstrongs I said hello."

Back in her room, Mia ate the breakfast off the Majestic's room service tray and stared out the window as she considered how her welcome had cooled.

Prue's theatrical speech at the Ace High.

Sarah and Jordan backing away.

Even Grant's surprise invitation to dinner.

The Armstrongs were doing their best to keep an eye on her movements in town. Why they would go to the trouble to alert their neighbors to her presence and the approved line of questioning was difficult to misunderstand.

"What don't they want me to find out?" Mia picked up her phone and wished the lodge had already undergone the Wi-Fi installation, but the small screen would work for a quick search. When entering Grant's name didn't turn up any recent news items, she slipped the phone into her pocket.

Mia turned pages in the cookbooks without reading, aware of the faint vanilla scent wafting in the air. There was a clear explanation this morning. When she landed on a spread with Sadie Hearst grinning from the pages, Sarah studied her face for any resemblance to Jordan and Sarah. She couldn't explain which features were familiar, but the sparkle in her eyes leaped off the page. Sadie's grin was contagious and she looked perfectly at home behind the stainless steel bowl of a large mixer. The recipe on the page was for Lemon Drops, a sort of twirled cookie made of two doughs that had to taste absolutely delicious.

Mia didn't cook, but there was something about Sadie's encouraging smile and the need to have one of those cookies that blossomed immediately. It made her wonder if Sarah and Jordan would let her test her skills against the Cookie Queen's recipes as long as she cleaned up whatever mess she made.

When she realized how far she'd wandered from her original plan for the morning, Mia slumped back against her chair. She'd gotten no helpful information from Sarah or Jordan or her halfhearted phone search.

Asking around the magazine's newsroom to see if anyone had heard any new whispers about Grant was an option, but it was the final, last-ditch choice. If there was a story to tell here about Grant, she wanted to be the one to get it. Bringing it to her mother to publish would be proof that she could deliver big wins for *The Way West*.

She pulled up the results of the Nationals competition from December to see who had benefited from Grant's retirement. She didn't follow the circuit standings closely but none of the names seemed unusual. *The Way West*'s summary featured a large action photo of Trey McClintock bent low over the back of a bucking horse. She scanned the article, but there was no whisper of a question about Grant's absence. Then she noticed the photo credit.

"Well, Casey Donaldson has made it to the show," Mia muttered to herself, uncertain how she felt knowing that the guy who'd been one of her least favorite photographers to work with had realized his goal of getting more than fried-food-and-craft-show assignments. Mia could remember long days of complaints when she'd worked with Casey. "But he did get good photos."

Did she still have his number? She scrolled through her contacts. His name didn't come up but there was an entry for Do Not Answer Photographer.

She considered her options. "Should I open this door, or…"

How important was getting this story? Did it matter enough to put herself back on Casey's radar?

A picture of her mother's shocked face as she read the story that Mia scooped right out from under her experienced news writers flashed through Mia's mind, so she punched the number before she could talk herself out of it.

"Please don't answer. Please don't answer. Please don't answer," she whispered as the phone rang.

On the third ring, just as she was composing her cheery voice mail in her head, Casey said,

"Mia Romero, I was thinking about you and here you are. What are the chances?"

Mia wasn't good with math calculations like that, but she hoped he was lying.

"No way. That must be what made me pick up the phone this morning. Where are you in the world today?" She stuck her tongue out, grossed out at her perky delivery.

"Got downtime before I head to Utah next weekend. Should I swing through Billings on the way? We could grab dinner." He made some weird humming noise. "Catch up."

"Actually, I'm in Colorado, working on a story. I was doing some research and saw the amazing photo you took of Trey McClintock at the Nationals. I couldn't let it go without passing along my congratulations. You have come a long way." Mia didn't want to overdo her praise, but she had a feeling Casey would accept this as his due.

"Yeah, years of kids showing off their fat goats and grandmas with their prizewinning pies was good training, I guess. So, dinner? I'm in Denver now. This was truly meant to be," he said.

Mia cringed, disaster looming. "Wow, I wish I'd called sooner. I'll be on my way back home on Monday, and I'm buried in research on Western Days until then." She glanced around the empty hotel room. Nothing was burying her here.

The pause that followed convinced Mia that

he was regrouping. Better she should try to re-direct, so she asked, "What was the unofficial story at Nationals? Anything exciting happen?"

The longer pause that followed her question made her wince. Had she shown too much of her hand?

"Well, there was a whole thing about one of the barrel racers hitting on a married judge, but that was more of a laugh than real news." He sighed. "Seems like everyone wanted to talk about Grant Armstrong missing the competition but no one knew anything about what had gone on with him, so it never went very far."

Thinking fast, Mia said, "I read about the new-est phenomenon. What was her name?" If he was on the trail of her real reason for calling, this might throw him off the scent.

"Annie Mercado. Yeah, she's one to watch, for sure. You doing feature stories, Mia? That's new. We should definitely reconnect if you're going to need shots for whatever you're working on."

"Me? Writing news?" Mia chuckled loudly, hoping to keep him distracted from her mission. "You know how much I enjoy the craft show and parade circuit I'm on. Plenty of characters out here, but I'm sure there's a story in the works about her. I thought there might be some travel connection I could work in." She realized she was pacing tight circles in front of the sunny window and forced herself to stop. This phone call was almost over.

"I might be able to swing it if—"

"Oh no, someone's at my door, Casey. Gotta run, but I appreciate the dinner invite. We'll definitely catch up soon." Mia ended the call and set her phone down on the table. Did it feel good to poke for information from someone who didn't know her true intention? No. It would serve her right if she was ducking Casey for months. Mia pressed her forehead against the cool window and stared out at the lake. She was the one who needed a distraction from the dread that conversation had inspired.

"Without accomplishing a single thing," she muttered as she yanked on her coat and shoved her feet in her sneakers. Getting out of the lodge room was her only hope. Since she hadn't had an opportunity to explore the Majestic, she might as well take advantage of her solo time. Mia shoved her phone and her car keys in her pocket and picked up the tray. It was a new experience to be the only guest in a hotel, but that meant she had plenty of time to make note of the details. She'd learned that the lodge had been closed for many years before the Hearsts came back to town. The wood floors and trim were no doubt original, but the place had obviously been cared for. Everything had a timeless quality to it, as if the place was outside the normal world. As she paused in the lobby, the sweet scent of freshly baked cookies filled the air.

"Ha, Sadie, I guess I'm not completely alone, am I?" Mia studied the large painting of the Rockies as she decided how she felt about ghosts. "If they are real, one that smells this delicious is okay with me." She continued through the restaurant, where it was clear the Hearsts had been making plans. Tables were neatly arranged with chairs turned over on top to make sweeping and mopping the room easier, but the place was spotless. If they found a chef today, they could start serving meals in the room tomorrow.

"And the place would be packed. Look at that view." Wide windows lined the front of the dining room, letting warm sunlight filter through the trees. The lake was perfectly framed, glittering in the distance. Determined to get a closer look, Mia hurried into the kitchen. A magnet stuck to the dishwasher said Dirty, so she rinsed her plate and silverware and slipped it all inside. Several different ceramic pieces lined the countertop. There were three pie keepers, one blueberry, one cherry and one apple. A large cookie jar shaped like a cowboy hat with a red-and-white gingham band was lined up next to a canister set rimmed with the same gingham. Mia picked up one of the canisters to see that it had been made by the Cookie Queen Corporation. "Sadie, you were the real deal, weren't you? A celebrity chef. I had no idea."

There were cardboard boxes stacked next to the counter and more were arranged neatly beside. At a quick glance, Mia could see notes about a TV schedule, doodles of funny horses and cows along the margins, file folders that were labeled with recipe names, and a few photos of completed cookies. The open box on top contained more paperwork, old calendars, and Mia realized she was looking at a bunch of Sadie's papers. When she pulled out the first recipe folder, the top sheet showed a handwritten recipe and contained Sadie's notes as she tested it. There were minor adjustments made to ingredients here and there and comments for each change. If she was reading the notes correctly, Sadie had tested this recipe for No-Bake Bear Paws four times, and she hadn't been satisfied until she'd added pumpkin spice at the last step. The last bit of writing said "Scrumptious."

Sarah and Jordan had so much of Sadie's materials to work with, not just for redoing the lodge but for a book. Even her work files were scattered with drops of Sadie's enthusiasm and personality.

Whoever worked on a biography of Sadie Hearst was going to enjoy every minute.

What would it have been like to work for Sadie? In her mind, the headquarters for the

Cookie Queen Corporation was filled with people wearing overalls and straw hats or aprons and chef hats, for some reason, and everyone was very happy.

That couldn't be right. A job was a job, but there had to be a special Sadie touch to the place.

She pulled her phone out of her pocket to make a note to contact Michael Hearst, CEO of the Cookie Queen Corporation. Mia realized his input on Western Days would be negligible, but if the magazine needed new advertisers, this story could be the beginning of a beautiful relationship. Her mother would never believe Mia had pulled it off, but it would be a big win.

Then she made a note to find out why neither of the town's celebrities had any signage or historical markers or even a tourist trap making money by selling souvenirs. Why wasn't there a Home of Sadie Hearst sign as people rolled into Prospect? Or a statue of Grant Armstrong mastering a bucking bronco that visitors could pose in front of?

Cold, clear air hit Mia as soon as she stepped outside. There was something different about the atmosphere in the mountains, and she'd learned to appreciate how the light landed particularly at the high altitudes, even if her heart beat a little faster and her breathing was quicker, too. It was an effortless walk down to the water's edge.

Snow was still covering spots here and there, but it was easy to believe that spring would be coming soon. Mia followed the bank for a bit until she saw the closed marina in the distance. When the Hearsts reopened, this place was set up for success. The lake was crystal clear. Every single piece was in place for Jordan and Sarah. How could anyone walk away from a location like this?

Even if she failed to get the story on Grant Armstrong, she would look back on her short stay in Prospect fondly.

Since Mia had plenty of time before the Western Days meeting, after she explored the lakeshore, she opted to window-shop along Main Street. She hadn't seen much of the town, and discovering some of its history had increased her curiosity. The drive into Prospect took only a short while and parking next to the Mercantile made perfect sense, since that was her final destination. Mia hesitated as she scanned the storefronts from the sidewalk.

"Mia, it's a round trip. Either direction, just go." She was glad there were no crowds just then. No one had overheard her talking to herself. The invisible line that marked the end of the oldest section of town was easy to see, so she decided to check out the businesses surrounding the Homestead Market. The store had been built into the facade of the old livery stable.

Across the street, she saw a newer portion of architecture, storefronts with large plate-glass windows and charming red brick that were neat as a pin and made her think of mid-century modern homes. The largest was empty, but the faint gold lettering on the glass said The Prospect Post. The newspaper hadn't been a large operation when it was open for business, but it had covered the heartbeat of the town: what mattered to the people there. There were a few desks inside, but nothing much else to investigate. Imagining settling in to work there was easy, though. Telling the stories of her neighbors, a real community, would have been satisfying, Mia thought.

She shook her head to clear the daydream and continued on to the heart of town: the Mercantile, the Ace High restaurant and the bed-and-breakfast, Bell House, a beautiful old Victorian building. As she walked, it was simple to see why the people who had stayed in Prospect must love the place. There was so much history at every turn.

The line of storefronts leading to the theater was missing the obvious markings of the livery stable and the saloon, but there was a small plaque that described the Fashion Row of Prospect's heyday, during the silver rush. These buildings, where there had once been an exclusive milliner, a

cobbler and boot maker, a tailor who created fine
men's suits, and three competing seamstresses,
was empty, but there was a sign in one window.

Future Home of the Colorado Cookie Queen
Museum and Gift Shop, Mia read as she moved
closer to peek around the edges. In the shadowy
interior, it was hard to see anything clearly, but
the shapes suggested wood crates and possibly
displays being built.

That answered one of her questions about why
there was no sign for Sadie Hearst.

Prospect had been waiting for Jordan and
Sarah to come to town.

When she stopped to check her phone for the
time, anxious to be there on the dot for the Western Days planning meeting, a woman stepped
out of the historic theater, the Prospect Picture
Show, with a box under her arm.

"Oh, hi, I almost bumped into you, Mia. Sorry
about that." The woman turned a key in the door
and the loud thunk of a sturdy lock proved it was
secure.

Mia was sure her surprise showed on her face
when the woman smiled. "Sorry. We haven't met.
News of your arrival has preceded you, obviously. I'm Amanda. I bet we're both headed to
Prue's completely voluntary, and in no way man-
datory, meeting for Western Days." She tapped
the box she was carrying. "I'm delivering some

of the Sadie Hearst memorabilia we've had stored here at the theater to Sarah. There's no need for me to attend, per se, Prue has already given me an assignment, but I do like cookies."

Mia laughed. "I did receive a lovely, public invitation, so yes, that's my next stop."

Amanda matched her pace, the box resting on one hip. "I've been here so long that I've forgotten how weird it can be when someone you've never seen before calls you by name. The town's busier, in the summer months. I wouldn't have assumed then you were the magazine reporter I'd heard about."

"A Prospect transplant? It's nice to meet you. I had begun to think everyone here was hatched from the Mercantile," Mia said as they paused on a corner to check for nonexistent traffic.

Amanda chuckled. "I can see how that could happen, but no, my husband wanted us to live here, and then I never moved away, even after he was gone. It's a good place to call home. I have lived here long enough to have raised an adult daughter who is out conquering the world, though, so you might as well think of me as one of the old-timers."

Mia liked her easy personality. Come to think of it, she hadn't met a single person in Prospect who treated her with actual suspicion.

"Your theater is lovely. Plays the classic Westerns." Mia motioned over her shoulder at the marquee. "Too bad I'll miss next weekend's show. *Along Came Jones* is one of my favorites. I was half in love with Gary Cooper when I was ten, thanks to my grandfather's collection of movies."

"That role was different from the strong, silent, solid hero he usually played. Lighter. Your grandfather had good taste. So did young Mia." Amanda patted Mia's shoulder. "My first crush was a dancer in a toothpaste commercial. The silver lining is that I had very few cavities."

Amanda wrinkled her nose as Mia laughed.

"Before I married a man who inherited a historic movie theater that shows only Westerns, I didn't know much about those old silver-screen cowboys. Now? I have them memorized and I couldn't pick a favorite out of the lineup. Favorite villain? That one's much, much easier. Jack Palance. At every age, he made an excellent villain. I'll have to remember to set up a Gary Cooper double feature for when you come back into town." Amanda shrugged. "That's one of the benefits of owning your own movie house. I can take requests at any time. We'll get *Along Came Jones* back up on the big screen for you."

"That would be a perk," Mia agreed. "Will the new museum be opening soon?"

"During Western Days. If all goes according to plan." Amanda waved her free hand broadly.

"This whole town will be buzzing with fresh attractions. I have a lot of faith in Sarah and Jordan, but they have filled their plates, for sure. Sadie Hearst was a dreamer, but she also worked those dreams until they became her reality. Must be part of the Hearst family tradition to shoot for the moon."

They reached the Mercantile, and Mia opened the door for Amanda.

Mia wasn't sure what to think when she stepped into a short hallway. A display of pamphlets for local attractions was the only piece inside; there were two doors, one on either side. Amanda paused. "The Mercantile used to be one large open store, like what you expected when you stepped in, but when Prue and Walt divorced, she demanded to have her own space carved out. This was the solution. Hardware on one side, and her store, Handmade, on the other side." She frowned. "As a woman who moved to town and got carried away by her husband's career and family, I get Prue's need. Now that they seem to be reassessing their divorce, I wonder about what happens to this space. It was weird when they built it, but it'll be weird if they take it down, you know?"

Mia followed Amanda into Prue Armstrong's shop. She didn't realize how her head was swiveling from side to side as she trailed Amanda to the staircase, but she knew she'd have to find time to come explore Handmade before leaving town, if only to touch all the fabrics.

Then, before Mia was completely prepared, she was in the center of an extended open space where everyone turned to stare at her. Some of the faces were unfamiliar, but there was no question they knew her name, her job and her stated purpose in town.

Grant was slouched against the wall near the podium at the front of the room. The way their eyes locked was reassuring. As Mia settled into the back row near Lucky, she pulled out her tablet, to jot notes about the meeting, and considered a creative way to get Grant Armstrong alone.

So she could ask him questions.

Without an audience.

That was the only reason to plot private time with Grant.

Mia was especially glad no one could hear her thoughts this time. She didn't even believe what she was telling herself.

CHAPTER NINE

ON SUNDAY AFTERNOON, Grant was relieved when Mia stepped inside his mom's large room on the second floor of the Mercantile. He'd also been happy to see a decent turnout. The two things were related. Mia's appearance wouldn't have meant much without the rest of the crowd and vice versa. Since it was impromptu and his mother hadn't had time to compel as many folks to report for duty, he'd been concerned that attendance would be too low to convince Mia that this was a real planning meeting.

He should have known his mother would never waste an opportunity to prepare for the town's most important weekend of the year.

Matt had been thoroughly coached, because he was doing a credible job of taking the lead. The first order of business had been to announce Mia's presence in the room. She'd introduced herself by outlining her Western Days article and giving her email address in case anyone had a story they wanted to share with her about it. As she'd settled into her spot in the back row of the folding chairs he and his brothers had set up that morning, Mia met his stare and their instant connection snapped into place like a magnetic field existed between them. It was hard to fight.

His mother had named him head of the Cowboy Games Committee, an "exciting addition to the festival's lineup," before he knew that was the next order of business. Since every single one of his brothers had been placed in charge of a committee of his own, it was impossible to argue his way out of what seemed inevitable anyway.

"Grant, you want to tell everyone about what we've done so far to plan for the Cowboy Games?" Matt asked, his eyebrows raised.

Had he missed his first cue? Grant realized he was watching Mia again, so he cleared his throat and stood. "My plan is to set up a timed riding course. We're going to hire some help with this because we need experts making sure this is challenging but safe, and it will be an all-around skill competition with riding, roping and a shooting category. Every event will be scored, with a grand prize and then first, second, third places in each." Grant was speaking off-the-cuff, since he and Matt hadn't made it quite this far, but if they were hoping to attract talent, it made sense to pattern pieces after other official rodeo competitions. "Gonna need to offer monetary prizes along with trophies. I nominate someone else to be responsible for finding sponsors." He went to sit down but Matt gave him a small shake of his head, so he quickly reversed course. "In the park back here—" he motioned vaguely behind the Mercantile to the city park that was used for every town celebration, large and small, and everyone in the room knew exactly what he meant, except perhaps Mia "—we'll set up a minicourse for kids. I'm thinking we'll have a lasso station, maybe archery… We'll need to do more thinking on that, but if anybody has suggestions, I'll take them. I expect this will be prime real estate to set up photo opportunities for families, as well, so we'll need props."

It was clear Matt expected him to do more, but Grant hadn't intended to give a multimedia presentation or anything. He crossed his hands in front of him. "Any questions?"

"The park is the perfect size for the children's course, but have you two thought about where we'll hold the adult competition? I don't think we've got room in town." His mother bit her lip. "There's always the ranch, I suppose, but…" Grant knew very well his father and all of his brothers were loudly disagreeing with that option, even if none of them said a word. The disruption to their cattle business caused by a crowd of that size would be wrong and bad, and immediately shot down if anybody other than his mother had tossed it out.

"It's too bad the ghost town isn't accessible," Sarah Hearst said from her spot next to Wes. "That would be an excellent backdrop."

"It's also not safe. Those buildings need to be examined properly before we could let people loose up there." Jordan turned to Clay and smiled. "Right, Clay?"

Grant was certain they were communicating on a deeper level than the rest of them could hear when his brother wrapped his arm tightly around Jordan and murmured, "Jordan is right."

"What about Sam's hay field across from the high school?" Reginald McCall stood to make his case. "It's a real good space. Since the Prospect Rodeo Club shut down, no one's using that land or the barn."

Grant turned to Wes for confirmation that the rodeo club was no more. Coming to Prospect had been tough but finding that club and a group of kids who loved the competition in the ring as much as he did had put him on the path to the professional rodeo circuit. He was sad to hear it had closed.

Low chatter filled the room as everyone debated the merits of his suggestion until Matt raised his voice. "That seems to be a solid contender, Reg. Thank you. Grant can talk to Sam.

The next time we meet, we'll have more details to discuss, with an outline of the course and a budget. You can do that in a week, right?"

Grant had no idea whether he could or not. Budgeting wasn't exactly in his wheelhouse, but he had a lifetime of bluffing his way through questions he didn't know the answer to. "You bet."

Matt's lips were twitching as he nodded.

Almost as if he was aware how little Grant knew and how that had never stopped him from agreeing to a request. "Include tents for the competitors while they're waiting. Any construction we'll need for the course and targets. A fair price for using Sam's land for a month or so and any setup, teardown and repairs necessary." Matt offered him a pen. "Should you be jotting this down?"

Grant grunted. "Of course not. It's a budget. I got it." Then he sat down.

Wes leaned over. "I know my way around a spreadsheet. I'll be happy to help."

On the other side, Clay tapped his chest. "Construction. I got you."

Grant nodded and forced himself to relax. Somehow, in his mind, this megasized event was in the distance, too far away to be a big concern.

Having a plan and a budget in a week? That prompted a cold sweat, but he could count on his brothers to get him across the finish line.

He tried to relax, but then he noticed his mother's frown.

"Are we ready to move along?" Matt asked her uncertainly.

She nodded but it was not convincing. "I just…" She waved her hands vaguely. "I want to make sure our event is unique. Right? Have we got that piece yet?" She pointed at Grant. "I mean, we'll have our own rodeo star on hand, so that definitely helps, but lots of other places do riding and shooting competitions." She sighed. "Let's all consider if there's another way to do this, to make us stand out."

Grant exchanged a what-are-you-going-to-do-about-this? look with Matt, but he wasn't sure which one of them was the person responsible for the "doing."

"Moving on for now. It looks like Lucky has a long list of food vendors committed for the weekend." Matt held up a printed list and tapped it. "If everyone could be like Lucky, I would appreciate that. I love a good list and if you can turn it in early?" Matt fanned his face with the paper. "If she wasn't married already, I'd propose."

Laughter bubbled through the room. Grant turned to see what Dante thought about that, but he was sidetracked because Mia was seated next to Lucky. Her face as she and Lucky exchanged a look was captivating.

As soon as the thought filtered through his brain, Grant wanted to bury his face in his cowboy hat. *Captivating?* That wasn't a word he used, but it was the only one that fit. Mia's expression was so open. Her eyes gleamed and those lips curved… When she locked eyes with him again, he knew he wasn't the only one feeling the attraction.

"I got her first and it's a good thing. The whole town needs Lucky right where she is. She keeps the business running, so I'd have to fight you for her." Dante pressed a kiss to Lucky's lips. Grant wondered if Mia experienced the same pang of envy he did at the way Dante and Lucky were behaving.

"Fine, fine, enough of the personal affection, please." Matt flipped through the giant binder his mother had handed off when she'd volun-told him to run the festival this year. "How is the quilt show coming, Mom?"

"Right on track! We've gotten in a few entries for this year's juried competition. The deadline is in mid-March, so the early entries are a good sign." His mother smiled. "You're doing a fabulous job, Matty. Once we get everything ironed out, this will be the best festival yet."

Matt cleared his throat as if stalling for time to think. "Thanks, Mom. That means a lot." He tugged on the neck of his shirt before asking.

"Is there anything we need to discuss before we break for refreshments?"

"What about an update on the status of the Majestic?" Walt called out. "We gonna have rooms available for rent? I got a phone call at the hardware store asking for recommendations since Bell House is all booked up already."

"I'd like to know that, too. I can pass the information along to callers. I've already got a waiting list for any cancellations." Rose Bell was seated in her usual spot, right next to his mother, but she'd removed her usual Broncos jersey and hat, so it was hard to recognize her.

The fact that she was holding hands with Patrick Hearst, Sarah and Jordan's father, was something he was going to need to discuss with someone later at great length.

"Our only holdup is the restaurant," Jordan said, "but our most recent guest, experienced travel writer Mia Romero, gave us her stamp of approval, so I'd say we'll be open for business in time for the festival. Let's get it booked up." She inhaled slowly, held that breath and then released it. "Looks like we'll be hiring, too?" Her voice squeaked on the end, as if the nerves had taken over.

Sarah squeezed her sister's hand. "We were working up a plan of our own to get some interest going in the restaurant, a cooking competition that will be broadcast live on the Cookie Queen website."

Jordan ducked her head. "We are? You're moving forward with that?" She started fanning her face. "This, the lodge, a book, Sarah?"

Sarah wrapped her arm around Jordan's shoulder and squeezed her hard. "It's fine. I've overloaded Jordan with too many ideas all at once, but Michael's working with an LA chef to get us two competitors for a cook-off. We're going to shoot it at the lodge for one week next month. People were drawn to the Cookie Queen website to see Sadie's weekly recipe videos, so this will provide some new content. In exchange, Michael is supplying a location fee that should cover most of the siding repairs. By the time Western Days rolls around, the Majestic is going to shine." She waved her hands. "More on that to come, but I'm hoping that one of those cooks will jump at the chance to build their own kitchen at the Majestic."

Everyone in the room watched as Jordan inhaled deep breaths, held them and exhaled slowly. Eventually her face returned to its normal color.

"If the new chef's not ready to open by Western Days weekend, we'll offer breakfast pastries, coffee and juice and send everyone into town for everything else. Lucky's food vendors will offer plenty of variety." Jordan crossed her arms over her chest. "The Majestic is open for business."

Applause filtered through the room. It had been a long time coming and everyone understood what it meant to Prospect to have the lodge attracting visitors, even beyond Western Days weekend.

Grant was pleased that the meeting was going so well.

Until Jordan turned to face him. She smiled brightly. "I have the best idea for a business venture for Grant, one that will add some real shine to the Majestic's experience."

That didn't reassure him at all. He'd forgotten this part of being in Prospect. He ended up being involved in projects before he knew a thing about them, somehow.

Matt shrugged. "Any other updates?"

"What about the museum?" his mother asked. "Sounds like you might be overextended, Sarah."

Sarah rubbed her forehead. "You aren't saying anything I haven't been thinking. We've got all the displays installed, so now all I have to do is…set it up. Order items and stock a gift shop, while I also work with Michael on the displays at Cookie Queen headquarters, plan this cooking competition, negotiate sponsorship and prize money out of my cousin for these Cowboy Games, because everyone in this room knows that Cookie Queen should be an official sponsor, and help out at the lodge." Sarah huffed out a breath. "Every Hearst and Armstrong in the room and anyone else I can rope in will be involved, but it's all important to me and it will all happen before Western Days weekend."

Her expression was grimly determined.

"Let me worry about the gift shop," Prue said. "You and I can decide what to order, but I can handle the merchandising. I do well enough in my own shop. And Faye will run the cooking competition." Her delivery was so matter-of-fact, as if there was no doubt that it was the correct answer.

"Faye, who isn't here right now?" Walt drawled slowly from his spot at her side. "The Faye who is always in the Ace High because the place would fold without her?"

Prue snorted. "Looks like it's time to find a solution to that little problem, too." She nodded firmly as if it was all settled.

Grant could see that Mia's head was down as she made her notes. There was a lot happening in Prospect. Surely she'd have the story she needed without involving him in any way.

"The to-do list is long enough for now. We'll meet again next week with status updates." Matt held up the binder and banged it on the table in front him, like a makeshift gavel. "Let's have cookies."

Grant waited for the feeding frenzy to die down before he eased over to the counter of the small kitchen. For as long as he could remember, the second floor of the Mercantile had served as the unofficial community center for the town. It was used for potlucks, planning meetings, occasional dance rehearsals and choir practices, and soon monthly Sip and Paint nights organized by his mother and Patrick Hearst, the man responsible for the large landscape over the check-in desk at the Majestic and the soft smile on Rose Bell's face. Prospect was a small place, so the crowd that showed up for the different events never changed a whole lot, but it felt different today.

That had to be because he was so aware of Mia and her location in the room.

She'd already chosen a cookie and had retreated over by the windows.

It was a testament to his mother's acting skills and the success of her veiled messages that Mia was standing alone. Why did that seem so wrong?

The answer had something to do with how Sarah and Jordan were trying not to stare at her with worried expressions. Then he noticed Lucky doing the same, and headed for Mia. The urge to warmly enfold their visitor would overpower their caution soon, so Grant had to step in. For the town's good, obviously.

"Get enough to start your article?" he asked, leaning one shoulder casually against the wall. That was his intention. Misjudging the distance, so he landed awkwardly, meant he lost some cool points, but he couldn't acknowledge that now.

She nodded. "And these cookies are incredible. I wondered what made them palomino peanut butter. It never would have occurred to me to add white chocolate to peanut butter." Mia smiled up at him. "I guess that's why she was the Colorado Cookie Queen and I am not."

He returned her smile before he knew it was happening. "Do you enjoy baking?" Why did his voice sound like that? It was cracking as if he was a sophomore trying to ask a senior to dance.

Mia frowned. "I don't think so?" She shrugged. "I don't spend enough time in my tiny kitchen at home to practice, but these results are impossible to argue with. This morning I was paging through Sadie's cookbooks and fell in love with a lemon-drop cookie, so if I'm in town beyond tomorrow night, I may have to borrow the lodge's kitchen to give them a try."

"Good thing you'll be on your way home by Tuesday morning. The last thing you need is a cookie addiction, right?" Grant surveyed the room, well aware that he had more attention than he liked. Technically, no one was watching them, but every antenna in the room was tuned to his frequency.

When his mother popped up at his elbow, Grant did his best not to jump.

"You should take Mia over to the storage building, Grant." His mother pointed vaguely over her shoulder. "If you want to see pieces of the town's history, there's a nice collection in one place, Mia. And Grant needs to go through the various backdrops we've got stored. I know some will work for his sweet idea for the kids' photo opportunities." Then she clasped her hands together. "Oh my, I bet you've seen awesome setups in your travels. Please, you have to help us." Her firm grip on his arm convinced him his mother wasn't acting this time. She'd been struck with inspiration. "We need to pick her brain before she gets out of here."

Before he could answer, Reg McCall stepped up. "If you'd like to see this field and barn setup, I have a key. As the last remaining active sponsor of the defunct rodeo club, Sam told me to hold onto it. We made a few improvements after you left town, Grant. With some polish, it could be perfect for some kind of activity."

His mother's enthusiastic nods were easy to read.

Grant turned to Mia, but he had zero hope that she'd rescue either of them from this idea.

Mia smiled. "Do you think we can work both visits in this afternoon? I wanted to spend tomorrow morning at the library before I get my car fixed up."

Before he could answer, his mother said, "There's no time like the present. Grant, the two of you come by my apartment later. I'll make dinner." The way his mother blinked innocently while she waited for his agreement worried him. Was she moving Mia from opponent to possible matchmaking target in so obvious a manner? She touched his cheek. "Retirement has made you so helpful. Mia, I definitely want to discuss the history of Western Days with you."

Mia smoothed hair behind her ear. "Dinner sounds like a great time to do that, if you're sure you don't mind."

His mother's wry smile made him nervous.

"I love to cook for others. Ask anyone. We won't be disturbed and I have so many photos to show you." His mother turned on her heel before Mia could accept. "I'll see you at six!"

"I understand it takes a minute to catch up when my mother starts planning your life," Grant said as he touched Mia's shoulder. She was still staring at the spot his mother had already vacated. "She's always in motion."

Mia laughed. "Yeah, I get that."

"You two want to ride with me or follow behind?" Reg asked and shook the keys again.

"My truck's downstairs. Want to ride shotgun?" he asked Mia. Why was he so nervous as he watched her weigh her options and relieved when she nodded?

Before he realized what he was doing, he'd unlocked the passenger door and held it open while Mia climbed inside.

Like this was a date or they were a couple or something romantic was in the air. After he shut the door behind her, he reminded himself that this was part of the plan to keep an eye on Mia.

Nothing more.

Why was he struggling to remember that?

CHAPTER TEN

MIA KNEW THE afternoon had taken an unexpected turn because Grant seemed deep in thought as they followed Reg out of town. It was a short distance, but wide pastures immediately lined both sides of the road and Prospect's school campus, first grade through twelfth, was the only development as far as she could see.

"'Prospect School District, Home of the Wildcats.'" She read the large sign that arched over the entrance. "I wasn't sure what the mascot would be. Were you a proud Wildcat once upon a time? Football? Basketball? Math team?" She grinned at him.

"None of the above. I was always all about rodeo and horses and riding and getting out of high school so I could move on with my life." Grant pointed at the large structure a little farther down the road. It was more modern than Mia expected in Prospect, with red and white metal siding. "This is where I spent all my spare time."

"Ah, the rodeo club." Mia frowned as she tried

to pull up anything she knew about high school rodeo clubs. It was a sparse pool. "That's where you learned everything you needed to be a winner?"

He glanced over at her before he parked. "A lot, yes, but it was really what kept me here in Prospect until Walt and Prue could domesticate me a little." The corner of his mouth curled as he made the joke about himself. "It was pretty helpful to be a little wild and lack the ability to think things through when I was learning to stick in the saddle."

He slid out of the truck and Mia hurried to hop down to join him and Reg near the barn doors. She didn't want to lose this thread of the conversation.

"Reg, how did you get involved with the rodeo club?" Mia asked as she regretted not bringing her recorder. She pulled her phone out and waved it. "Okay for me to record our conversation?"

Reg's enthusiastic "Sure thing" interrupted Grant's more restrained shrug, so she started the recording even though she had no idea why.

"Grant and I were in high school together." Reg clapped Grant on the back before stepping inside to flip on the overhead lights. The wide open space lit in a wave, and Mia was impressed with the shape of the barn and the amenities. "I was never as fearless as he was, which is why I run the doctor's office and he rides on the circuit." His good natured grin was accompanied by a wink, so Mia got the impression that Reg was happy with how his life turned out.

It was clear who her best source was going to be, so Mia moved closer to Reg. "What kind of things did you do in the club?"

He waved his hands. "Pretty much what you'd imagine. We had some guys that would come in and work with us to improve techniques, we learned how to take the best care of our livestock, we trained for state competition. There were fundraisers and exhibitions. We always rode in the Western Days parade. It almost kept us all out of trouble." He raised his eyebrows at Grant and Mia wanted to know so much more about the trouble.

"After Grant graduated and started winning, he made some sizeable donations to help us improve the amenities. Better lighting, stuff like that." Reg pointed at a large sign leaning against a line of empty stalls. "Amanda Gipson's daughter, Carly, painted this for us before she graduated. Did you know Carly?"

Grant shook his head.

"I couldn't get that girl on a horse for love nor money, but she was the best organizer I ever had. Good thing she was in love with my top team-roper, I guess." Reg sighed. "I miss the club these days."

"Why did it disband?" Mia asked as she watched Grant pace slowly down the aisle between the stalls.

"Our original sponsors are a little," Reg coughed, "gray now. Sam retired and dropped out. Walt had some health issues so he had to take a break. One or two of the guys from our years might be interested, but I haven't found the right spark to get it back up and running yet."

Mia met Reg's stare and could read the message he was broadcasting silently but so loudly there was no way to miss it. She glanced over her shoulder.

"A spark, you say?" Mia said. "Like what?"

Her lips twitched as Reg ducked his head in thanks. "If we had a big rodeo star move home and agree to help get this club back in business, I am certain I could find more help and the kids would jump at the chance."

Grant slowly shook his head as if to say he wasn't falling for it, and Mia was amused all over again at how he might put up a fight, as he had wanted to with his mother, but even she could see this writing plainly on the wall.

His involvement in the reborn rodeo club was only a matter of time.

Reg wasn't quite finished with his pitch. "Grant and I both know Travis wasn't much for competition, but I've heard through the grapevine that his foster sons, Damon and Micah, are already comfortable in the saddle. If I could get two or even three of the Armstrongs to agree to step in, we'd be set."

Grant tipped his head back to stare up at the ceiling. Mia followed him and was impressed again with how well kept the barn was. "I think this might be the cleanest barn I've spent any time in."

"When you have kids to keep busy, you come up with plenty of chores." Reg pretended to pick up a whistle and blow it. "I coach flag football, too. You should see how nice the practice field is."

Satisfied that he'd completed his outline for the new and improved Prospect Rodeo Club, Reg motioned them out and turned off the light. After he locked up, he said, "I know Sam will be amenable to renting out the spot for your Cowboy Games. If you need to check out anything else to make your plans, you can let me know." Reg held out his hand and waited for Grant to shake, which he did. "Sorry for the ambush, but that club meant a lot to me."

"Yeah, me too." Grant ran his hand over his nape.

Mia leaned in. "When I met Sam yesterday, I got the impression he was a man who would be interested in renewing the club." It was easy to remember his happy face when he'd talked about his doctor encouraging him to get out to work some.

"Yeah, he has regular chats with Dr. Singh." Reg shrugged. "I can believe he would love to have the club to talk about again."

Grant held his hands up in surrender. "I will think about the club. That's all I can promise right now."

Reg clapped loudly in satisfaction. "You always were a smart one, Grant. I know you'll see the benefits to the kids of this town."

Mia bit her lip as she watched Grant struggle in the face of such enthusiasm. He had his concerns, but the size of the wave was eventually going to wash them away. She hadn't known him long, but every interaction she'd had with him convinced her that he had a hard time letting people down.

"Thank you for showing me the barn. You're right." He motioned with his hand toward the pens and the large, fenced paddock next to them. "This is the right space for whatever we come up with."

"So, no actual livestock roping or herding," Mia said as she stared out over Sam's property. It wasn't impressive in the spring, but it was spacious. They'd have room to park trucks and horse trailers, set up tents for competitors and rope off an area for spectators, in addition to any course they set up.

"No, we aren't prepared to launch a rodeo," Grant turned to grin at her over his shoulder, "and please don't even hint to my mother that we have that ability. We don't. I don't."

Reg hurried back to his truck, whistling loudly.

Mia tilted her head to the side. She didn't recognize the tune.

"'You Can't Hurry Love.'" Grant rubbed his forehead. "That's the song he's whistling."

"Thank you," Mia exclaimed, "that would have bothered me for days, until I woke up in the middle of the night with the song name in my head."

His smile was attractive, as always, but she could tell he had a lot on his mind as they slid into the truck. This time he let her get her own door, which was the smartest choice, but she missed that old fashioned sign of respect.

One of those sweet things a cowboy might do for the woman he was courting.

Courting? When Mia realized she'd stepped back in time to pull that word up, her eyebrows shot up. Luckily, Grant was still deep in thought over everything Reg had laid out about the high school club.

She cleared her throat in the silence as they went back into Prospect. "How long will it take you to get comfortable with this idea of leading the rodeo club for Prospect's next generation?" When his hands tightened on the steering wheel, she swallowed the smile that bloomed. He could see it was inevitable, too. When had she learned to read him so clearly?

After he parked next to the Mercantile, he turned to face her. "Think you've got a read on me, don't you?"

"I've met your family, traveled your home-town, understand your career, and seen firsthand how you treat me, an adversary who might dis-cover something you don't want to see the light of day." Mia shrugged. "I can't complain about your treatment. Changing my tire, finding me a place to stay, saving me from being the awkward wallflower standing all alone. A club that meant so much to you? One you can rebuild by doing things you love?" She squeezed his arm and let him take her hand instead of pulling away. "This is an equation anyone could solve."

"There's a variable you're still missing," Grant said as he slid out of the truck. Mia followed him to a building across the street from the Mercan-tile and waited as he unlocked the door.

"I can't believe you've got me making math analogies," he muttered.

Mia grinned as he opened the door. When they stepped inside, she could see what appeared to have been an office space at one point. He mo-tioned at another door. "This is the bank vault. My mother has a storage system for all the quilts that have won the Western Days quilt show over the years, stored in sealed plastic containers and labeled with the winner's name, the quilt name, and the year. She rotates the quilts on display at the festival each year and the records rival a Fortune 500 company's accounting system." One corner of his mouth tilted up. "You do not have security clearance for that room."

Mia knew she was getting closer to hearing his whole story and considered her options to find that missing variable. Her only solid choice was the direct one.

"If you'd tell me whatever it is that you don't want me to find out, whatever it is that is important enough to involve the whole town to keep quiet, I'd be able to write a much better feature on Western Days." Mia's eyes held a challenge.

If this terrible, secret thing was no longer between them, what would change? Mia wasn't sure, but there was something about him that made the answer important.

And if she was reading Grant's face correctly, he was seriously considering…something. She couldn't say for sure that he was weighing his options in laying out the truth about…whatever it was he was hiding, because his dark eyes were hard to read, but he wanted to trust her with something. She followed him to the jumbled back wall of the large open room.

Grant pulled his hat off and set it down on a table there. Did he do that hair-ruffling thing to confuse her on purpose? If so, he was diabolical, and if not, he was too powerful for his own good.

"How much did you know about my background before you rolled into town, Mia?" He studied her face. As much as she was testing the waters between them, so was he.

"Not much. I knew the name and I had seen photos of you, but I don't follow the standings closely. The magazine's staff is pretty small. We rely a lot on freelance writers and photographers, but I overhear phone calls, meetings, things like that. I never put Grant Armstrong in Prospect, Colorado, until we met on the side of the road." Mia paused as she considered what that meant to her news-tracking skills. If she was a real reporter, would that connection have been immediate? "While I was thumbing through the most recent copy of *The Way West*, on newsstands this week, I noticed the advertisement for Western Days." She held her hands out to demonstrate that it was a splashy two-page ad. "The centennial festival, back and bigger than ever. I needed a story for the May issue. It seemed like the universe was sending me a road sign. I pay attention to those gifts, right?" She turned on her imaginary blinker as if she was exiting the highway.

"Plus, I was supposed to finish my college degree this semester, but I forgot to register. My mother was vocally unhappy about that and I'm honestly tired of having the conversation, so it seemed a perfect time to hit the road to do research."

He frowned. "You forgot to register."

"I don't need a degree for the job I'm already doing. My mother views it as a way to prove I can run the magazine. An exciting story could do exactly the same thing and boost advertising dollars at the same time." She shrugged, certain he was picking up on her hints.

"You want to write. You don't want to go to school." Grant took a step forward. "I get that. My whole life improved once my high school diploma was behind me and I could live life instead of studying."

"I actually like the studying part," Mia confessed, and giggled when he frowned at her as if she'd switched languages suddenly.

He started pulling dust sheets off so they could see what was underneath. "Do you want to run a magazine?"

Mia watched the muscles in his back work as he moved down the long line. Of all the Western Days work assignments, this one had some perks.

Then he turned to stare at her and she realized she had dropped the conversational ball. "Maybe not, but what else can I do? Let the magazine my

grandfather built and loved just…disappear?"
Understanding lit his eyes. That made it harder
to face him. She inhaled slowly. "I'll pay bills
and file taxes and paperwork and so many mil-
lions of tiny, similar, annoying paper cuts to keep
it going."

To avoid showing Grant more of her own soft
spots, Mia stood and wandered over to the closest stack of large wooden pieces. It was a horse
with what had once been a flowing mane attached. "If you have a wig around, this would
be a cute backdrop for your kids." She flipped
through the smaller pieces until she uncovered
the final one. It was big, maybe six feet tall at
the highest point.

"Is this a schoolhouse?" It was painted to suggest a log cabin, but there was also a large bell
at the top. In the dusty recesses of her brain, she
remembered some kind of TV show or movie
where the teacher tugged on a rope to ring a bell
and call the kids to school.

"Yeah. It's big enough that it could work for
something." Grant moved closer to hold his
hands out to get an idea of the width. "We'll
have to brace it to get it to stand tall, but it might
be perfect."

Mia gazed down the length of the storage room.
"I bet there are other gems in here. Want to keep
going, or do you want to bare your soul and your

secrets to me?" The side-eye he shot her was so unexpected that she chuckled aloud.

It felt good.

"Fine. We'll keep going." Mia wasn't sure exactly when she lost focus on slipping under Grant's skin, but a couple of hours later, they had created stacks of pieces that might be reused. There were multiple horses in different styles, but Grant suggested repainting them all to try to use every one. In addition to the school house, they found a large covered-wagon backdrop, and a jail with a forlorn prisoner peeking through the bars in the windows.

"Western Days was darker than I remembered, I guess." Grant shook his head as he tapped the miserable face. "Probably a cattle rustler. Nobody likes a thief."

Mia was laughing along with him, but she was also watching him closely enough to see the emotions flit across his face. Amusement was replaced by... The closest guess she could come up with was worry.

Their conversation had been easy. As if they were old friends.

"I've been in the magazine a few times, here and there." Grant gripped the jail cutout and moved it to their "use" stack. "You're pretty sharp. I'm having a hard time convincing myself meeting you on the side of the road was a happy accident."

"If you're about to accuse me of flattening my own tire to lure you into my web, please join me in the real world, Grant." Mia sighed. "I've always been luckier than I deserve. I've confessed being a college dropout, my general lack of ambition and hard-hitting reporting ability. Does it help to know it's the second time I've quit a degree close to the end? I'm only on the fringes of the news department. She protects the magazine and me, mainly by keeping us separated." She leaned forward. "But for the life of me, I can't remember seeing a single feature on Grant Armstrong or his close-knit family of adopted brothers living in Prospect, home of an exciting local festival."

Mia wrinkled her nose. "What you don't know is that whatever it is that you don't want told… There's not much chance my mother would let me be the one to write about it anyway."

That caught his attention. "Even if you uncovered it? Why is that?"

"A lifetime of never hitting the mark?" Mia knew that telling him this was another roll of the dice. If she wanted to be the reporter he trusted to tell his story, impressing him with her skills and experience would have been a smarter route. "I don't know if a successful, championship rodeo star can understand this, but my mother had high expectations for her only daughter. Instead, she ended up with one who can't change her own flat tire or get a college degree."

"I can only do one of those things myself." Grant grunted. "I'm guessing that's more common than not. Your mother good with a jack, is she?"

Mia shook her head. "No, but she finished the degrees her father asked her to do and she stepped up to learn the business side of the magazine right after. She would tell you that success requires sacrifice, doing things you don't like to earn rewards later."

He brushed a smudge of dust off her cheek. "Yeah, seems I've heard that sentiment around here a time or two."

"Of course you have. Reading a decade of newspaper articles has shown me the Armstrongs understand that." And it wasn't that Mia wouldn't make sacrifices for the things that mattered to her, but she wanted those decisions to make sense to her. A college degree she didn't need would show obedience but how would it change Mia's life? The magazine was her past and her future, no matter what happened this semester in health and wellness.

Mia leaned forward to touch his arm, certain she was going too far. "Stay with me. I know she loves me, right? She will tell me she did all that hard, boring work because she loves the magazine and her father and me. Even though she doesn't understand me, I believe that my mother loves me. Sometimes I can't understand why."

Mia knew she'd jumped right into the over-sharing deep end. There was no way she was coming out of this conversation with his trust, but then he clasped her hand and held on tight. Since she knew clinging to this bucking ride would turn into real attraction if she wasn't careful, Mia almost pulled her hand free.

But it was nice to have his warm, reassuring hand wrapped around hers.

"Out of all the things you could have said, I don't know how you picked the single collection of words to cut right through all my defenses. You know your mother loves you, but you aren't sure why." He traced his thumb over the back of her hand absentmindedly while Mia did her best to ignore the effect his light touch had on her nerves. She was comforted and energized at the same time. "I could say that about my whole family sometimes. Worse than that, it's my own fault. I've spent a lifetime being a burr under their saddles, agitating when things got too quiet around here. How do I have the right to ask if they trust me now?"

He narrowed his eyes at her. "We may need to go back to that 'off-the-record' status if I start to cry into my hat, confessing my innermost wounds."

Mia couldn't stop the blooming smile. "As long as you swear not to tell my secret, I won't tell yours. We have made these messes, haven't we? We'll have to muddle through on our own, but it's nice to have company on the journey."

He stared down at her hand, tracing one finger back and forth. "When you're building a brand as a bad boy, heartwarming stories of the amazing couple who adopted you from the foster care system and the impressive brothers who round out the rest of the family don't fit the tale."

Mia wasn't sure why, but she believed this was a piece of the puzzle she was trying to assemble. She needed more pieces to fill out the border. "Who decided being the bad boy was the right way to go?"

Grant tipped his head back. "Which time?" His wry grin landed somewhere in her chest with a warm splash. He was nearly irresistible like this.

"When I first showed up at the Rocking A, Wes and Clay were settled. They were solid, you know? Smart. Conscientious. Good in school. Travis and I arrived not too far apart, but he was mostly an alley cat at that point, roaming around on his lonesome…unless I prodded and made him square off against me. I wanted him to be my… What's the right word?"

"Friend?" Mia asked and laughed at how he grunted in response.

"You didn't want to do this all alone. I get that. You and Travis could tackle it together and have each other to lean on." Mia moved closer and tangled her fingers through his, intent on keeping Grant talking.

"I couldn't be all open with my emotions and ask him to be my friend because I was lonely and worried about this new place. As a teenage boy who'd grown up where being seen was dangerous and no one ever complained or cried about it or they were sorry." Grant rolled his eyes, inviting her to laugh with him, but Mia couldn't. It might be something he could poke fun at now, but it was so easy to imagine how scared she might be in the same spot. "So I picked at Travis until the older boys decided to 'teach' us or 'guide' us, which meant being disgustingly good examples of all that is right in the world, and then Travis joined me—the two of us against the model boys." Grant covered his heart with his hand. "Fortunately, I was very good at provoking reactions. Always have been, most likely always will be. Never met a dare I wouldn't take or an argument I wouldn't fight or a horse I couldn't ride."

Mia wasn't sure what reaction he expected, but his stillness told her he was waiting for something.

"And you took all that from Prospect to the rodeo and you started winning." Mia tilted her head back. "Why would you change it then, since it was working?"

He pointed at her. "Exactly. That wise-cowboy philosophy says 'if it ain't broke, don't fix it.'"

Mia pursed her lips. "Did a cowboy come up with that?"

Grant wagged his head. "If it wasn't a cowboy who started it, we definitely perfected it. So, when Red Williams started working with me, training me on how to talk to interviewers and when to make a statement by way of a splashy spectacle to keep everyone's attention, I listened. I was good at being bad, so the bad boy character was the right way to go." He grimaced. "Guess it's not a character, now is it? Genetic, most likely."

She had no idea where this trail was leading but they were getting close.

Mia knew that because his muscles were tense as she held on to his hand.

"Could be," Mia said slowly. "But I keep telling myself that I'm in charge of where the road takes me. Someday, I might need that college degree. There's nothing that has convinced me yet that I can't get it if I need it. Figuring out my job and my mother... That problem's harder, but it doesn't mean I should change who I am to please her." She realized she was getting offtrack and shook her head. "But I don't know that a bad boy would be digging through dusty storage to find pieces that could be reused for a kids' photo op and a competition that he's been forced to organize to help his hometown." Her lips twitched as he frowned at her.

"Even that cattle rustler in the jail had a hometown, Mia. Not sure that's a solid character witness."

Mia giggled in relief. Things had gotten so serious between them that it felt good to return to solid footing. "My stomach is telling me it's time for dinner. Do we have enough backdrops here to please Prue?"

When he nodded, she turned to head out to the sidewalk and waited for him to lock the door behind them. The fact that he never let go of her hand meant something, but Mia was too afraid to consider what it might be.

CHAPTER ELEVEN

GRANT HAD NEVER expected to spend so much time with Mia after the planning meeting at the Mercantile, but as he walked with her toward his mother's apartment, he realized how much he'd enjoyed her company. Dancing around the story between them was getting harder.

Because he wanted to share the whole truth with her.

The way Prospect's old town took on a romantic rosy tinge as the sun set didn't help that. Shadows lined the street and it was so quiet. They might be the only two people in the world. Since her fingers were tangled with his, that thought filled him with… Peace. It was the only name for the emotion that Grant could find. Had he ever experienced peace like this?

Mia brushed her free hand down the front of her oversized sweatshirt. "At times like this, I regret not packing for a longer trip. Luckily, I brought every baggy sweatshirt that I own, in order to make a sloppy first impression. My mother would be proud of that, too."

The way she blew out a raspberry and held out her arm made him think she was making a joke at her own expense. "You're dressed exactly right for the job you're doing. We were just digging through a century of dust back there."

She brushed bangs off her forehead. "When I come back for Western Days, I'll bring my good jeans. The whole town will be impressed then."

"I like this Mia." He squeezed her shoulder. "But you can count on me to say that about whichever Mia you show me next, too."

She froze as she watched his face. Then she exhaled so loudly her bangs ruffled. "Grant Armstrong, cover-model cowboy, likes my sweatshirt? This is some kind of tactic, right? You're trying to throw me off the trail of what-ever it is you're hiding." She tapped his chest with one finger. "I'm on to you."

He wrapped his hand around the poking fin-ger. "I was about to accuse you of sneaking under my guard by being all cute and soft and aggres-sive with that pointer finger, so now where do we go?"

They were both smiling when she stepped back.

Mia opened her mouth to say something but must have thought better of it. He immediately wanted to know what question she'd reconsidered. "You can ask it, whatever it is. I might not answer it, but asking won't offend me." He wanted to tell her about himself. It was a weird urge and it could get him into trouble if he wasn't careful.

"Prospect is special. Do you have other family elsewhere?" Mia asked and then wrapped her arm around his. "I'm sorry. You don't have to answer. I don't know much about the foster care system."

He questioned whether this was something he wanted Mia to understand. Since his family's reaction to his secret was top of mind still, he said, "I do have an older brother, but we were separated when my mother was sent to jail for her third driving-under-the-influence charge. He was already eighteen, so he didn't go into the system. I did, and I made sure to make three different families regret my stays, mainly by running away. When I got caught, I got a fresh start. And the only time I didn't run was at the Rocking A. Most of that was Travis's fault." He shook his head at her muffled laugh. "It's like once I met the kid, I forgot how to be wild all on my own."

"Sounds like you owe him. A lot." Mia squeezed his arm.

"I do." Grant owed them all so much. "It's the kind of debt you never repay."

She stared into his eyes and he wondered if

she would pursue that unintended bit of honesty or do them both a favor and let it go.

"Family who will not stop supporting us or loving us. How did we get so lucky?" Mia asked.

It was a good question, one he didn't have an answer for, so he returned to the business at hand. "Cowboy Games. Some kind of riding course, target practice. What do you think?"

Mia chuckled. "Your mother likes to aim for the stars, I know. It seems like that place is perfect for a competition. If you had a rodeo club in place, they could help you run it, too."

Grant groaned. "Relentless."

Mia bumped his shoulder with his. "Just saying."

He sighed and produced his phone to tap out notes. "Cowboy Games first, rodeo club later. Maybe. I need to get Sam's buy-in first, then talk to the school administrators." He rubbed his forehead. "Oh, and can't forget the budget spreadsheet."

Mia was quiet as she strolled slowly along the fence line. He could tell by the way her face changed swiftly that she was deep in thought.

"An obstacle course with target shooting, using the backdrops we salvaged, may save you a bit of extra construction." She bit her lip as she faced him.

"Doesn't sound very impressive, does it? I'm

not sure how we're going to attract a crowd of stars like my mother hopes, especially in two months."

She nodded but didn't explain whatever it was that caused her eyes to momentarily light up before she shook her head.

Grant was surprised to discover that he didn't like that, being shut out of whatever inspired thought lit her eyes like that. He wanted Mia to trust him with those sparks.

To get there, he'd have to tell her everything. Grant forced himself to let go of her hand as he raised his own to knock on his mother's front door. Whatever came next between him and Mia would be decided by his own choice to trust her with the story that had been keeping him awake at night for months.

So much of where he went from here depended on the answer to one question.

How much faith did he have in Mia Romero?

MIA WAS STILL staring at her empty hand when Prue Armstrong yanked the door open. The wreath covered in pink-and-red hearts swung wildly before Prue caught it. "All right, Valentine's decorations. Settle down." Then she waved them both inside. "Come in, come in. You kids ever wonder why we have mistletoe for Christmas but nothing for kissing around Valentine's Day? That's a missed opportunity right there."

She hurried back to her small corner kitchen and picked up a ladle. "Been craving a nice beef stew for a week or so, and this morning I gave in. Dumped everything in my slow cooker first thing so I'd be sure to have a hearty dinner. Might not be fancy enough for guests but it's right for family."

Family? Mia raised her eyebrows at Grant but he only shook his head in resignation.

Prue pointed at two seats across the counter from her. "Only got seats for two, but that's fine. Perfect for romantic rendezvous when I need 'em, and tonight I'll hop up on the counter."

As Mia slid into the chair, she noticed Grant's hand was loosely clenched, like hers.

Mia missed the warmth of his palm next to hers. Was he experiencing the same sensation? As if they'd both discovered something new and neither wanted to return to being empty.

"How many romantic dinners for two are you having, Mama?" Grant drawled. Mia hid her smile by picking up the digital frame that was scrolling old family photos. He took his job as the troublemaker seriously.

"Stay out of my business, Grant. Did y'all accomplish a lot in the storage room?" his mother asked as she dished up dinner and plopped a hank of crusty bread on each of their saucers.

Grant started naming an inventory of the pieces

they found to use and the trip they'd made to the high school. As he answered his mother's rapid-fire questions, Mia studied the photos. Intrigued by a group shot of four teenage boys, she pulled it closer. Each of them was lanky, long arms and legs, as if they'd sprouted up quickly and the rest of their bodies had to catch up. If she looked closely enough, it was easy to pick Grant out from the quartet. Clay and Wes had wider grins, Travis stood apart from the group and Grant had his arm wrapped around his shoulders as if he was anchoring him in place. They were heartbreakingly young in the photo and had already been through so much. The desire to ask a million different questions about his childhood surprised her.

Before she was ready, the photo advanced. She lost track of whatever it was that Prue and Grant discussed as she watched ranch photos morph into school pictures and candids of each boy. Matt eventually joined the family, and Prue and Walt were scattered throughout. It was a slide-show of the Armstrong family through the years, and Mia was charmed.

Whatever story she'd told herself about them based on the newspaper clippings and her brief encounters was fully illustrated as one frame followed another. Small-town neighbors. Prospect leaders. Good kids who became successful men. A loving couple who changed the lives of their sons for the better.

The most recent photos were from Christmas. Sarah and Jordan appeared here and there, along with a beautiful redhead she had yet to meet. Then a picture of Grant shuffled up. There were two younger boys, each one hanging over Grant's shoulders as he propped a T-shirt over his chest. Funcle was in bold letters with The Fun Uncle underneath. The kids were proud of their gift, and the broad grin on Grant's face changed his appeal from brooding and handsome to too much.

Way too much handsome.

There was no cowboy hat or serious expression. His happiness was on full display, right there in that moment.

She loved this photo because she knew there was probably not another one like it.

"When the renovations commenced at the ranch, my boys took down a lifetime of photos. I had them lining the hallway in my house. In my husband's house? My ex-husband left them up after I moved out?" Prue shook her head uncertainly and dipped her spoon back into the bowl. At some point, she'd settled herself next to the sink and seemed comfortable there. "Anyway, they gave me that rotating picture frame, most likely to keep me from hanging all those photos up somewhere else that would contribute to the scarring they still carry from their awkward phases."

"I was wondering which of the brothers was the funcle. I would not have picked Grant." Mia wrinkled her nose at him.

"That is because you have not seen my gaming system." He pointed at the frame. "As soon as I can wrestle it away from Damon and Micah, I will show it to you."

Mia reluctantly set the frame back down and picked up her spoon. Then she noticed that Grant had finished eating. Had she been looking at the photos for that long? "I'm sorry. I missed some of the conversation." Her first bite of the stew landed with a swell of pleasure. "Whoa. I should have been paying closer attention to the food."

Prue laughed. "No harm done. Besides, I'm proud of my boys. Warms my heart to show them off. That little smile on your face as you watched the slideshow was the kind of reaction I need."

"Even from the dangerous reporter in town?" Mia ate two bites before she could add, "Travel writer. I'm not a reporter. Yet." But I could be, she tacked on mentally. If she got the chance, she could do something great.

She managed to tear her attention away from dinner long enough to find Prue watching her closely.

"Mia has some inspiration for our Cowboy Games, Mom," Grant said as he hooked his arm over the back of her chair. "Don't know what it is, but I can't wait to hear it."

She'd intended to keep her ideas to herself. After too many story pitches that had been shot down or co-opted, she'd learned to pick and choose her opportunities.

But the way both Prue and Grant were waiting convinced her to go for it.

"Fine. Have you ever thought about building a 'Western competition unlike any other'?" She waved her arms grandly to punctuate her idea.

Grant tipped his head to the side. "I wouldn't know how to go about building one of those, so no, I haven't."

Prue leaned forward. "I am intrigued. Go on."

"Cowboys expect horse riding and shooting." Mia raised her eyebrows. "What if you gave them something else entirely? Wild-card events? I was trying to think what might make Prospect's Western Days stand out from all the other small towns scattered across the West, who have parades and craft competitions and livestock shows. Like you could have a relay race scattering hay bales. On foot. Or you could do a Dutch-oven cooking contest, best meal and cup of coffee wins so many points. Western life wasn't only about cutting herds and sitting on a horse." She shrugged.

"Western life had a whole list of hard work that is ripe for competition."

Grant studied her face as he thought about her suggestion.

"Repairing a fence. Mucking out a stall. Breaking ice in the pond. Chopping wood for the fire. Washing clothes in a tub and hanging them on the line in the shortest time. Best cowboy serenades around the campfire." She counted items off on her fingers as she named them. "Instead of professional cowboys who ride the rodeo circuit, you could recruit real men and women who work cattle and award good prize money. Coed teams, even. The judges could be stars instead."

"Turn our idea on its head," Grant murmured.

The Armstrongs' long pause triggered the uncertainty again. Mia scraped the bottom of her bowl with her spoon and wished she hadn't eaten quite so quickly. Now she had no reason to pretend not to be paying attention.

When Mia's nervous swallow made an obnoxiously loud gulp, she wanted to disappear in a cloud of embarrassed smoke.

"Or not. Just spit balling. That's a thing I do, throw out ideas that no one asked for. People don't generally appreciate it, either." Mia shrugged. "Don't worry about telling me all the whys and hows this won't work. Not necessary."

"That's the thing... I think it will. It might even

be genius. No one in Prospect wants to do things the same way other places do if we can help it." Prue's beautiful grin convinced Mia her idea might be the winner all three of them wanted.

Grant squeezed her shoulder and the instant shot of heat filled Mia with a jittery, excited awareness.

The admiration on his face was overwhelming. He murmured, "I might be coming around to your way of thinking about how this universe works if you let it."

Her eyebrows shot up. "No way! Not practical Grant Armstrong?"

"I can't deny your timing is suspicious," he said as stared into her eyes, "but you are proving to be the kind of gift I had no idea I needed, Mia Romero."

The flush that immediately covered her cheeks was embarrassing, especially when she glanced over at Prue to see Grant's mother watching her closely.

"Seems like the travel writer had some good input. I love it." Prue leaned back to cross her arms over her chest. "Might have changed my opinion on Mia Romero, too."

Mia straightened in her chair. "In a good way?" She wasn't as experienced with someone accepting one of her ideas and giving her credit for it at the same time.

Prue laughed and winked at her. "Only one little thing stood between me and you being the best of friends, honey." She motioned with her head toward Grant. "Overcoming that was never gonna be easy, but I underestimated you."

Mia grinned at Grant. It sounded like his mother was ready to pick Mia over her son. It was unclear how one good idea could accomplish that, but while she was sitting in Prue's kitchen and contemplating asking for a second bowl of stew, Mia wasn't going to ask difficult questions.

"In fact, I think you should tell her everything, Grant." Prue opened a large container from the shelf near her elbow. "About why you left the circuit."

Grant hesitated. Was he about to argue?

His jaw clenched and his mother added, "Give her a chance. Let's see what she says."

Then he raised his eyebrows.

Prue held up her hands. "Me? Part of the wallpaper. You won't even know I'm here."

Mia worried about making too big a reaction and scaring the moment away, so she shifted slowly in her seat to face Grant directly. "Give me a shot. I'm listening."

She reached for his hand and forced herself to wait patiently.

The loud clatter of the plastic container on the counter didn't interrupt their moment, but

Grant's lips twitched as they shared some amusement at their "invisible" audience.

"The Bad Boy of Bronc Busting." Grant scratched his chin. "All thanks to Red Williams. He taught me which bars to skip, which women to avoid, which questions to answer and how, and at every step, his advice paid off." Grant cleared his throat but he didn't let go of her hand. "Rodeo's kinda like one big, dysfunctional family, right? You're all traveling from one stop to the next, but the faces don't change that much. You get to know each other. Trust each other." He huffed out a breath. "And I was as successful as I always knew I would be. Growing up, I'd have told you I was going to win whatever event I entered."

Mia wasn't sure where he was going with this, but the pain on his face worried her. "And you were right, but you decided to leave because…"

"I left because I recently heard my mentor, my manager, the man whose steps I followed almost like my own father… I overheard him and my best friend discussing this scheme they had been running to get me to the top by convincing other riders to…falter. Lose just enough time on their rides that Red and Trey could also bet on my first-place finish and come out with a nice payday all around. I don't know how many people were involved, but Trey was worried it was about to come out. Red reassured him that it would be easy enough to convince the world the scheme was all my idea. That's what a bad boy would do, right? Cheat to win?"

Mia laughed because she expected there to be more to the story. When he remained silent, Mia said, "And you were thrown out or threatened with possible charges because you punched him in his lying mouth. That's the end of the story?"

Grant shook his head slowly. "It's like the boy who cried wolf. I've done a bunch of silly stunts. I'm convinced they're right. People would accept their version over mine."

"He thought his family would believe that he was involved with such a grift," Prue said, scoffing from her spot at the counter. She'd moved closer to lean her elbows and rest her chin on her hand. "Didn't tell us what was going on until this suspect travel writer rolled into town. We needed to know if you were here snooping for proof for that story while also handing you a barrel of Chamber of Commerce advertising for the town and Western Days."

Mia closed her eyes as she realized the universe was pulling strings again to land her in exactly the right place at the right time. "I only came to research Western Days. Then all your espionage and public theatrical displays tipped me to the existence of something else."

Prue plopped the plastic container now filled

with stew on the counter. "This is for you. Take it out to the Majestic and have another bowl with Sarah and Jordan. I'll wrap up the bread to go with it."

Mia watched as Grant rolled his head on his shoulders to try to relax.

"What next?" Mia asked.

"What do you suggest?" both Armstrongs asked at the same time.

Grant frowned at his mother and she held up her hands in surrender.

Mia bit her lip as she reviewed their options. "Do nothing, because the story will come out or it won't, but then you'll have the threat of discovery, and an investigation always looming and what would happen to your wins and your record. You're innocent, so there's no proof of your involvement, no matter what story Red might spin. If you don't expose Red, he may still be running the scheme, keeping other good riders from winning fair and square. You Armstrongs strike me as men and women who dislike cheaters like that." She watched the photos slide by in the frame as she thought some more. "Or you can strike first. Tell the story to someone who will publish it in one of the industry's most respected magazines for rodeo news. Investigating might take time, but you could have your truth out there in the next issue of *The Way West*."

Mia watched how his frown changed from worried to dissatisfied to concerned… It was a lot of movement for one frown. "You wanted a third option, I'm guessing."

"I came up with those two on my own." His disgruntled mutter was punctuated by a squeeze of her hand and his mother's snort.

"Now that I know the background, there might be a third," Mia said. "If the right person investigated the story, you might be able to avoid being connected to it at all. I hear the next big competition is in Utah." She bit her lip as she wondered what kind of excuse she could invent for nosing around behind the scenes.

Then she considered how much trouble it would be to dodge Casey Donaldson the whole time she was hunting for sources.

"Too bad you can't hang around, Mia. I love your idea for the games. I bet the two of us could put up some real big shenanigans by April. People would talk about Western Days in all fifty states, Canada and Mexico." Prue put the leftovers in a tote bag displaying the name of her shop, Handmade. "Come into the store before you go. I want to say goodbye, 'mkay?"

Mia nodded and accepted Prue's hug.

"This was lovely, Prue. Thank you for giving me a chance to win you over." Mia hated to leave, but she was so relieved that she and Grant and every Armstrong and Hearst by association had cleared the suspicion they had about her. She was also sad that she would be leaving town so soon.

In the back of her mind, she was churning through ideas to convince her mother that she needed to go to Utah instead of returning home and how she would wriggle her way into Red Williams's inner circle from the travel desk. The universe would have some heavy lifting to do to make this story come together quickly.

As they slowly walked back toward the Mercantile, where they'd both parked before the meeting, Mia and Grant were silent.

"I'll follow you to the lodge." Grant nodded as she started shaking her head. "I live next door, Mia. This is not out of my way. Even if it was, I want to make sure you're safe."

Mia sighed. "Fine. Thank you. I do tend to trust things to work out. Sometimes it would be nice to have someone watching over me to make sure they do."

"I know what you mean." Grant stepped forward until they were close enough to touch. "Thank you for listening."

Mia smiled at him. "All off-the-record, of course."

"I hope you mean that." His lips curved before he pressed a gentle kiss to her lips. When she wrapped her arms around him, he kissed her again, deeper. It was a new kind of kiss for Mia, one that she wanted more of, one that spoke to his steadfast character and meeting her where she was. They fit.

"What a kiss. And from a man who doesn't fully trust me," Mia said softly. That little wrinkle should absolutely bother her, but she trusted him, so her own lips were ready to go.

If she wasn't careful, her heart would follow.

He urged her into the car. "Right behind you."

She was dazed as she started the ignition. There was no denying the new feeling of trusting Grant Armstrong to keep her safe.

Mia wished she had time to get used to it. When they reached the lodge, he pulled up next to her and rolled the window down. "Have a good night, Mia. Thank you for everything you did today."

She wanted to get out and kiss him. It wouldn't be too hard. She'd have to stretch, but it was possible. Or she could go around and hop into his front seat and kiss him there.

"We both have plenty to think about tonight," Grant said softly before one corner of his mouth curled up. He wasn't a big talker, but the more minutes she spent with him, the easier it was to read his eyes. He was thinking about kissing, too.

And they both understood why it wasn't a good idea. She'd be headed out of Prospect the next day…or she could stretch it another twenty-four hours? Thirty-two?

Jordan was framed in the lodge's doorway. Her audience convinced Mia to slide out of her car. "Good night, Grant. Let's talk tomorrow."

He nodded, and she went inside.

"Is that Prue's beef stew?" Jordan asked as she took the tote bag. "And I smell bread."

Sarah poked her head through the opening to the restaurant. "We have bowls."

Mia laughed as Jordan towed her toward the restaurant's kitchen, where they heated up the stew, divided it and the bread evenly, and then moved to one of the tables with the best view of the lake. Moonlight gleamed across the dark water. "Even the night view is spectacular," Mia murmured.

Both sisters agreed, but they didn't take a break from eating until spoons were scraping the bottoms of the bowls. Then Sarah propped her elbow on the table. "Grant told you everything, right?"

Mia blinked as she tried to figure out how Sarah could possibly know that. "Did Prue call you while I was on the way home?"

Jordan grinned. "Home. I like that." She patted Mia's hand. "No, Sarah tried to convince the family that you would be a help in this situation, while we were arguing over breakfast at the Rocking A. She generally believes the best about people."

Mia leaned back. "But you had your doubts?"

Jordan pursed her lips. "Not doubts, exactly, but I'm careful about who I trust with my family. I wanted my sister to be right, if that counts for anything."

Mia finished her bread as she considered that. "Okay. I'll accept that."

"Sure am glad I don't have to keep my distance from you anymore. It's been a struggle." Jordan wiped her brow dramatically.

"It was one meal, Jordan. What an epic battle," her sister drawled.

"Thank you." Jordan pretended to bow.

"I didn't enjoy it, either. I almost called my mother." Mia stared up at the ceiling and pondered the horror that might have unleashed. Calling Casey had been bad enough.

They all giggled at Mia's tone.

"I wish I had better options." The urge to share how much she wanted to be the hero for Grant and the Armstrongs surprised her. She hadn't known Jordan or Sarah for long, but she believed they might support her slowly evolving plan to head for Utah, wait for the universe to unravel the cheating scandal while she was there, and write up the most amazing expose that reignited the magazine's readership, exonerated Grant clearly from any part in the scheme, and made it possible for her to kiss Grant without either one of them having to navigate any trust issues.

It was a lot to ask from a travel writer, but the part of Mia that expected things to work out was almost sure it would happen exactly that way.

Mia picked her bowl up and followed Jordan and Sarah into the kitchen. The vanilla scent that accompanied her trip this time didn't bother her. In fact, it was building her faith in the existence of the Majestic's ghost.

After the dishes were loaded in the dishwasher, Jordan wiped her hands on a dishcloth. "Tonight let's brainstorm a way to keep Mia in town. I don't want you to leave."

Mia loved the warmth that filtered through her to hear Jordan say such a thing. It was sweet to be so welcome. Her mother would say Mia should be in Billings, but they didn't spend much more time together when that happened.

They had made it through the lobby when Sarah said, "Oh, I already know the answer to that one."

Mia stopped in her tracks. "You do?"

Sarah grinned. "Yeah. All it'll take is one hard-headed cowboy."

It was impossible to misunderstand what she meant.

"I can't leave the magazine. To hear my mother

tell it, she's only keeping the magazine open for me, to pass it along. And I like *The Way West*. I was meant to write." Mia believed that completely.

"I don't have an answer for the magazine, but you can write anywhere, especially if there's a cowboy next door who keeps you coming back. What if the universe is already working that out, Mia?" Sarah wrapped her arm around Mia's shoulder. "If Sadie were here, I would suspect her of leading us all to this spot. I can't figure out how she's doing it now, but I'm also not putting it past her."

Jordan chuckled under her breath. "Sadie always was two steps ahead of us, but managing this would be impossible even for her." Then she stopped. "It would be, wouldn't it?"

Mia shrugged. "We'll wait patiently for more information from whoever is pulling the strings."

Sarah smiled. "Waiting. It's a nice concept, Mia, but I've never met a Hearst who excelled at it."

CHAPTER TWELVE

GRANT WAS STILL thinking about his conversation with Mia from the night before on Monday morning. The day had dawned crisp and cold; it was a relief to give up on pretending to sleep. The old bottom bunk he'd claimed when he'd returned home was never comfortable, but going back and forth in his mind about trusting Mia had battled with the memory of her kiss until he was worn out.

He'd expected everyone to accept the worst about him, and it turned out no one did. Apart from himself. At some point, he was going to have to come to terms with that fact.

But that was a long-term project.

Unfortunately, that didn't mean there would be no consequences if the story broke. Unless he proved his innocence completely, his history would always cast a shadow. Some people would probably always wonder if he'd been a part of the cheating scandal since he'd benefited from it.

That shadow would attach itself to the Armstrong name, too. That was unacceptable.

His sleepless night had picked up a third item on the list of things to worry over. First, his career.

Second, Mia, who'd separated herself from the problem of keeping Red's scheme under wraps to rightly stand on her own two feet and asked a different kind of question. He had a strange, empty spot in his chest, brought on by telling her good night the evening before instead of kissing her again.

And now, third, he was considering all the things he could do to help kids through the Prospect Rodeo Club if it was resurrected.

He wanted to give that a shot because it had meant so much to him as a youngster. That club had given him a place to shine, build confidence and helped make him who he was.

But it was easy to imagine it crashing in flames if his star was tarnished by cheating.

To find a distraction, he offered to drive Micah and Damon to school. The way Travis and Wes had stared at him, with their dropped jaws, from their spots at the breakfast table, still rankled.

After seeing the boys on their way and avoiding most of the other parents, it struck him that he had another stop to make. "I'm helpful. I volunteer to do nice things," he muttered to himself as he opened the door to the Mercantile.

Grant tapped his hand against his thigh as he made the short journey into his mom's store. As always, it took him a minute to adjust to the collection of color and texture that surrounded a person upon arrival. When they were growing up, Grant and his brothers were taught the basics of needlework by Prue, but beyond reattaching a loose button, he had missed out on the sewing gene.

That didn't mean he missed how much work and skill every piece in her shop took. He paused to scan the walls. There were two new quilts and an embroidered sampler with Bless This Mess in the center. Prue Armstrong was a one-of-a-kind who enjoyed collecting unique patterns.

"I hoped I'd see you today. Tell me what happened after you left the apartment." She didn't stop talking as she wrapped her arms around him and held him in place for a comfortable minute. That was one thing he had immediately loved about Prue. Before he landed in her care, hugs had been scarce in his life. His father had left when Grant was a toddler. There were a few pictures, but Grant couldn't remember anything about the man clearly. Once Grant had gone into the foster care system, he lost track of his mother, too. Prue and Walt had given him everything and he hadn't missed one day at home without a hug since.

"I followed Mia out to the Majestic and I drove home." He met her stare and did his best to leave it all there. "The end."

"Not even the last chapter, my boy. When are you two getting together so Mia can start writing up something for the magazine? Don't tell me you're still not sure? I can't believe you've managed to sit on the truth this long. She'll do a good job."

Grant motioned to a poster advertising Western Days. "She's already got a story, remember? She may decide to stick with that." He recalled how she spoke about finding the one big story that could change the way her mother treated her and knew that Mia was committed to doing both as well as she knew how.

His mother peered at him over the rims of her reading glasses. "You'll never get that whopper past me. You're wasting time. Sounds like you have a perfectly valid reason to be tracking down that pretty magazine writer." She shooed him toward the door. "Don't let me keep you."

Grant laughed. "Don't you want to lay groundwork for wooing the 'pretty magazine writer' to stay in Prospect, marry your black-sheep son and contribute to the growing Armstrong-ization of this town?"

Prue smiled slowly. "Well, now, that hadn't even occurred to me. I ought to let you tell on yourself more often." She braced her hands on the table in front of her. "Thinking of long-term possibilities, are you? Perhaps you should start with a kiss first. See where it goes." The tense silence between them stretched out until her eyebrows shot up and she exclaimed, "Oh, my heavens, you kissed her!"

Her volume registered, and she clapped her hand over her mouth.

The door swung open wildly and Walt stepped inside. "What's all the noise? Surely he's kissed someone before?"

Grant was prepared to stonewall both of his parents on his kissing history and then his phone rang. "Saved by the bell," he muttered as he saw Matt's name on the display.

"Where are you?" Matt asked.

"I'm at the Mercantile. What do you need?" Grant moved to the window to see his brother's truck parked in front of the storefront he'd been using as a veterinary office in town.

"I've been volunteering with this animal rescue group, and they have a case of animal neglect, a horse over near Leadville. I agreed to evaluate the horse and foster it at our ranch, but I'm not sure how easy it will be to get the horse home. Can you help?"

"Of course. I'll meet you at the barn to pick up the horse trailer." Grant hung up immediately. Matt would be anxious to leave right away. "Matt needs me to assist with a horse, a rescue. Are we rescuing horses now?"

His dad shrugged. "Different kind of fostering, but it seems to fit in pretty well. Can't see anybody having a problem with that."

Prue blew him a kiss. "Imagine if you weren't here, Grant. Who would lend Matt a hand?"

Grant shook his head. "There's a list of at least twenty people I could name who would help your baby."

She shrugged. "Not a one of them would be as helpful as you."

Grant squeezed her close and then clapped his father on the shoulder before he trotted out to the truck.

Matt blew past him on the way out of town, so Grant pressed the gas pedal a little harder and managed to hop out of his truck as Matt was backing up to the trailer hitch.

He took over while Matt hurried into the barn to grab rope and gloves, whatever he thought they might need to put the horse in the trailer.

"Ready?" Matt asked as he trotted back out.

"Yeah." Grant jumped into the passenger seat and they were on the way, Matt driving as assertively as usual.

"What's the story about the horse?" Grant asked.

Matt shook his head. "Apparently, his owner died and the family hasn't done anything to take over the horse's care. Probably too old to bring much for sale but starving him to death…" Matt bit off the rest of his sentence.

Grant didn't need to have the blanks filled in. Every single one of them had been raised to care for animals, but Matt had been born with the sensitive soul to feel their pain.

"How did you hear about the horse?" Grant asked.

"I've been working with an animal rescue organization. They focus on abuse and neglect cases, especially hard-to-place rescues like this one." Matt shrugged. "I started while I was still in vet school."

Grant gripped the dash as they rattled around a curve. "How come you don't toot your horn over the breakfast table?" Was he trying to keep his charity work secret?

"Nothing to brag about. It's part of my job." Matt grinned at him. "But now and again, I need help. That's where you come in."

Grant considered that as he watched his brother maneuver the road's curves. He was happy to help, of course, but it bothered him that this was the first he'd heard of Matt's extracurricular activities. They all gave him grief over his handsome face and the attention it got him.

All this time, he could have been annoying Matt by poking at his heroic work to help animals. It was wasted hours that Grant resolved to recapture as soon as he had his family all gathered around the kitchen table. Surely he could work in Dr. Dolittle somehow. "I wanted to tell you this great suggestion for the games." He gave Matt the shortest version of Mia's idea and was gratified that Matt was as impressed as their mother had been.

"I love it. If we have to, we can field enough teams from Prospect alone, no need for outside competitors, although that would certainly help spread the word for next year." Matt sped up as they came out of a curve. "Smart and beautiful. It's a miracle she's still single."

Grant swallowed the immediate response that rose up because he knew when he was being baited. That didn't mean he was smart enough to avoid the trap completely. Matt interpreted the silence correctly and chuckled. "Maybe she's not exactly single anymore. Does she know that?"

"There's a whole lot of world between her job and her place in Billings and mine here." Grant yanked his hat up before resettling it. He wasn't going to ask this, was he? "Got any advice on tackling that problem?"

Matt scratched his chin. "I believe one of our happily matched brothers might be more help, but…" He glanced briefly at Grant. "The two of you have proven you can come up with solid ideas when you work together. Try that again. Talk to her. It's okay if she's the smart one in the couple. That was bound to happen anyway."

Matt's evil grin surprised a chuckle out of Grant.

"Have you decided how to handle telling the world about Red?" Matt asked.

Grant sighed. "I want to get the story out. It's the right thing to do for everyone riding on the rodeo circuit. If I can't make my case well enough, there might be some gossip about me, about us, that I can't shake." He wouldn't have to explain how much that bothered him to one of his brothers. They understood.

"In your boots, I'd want the same thing, a little bit of justice," Matt responded. "Maybe you can't get even, but you can get a lot of satisfaction by telling the truth."

"I should have yelled loud and long as soon as I overheard Red and Trey talking, saved us all a lot of angst," Grant muttered.

"Yep." Matt's easy agreement landed on top of the ache in his chest that had replaced the hot burn of anger. "If you were a real bad boy, like your 'brand,' you probably would have punched first and ironed out the consequences later."

Instead, he'd been afraid and a little ashamed. He might even have believed he deserved whatever happened next.

Matt glanced over. "I'm glad you're here to help

with this, Grant. I'm glad you came home, no matter what sent you to us. We missed you."

Unexpected real, raw emotion between him and his brothers always made them awkward, so Matt cleared his throat.

"How glad? Are you glad enough to, say…" Grant inhaled as he considered what came next. As soon as he put the words out into the world, they would take on a life of their own. "Would you be interested in a role as advisor for the new and improved Prospect Rodeo Club? If Reg and I can get it up and going?"

Matt tilted his head to the side as he considered that. "On one condition." He held out his hand to shake.

Grant waited. It was never a good idea to agree to an Armstrong bargain until all the details were known.

"We wait until Western Days is all wrapped up before we start recruiting members." Matt offered his hand again.

Grant immediately clasped it. "And the club will be ready to serve for next year's festival."

Matt groaned. "Do you think I'm now stuck with doing this for the rest of my life?"

They both immediately nodded and Grant chuckled.

He was surrounded by people, smart ones, who were telling him to stand up and fight.

Dealing with the fallout after the story went into print and was out there for the whole wide world would be hard, but he could work through any concerns his neighbors had.

And Mia...

Well, they'd have to collaborate on the story first and figure the rest out later.

CHAPTER THIRTEEN

RESEARCHING SADIE HEARST had been Mia's first order of business when she'd settled at the table in the center of the church-turned-library. Thanks to fast internet and remarkably few interruptions, given it was a Monday morning, she'd jotted down notes about Sadie's first public-access cooking show and the almost magical way she'd parlayed that regional popularity into the early days of celebrity chefs with their own television programs. Mia knew all the basics: the year she was born; number of siblings; date of her death; broad descriptions of how she'd left her modest empire to her nephews and their children, a large, varied group spread out all over the United States, including the Hearst sisters.

As she surfed through all these web pages, Mia couldn't shake the notion that Sadie was impatiently waiting nearby for lightning to strike, for Mia to find something important. As if it was waiting for her, Mia, when she should be focusing on Grant's story or Western Days' lore.

Getting sidetracked by more and more ideas was a hazard Mia faced often enough that she wasn't surprised, but the undercurrent of excitement that fueled her work now was different.

Then she found a news story about Sadie's first cookbook, an international best seller filled with cookie recipes that she'd learned from her own mother, her neighbors and the people who'd made her who she was. The reviewer was both confused and charmed by the simplicity of the collection and parlayed it to a description of the personality driving the book's success.

The writer's theory was that Sadie herself was a secret ingredient that no other chef could match. All of the bits and pieces of Sadie's background had created something that was one of a kind.

Mia glanced up at the beautiful sunlight pouring in through the multicolored glass windows as she realized she'd found it, the project she was meant to tackle next.

A book about Sadie Hearst's life started to outline itself in her head.

Those first recipes had seemed to follow along with the places Sadie visited, the events in her early life and dreams she chased. The reviewer quoted one interview, where a talk show host asked Sadie if she knew how lucky she was to make it from her little hometown to the national stage, so Mia hunted up the video clip.

The male late-night talk show host seemed to imply that Sadie might be overwhelmed or out-classed in the kitchens of New York City or in front of Hollywood cameras. Mia was offended on Sadie's behalf, but Sadie was gracious and beautiful as she demonstrated the proper way to divide chilled dough into a dozen balls. Her laugh had been so light and genuine in response to his question. "Luck, you say? My daddy used to tell me 'luck ain't nothing but hard work and good timin'' and he was never wrong. The timin' is in somebody else's hands, of course, but I don't mind working at what I love while I wait for luck to show up."

Then she'd frowned at the man. "If you want cookies to eat anytime soon, you're going to have to give work a try, pardner. Spread these out evenly on the cookie sheet." Her can-you-believe-this guy? shake of her head at the crowd got laughter and applause.

Her warm eyes as she nodded at the camera and said, "Timing *and* hard work. Remember I said that, you hear?" caught Mia.

There was something so familiar about Sadie, pieces she recognized from Sarah and Jordan and their father, Patrick, but Mia knew in her heart that Sadie would have agreed wholeheartedly that someone or something put Mia where she needed to be. She and Sadie had that in common.

Mia wanted to keep digging to get to know this incredible lady.

"I can't believe there isn't a whole collection of philosophy books or humor books to join Sadie's best-selling cookbooks," Mia murmured as she stretched the knotted muscles in her lower back.

"Well, now, that would have been a money-making idea, to be sure." The petite redhead, Lillian Schultz, had introduced herself as the official librarian when Mia walked in, but she'd been occupied with rearranging her desk and going through book requests that had arrived over the weekend while Mia worked. "Sadie was a true original. You couldn't help but love her."

Now that Mia turned to face her, she could see that Lillian had transformed the bare-bones desk Sam had sat behind into a display of… "Are those crocheted dolls?" Mia bent closer to study a couple that were posed front and center. The period attire and the embroidered features on the man's haughty face added up to one simple guess. "Is this Darcy and Elizabeth? In crochet? I had no idea that could be done!" She leaned closer to see a tiny letter-sized envelope clutched in the woman's hand.

Mia wasn't sure how it could be accomplished but there was no denying the talent or Lillian's delight that Mia had identified the correct fictional characters. "I'm inspired by my favorite books, of course. Can you guess any of the others?"

Mia moved down the line, half bent to catch all the details. "Overalls. Straw hat. Mischief on his face. Huckleberry Finn?"

Lillian nodded. "I would have also accepted Tom Sawyer. I have a raft to put him on, but Sam hates all the clutter, so I take all the dolls down on Friday afternoons and put them up when I come in on Mondays. Recently, I've cut back on my desk decor."

This was cutting back?

"Is this a seersucker suit?" Mia asked. Lillian nodded. "Glasses, seersucker… It's not a lot to go on but this reminds me of Atticus Finch in the movie." Lillian clapped. The next one was harder. The figure was wearing a dilapidated cowboy hat and boots, a dusty overcoat and a stoic expression. "I'm going to need a hint for this cowboy."

Lillian tsked. "My goodness, he's the one who started it all for me. Famous book by Larry McMurtry?"

Mia only knew one. *Lonesome Dove*. She'd seen parts of the TV adaptation, but it had been years.

"Exactly. That's retired Texas Ranger Woodrow Call. I wanted something to get my patrons asking about this Pulitzer Prize-winning Western. I knew they'd love it, and I am a fan of the book, the series, the adaptation, both Woodrow and Gus, and the actors who played them." Lillian fanned her cheeks with one hand.

Mia grinned as she proceeded past Harry Potter with a tiny wand, Dorothy Gale from Kansas and her little dog, and Sherlock Holmes complete with a signature deerstalker. At the end, she said, "This is quite the collection. Who's next?"

Lillian bit her lip. "I'm having trouble deciding. Which one would you choose—Holly Golightly for a very fashionable addition from *Breakfast at Tiffany's* or Brienne of Tarth? I've been wracking my brain for a good fantasy character. I could put her in a suit of armor which seems like a fun challenge." Lillian bent and studied her collection.

"They're both great characters." Mia had her doubts about the "fun" part of crocheting armor, but it was a wonderful hobby. "How long does it take to make one?"

Lillian jerked upright as if she was shocked. "Oh, now you sound like my husband, Mia. Don't ask those kinds of questions. If I think about the time I spend on these for too long, I begin to worry about all my choices, you see? My husband is pondering his retirement, and I'm encouraging him to put it off. I don't need him hanging around under my feet while I design my pieces." Her warm smile convinced Mia that she was teasing.

"What does your husband do?" Mia had spent idle minutes considering what kinds of jobs were available in Prospect.

For no particular reason.

Definitely not because the idea of leaving town was filling her with dread.

"He manages the sporting goods store in Fairplay. Makes the thirty-minute drive every day, so I do understand his readiness to stay closer to home. I asked Sam to write down a good list of reasons to keep working." Lillian grinned. "Just in case my husband happens to ask."

Mia nodded. "Sam was a big help on Saturday. I asked about books available on the town history. None?"

Lillian pursed her lips. "No, none in this collection. We do have a copy of a paper Clay Armstrong wrote when he was a college student about the architectural methods used in building the old ghost town, Sullivan's Post, up above the lodge. I'd be happy to show that to you. It does have some good history, thanks in part to Sadie's contributions. It's like she's the thread that runs through every part of this town."

Mia agreed as Lillian summed up the point she'd been coming around to during all of her research. "She certainly does. I wonder why she never came back home."

Lillian fiddled with Huckleberry Finn's hat.

"I imagine she loved her life, no matter where she lived, whether here or Los Angeles or even New York City. I didn't know her well, but that's the impression she gave me. Happiness isn't in a place but a person. Sadie probably chose happiness no matter where she hung her hat."

Just then, a biography of Sadie Hearst became Mia's new goal in life. A goal she wanted to accomplish, a goal that meant something to *her*. If she could capture that personality on the page, she would have accomplished something worthwhile.

But first, she had other projects to finish. Grant's story had been percolating in the back of her mind all morning, too.

When her cell vibrated to indicate that she'd received a text, Mia picked up her phone.

Tires are in!

"Oh, good, it looks like I can head over to the Garage. It'll be good to have real tires instead of that spare." Mia put her laptop away. "When I come back to town, could I check out Clay's paper? It will be a few weeks till then." She wasn't sure what the paper would tell her, but she was interested in finding everything she could about Prospect, especially if it had Sadie Hearst's fingerprints on it.

"Yes, ma'am. I'd also suggest talking Clay into

taking you on an official tour around here and up at the old ghost town. He's got a big, successful business right now, building houses, but he's an expert on the town's architectural history. Do you ride?" Lillian asked.

"I do. I'm no superstar like Grant Armstrong, but I do enjoy time in the saddle." Mia finished packing her bag and waited to see if Lillian would take the prompt.

One way or another, Grant's story had to be told.

"I'll never forget the first time Grant came home to be the grand marshal for the parade, riding on his glossy black horse." Lillian pointed to the Texas Ranger in her lineup of desk characters. "There's the beat-up-saddle-tramp version of the cowboy, right? Grant Armstrong is the other archetype. Powerful. Movie-star handsome. So wild you know you'll probably never tame him, but you can't help but try." Lillian smiled warmly. "Grant was my husband's favorite rodeo cowboy—the hometown boy, of course, but he's more of a bull-riding fan. I don't get the obsession." Lillian shrugged, a blank look on her face. Mia wondered if Lillian's husband had the same expression when he talked about Lillian's dolls.

Amused and grateful at how generous Lillian had been with her time, Mia said, "I'll stop in next time I'm in town. Thank you for all your help today."

Lillian returned her wave as Mia headed for the door. She was sorry to leave the quaint library and its helpful staff. Telling herself that she could always come back helped a bit.

Before she got in her car to drive to the garage, she stopped at the historical marker that Sam had mentioned, outlined in bronze. As she pulled out her phone to take a photo of the dates on it and the building, it rang.

"Hey, Mom, I'm still in Prospect." She tugged her wool coat closer to her neck. The breeze was sharp.

"Casey Donaldson called to ask if we needed him to swing through Prospect while you were there. He was close, so I told him to do it," her mother explained.

Mia pressed her hand to forehead. This was not what she wanted, especially now that she knew the story. "Why? What is he going to shoot? There's nothing ready for Western Days yet."

Her mother sighed. "Casey had an angle I wish you had suggested. Grant Armstrong. His family is right there in Prospect. We can ask the question about what happened to him, even if we can't find him. If you had pitched that, along with your travel idea, we could have run with it. Casey wondered if I might want to do a background story that calls out the mystery of the cowboy's sudden departure from the circuit, Armstrong's rise to the top and theories about why he left. Even if we can't dig up the man himself, we can ask the question and then do a couple of paragraphs about his hometown and his history and call it out on the cover. You could have written it and gotten a news byline, but you were focused on the festival. This is why I can't let go of the reins here, Mia. You see that, right?"

The unfairness of the accusation landed first.

Was it true? If Mia had pitched that story, would her mother have allowed her to write it?

Or would she have taken the idea and given it to a trusted, professional investigative reporter?

Mia moved over to her car, ready to get out of this muddle. "That's pretty shady 'news,' Mother. Even a woman a semester short of a finished journalism degree understands that. You don't have any real facts, but you're capitalizing on this to sell magazines. Is that the way we do business?"

With heat blasting from the vents, Mia stared through the windshield at the church-turned-library and waited, disappointment weighing her down.

"If you had finished the business degree you started at eighteen, you would see that selling magazines is the first goal here at *The Way West*.

That means we can pay employees who do those very important stories. Every time I fork over the rent on this office space I wonder how much longer I'll be able to do that. That's the kind of thing that makes it hard to sleep, Mia." Her mother huffed a breath. "A story like this can pay the bills for one more month at least. Meet Casey and show him some spots in town to support this cover story. Then leave in the morning. Make him a reservation in town. He'll be there overnight."

Mia evaluated her arguments and discarded each option. If he was on his way, there was little hope that she could persuade her mother to change the plan. All she could do was support the Armstrongs in their strategy of closing ranks around Grant until he was ready to face the mess himself. "Okay, I'll do that."

"Good. I told Casey you'd meet him at Bell House around four." Her mother sounded suspicious, as if Mia had given in too easily.

"If you could get the story on Grant's reasons for leaving, who would you assign that story to?" Mia asked quietly. "What kind of writer do you want me to be?"

There was silence over the line. "Never mind writing, Mia, I want you to be a leader. Jesse Martinez. Now that's the writer you're looking for. A good managing editor would have him out on these news pieces, with Casey to get the shots, and then find a nice young college student or recent graduate to send in pieces about fun weekend festivals. Invest in the important stuff, Mia, and be here to manage all the moving parts. That's what I want from you. For you."

When Grant told his version of the cheating scam, he needed Jesse Martinez to write it up. That was helpful to know.

She'd also gotten the clarity she wanted.

The struggle to prove herself to her mother would never end, not while Mia was at *The Way West*. She'd loved every minute she'd spent with her grandfather, her hero and the one she'd based her understanding of cowboys and Western life on. That didn't mean she was the right person to keep his magazine alive, not if it made her miserable doing it.

Sadie's beautiful smile flashed in her mind, as if she agreed.

"We can talk about my future with the magazine when I'm home. Meanwhile, I'll get Casey set up in town." And make sure everyone in Prospect knew he was the intruder they'd been waiting for all along.

Her mind was racing as she worked through different approaches and punched the number for Jesse Martinez, a grizzled reporter who had spent his entire career watching rodeo change.

His reputation would add credibility to Grant's story if she could convince Jesse to keep an open mind. That would be the most important piece of the puzzle that she needed to fit before she left Prospect.

At first, she thought the phone had malfunctioned because the first ring was answered with a loud screech.

"Hello?" Mia said uncertainly before checking the phone display. Still connected.

"Give me that, you little polecat," someone muttered before Jesse said, "Mia? Everything okay?"

She understood the reason for the question. Her only phone calls to Jesse had been to deliver orders from her mother, ones she didn't want to handle herself. "Yeah, hey, have you got a minute?"

The screech was muffled this time, but Mia heard it. Whatever the source was, it seemed to be running away.

"Can I call you back? I'm babysitting for my daughter right now and my grandson is—" A loud crash covered whatever it was Jesse intended to say.

"Is there any way I can have five minutes?" Mia drummed her fingers on her steering wheel, determined to do something to help Grant.

"Okay, one sec." He must have covered the phone somehow, because his voice was muffled, but Mia heard him yell, "Babe, I need to take a work call. Ten minutes." Then there was the loud snap of a door closing. Firmly.

He sighed with relief as he returned to the phone. Mia pictured the bushy mustache that covered most of the bottom of his face and how on a windy day it would blow in the breeze. "Don't know how she could hear me over all the racket, but the house will most likely still be standing in ten minutes. What have you got?"

Mia bit her lip. "Have you ever heard any whispers about cheating on the circuit?"

"Oh yeah, every now and then, some disgruntled young'un gets upset because he can't shoot straight to the top, so the story kicks up that someone's messing around, but there's never any fire behind the smoke." He paused. "Why? You have a source?" He paused again. "Where are you right now?"

If she answered and he followed that string, it wouldn't take long for Jesse to untangle the answer she wasn't quite ready for him to have yet.

"If you could name anybody whose success seemed too good to be true..." Mia shook her head. That was the wrong tactic. She needed him to find the story first, with actual proof. Grant could be Jesse's confirmation, but no one would believe the story if he was the only source.

"Spit it out, Mia. Something may be burning

in the kitchen at this point. The smoke detector is going off."

Mia hoped that was a joke. There was amusement in his voice, but he was so crusty it was hard to tell. "How well do you know Red Williams?"

Jesse hummed. "Professionally, well enough. I've interviewed him once or twice. He likes to take kids coming up under his wing, sort of mold them." The silence stretched over the line as he considered the conversation. "Cheating. Fast-rising stars. Red Williams. What's the connection?"

Relieved, Mia relaxed in her seat. "Exactly."

Jesse grunted. "That's for you to know and me to find out, I'm guessing."

Mia smiled. "Yes, but the payoff? If you can find that story, I have a connection to answer one of the hottest questions on the circuit right now. I'll hand that over and you'll have the kind of story that will go far beyond *The Way West*. The only problem is that it's gotta happen quickly. Casey Donaldson is going to be awfully close to the source of the story, hunting for angles. If he manages to find the right one, we'll be scooped." And she knew Jesse and Grant together could tell the story better than anyone else.

She wasn't sure how many fans would still be listening if they weren't the first to speak.

"My wife is going to be airin' her lungs when I tell her I'm headed out to Utah." Mia would have worried, but he sounded more excited than concerned about his wife's emotional state.

"Call me as soon as you think you have something you can use," Mia said. "Or if you run into a dead end. We'll come at this from a different direction, okay?" She bit back the urge to tell the professional how to do his job.

"Why don't you meet me there? I have a phone interview set-up with this new hot-shot saddle bronc rider. I'll call and tell her I decided to come in person and bring you along for…a woman's perspective on her story," Jesse suggested. "Something about what you're saying makes this feel personal. We could tell everyone you're…" He paused as he weighed the options. "You're gathering hometown stories on rodeo's rising stars. That'll get a lot of doors open. Then we both step through 'em and poke around."

Mia bit her lip and mulled over the proposition. How long it would take to drive to Ogden, Utah, and what she could accomplish while she was there. The quick turnaround to get back to Billings to file the story.

All of that after riding herd on Casey while he was in town.

Letting Jesse go alone would be faster.

But he was absolutely correct. This was personal. And she wanted to make sure it was done right.

"If I won't slow you down," Mia said and waited.

"Text me when you get to town. We'll plot out our moves over a burger and see what we dig up. See you tomorrow." Jesse had ended the call before she was fully convinced she should agree.

Then she dropped her phone on the passenger seat and covered her face with her hands. Her easy, straightforward plans had just been scattered.

That was how the universe worked, though.

Being in the right place at the right time, over and over, was proving itself to be the key to her luck. Mia was certain this was the right track for her, for the magazine and for Grant.

But the clock was ticking.

At the Garage, she warned Dante and Lucky about the photographer coming to town while she built towers of blocks for Eliana and Selena. The twins clapped with extreme pleasure every time the slender stacks grew too tall and crumbled down. Lucky nodded her understanding while she rang up the total for the repairs. As Mia took her credit card back, she wondered if she should use it to catch up on the maintenance and any other repairs now…while her mother was still covering the credit card payments.

When she returned to Billings, everything would change.

Then she realized this might have been the "lack of adult survival skills" her mother had lectured her about.

Dante was swarmed by the twins when he came back into the office. "They are stern supervisors. You can't stop with the blocks until they are done and they are never done. Run away while you can, Mia."

Mia laughed. "They're adorable, but you have to stop feeding them whatever it is that is giving them this energy and then pass me the recipe because I could use a boost."

"You are welcome to return to babysit at any time. The pay is not great, and neither is getting up off of the floor after hours of entertaining these two," Dante said as he held the door open for Mia, "but you will have our eternal gratitude. We only offer that deal to special family members."

Mia waved, but she was touched by his words. They had taken good care of her. What if being "safe" as her mother wanted had more to do with the people she surrounded herself with than a guaranteed paycheck?

"Why not both?" Mia mumbled as she started the car and drove over to the Ace High. Her plan to get the word out was based heavily on the first informational campaign she'd witnessed in town. There was no need to do a dramatic reading in the center of the dining room, since she'd seen Faye herself in action. The woman who knew and saw everything that happened in Prospect would be enough for this task.

Especially since she was standing behind the host station as soon as Mia entered. A petite older woman was shaking her head angrily as she walked away when Faye said, "Hey, sit anywhere you like. May take a minute to get your food because the chef is in a mood." Faye held both hands out. "She's always in a mood lately. Evidently, she can't work like this. She needs freedom." When she realized she was saying too much, Faye's mouth snapped close. "But there are no bad menu choices. Trust me on that."

Mia checked the time. Casey was supposed to arrive at Bell House in less than two hours and she had to get to Prue Armstrong. "If it's okay, I'll swing back through during the dinner rush. I'll have someone with me."

"Grant again?" Faye winked. "Is he still underfoot?"

"Yeah," Mia said as her lips twitched, "he's been sticking pretty close."

Faye's grin bloomed slowly. "Well, around here, the next step is love." She sighed and leaned closer. "Between you and me, there's not a bad

Armstrong in the bunch, even if Grant is probably the orneriest one of the five. I take my job as honorary Armstrong seriously, and I've done my best to keep him humble. He's always been a star, you know."

Mia said, "It's working. Grant understands your power, especially with control of his favorite restaurant." She was amused to see the twinkle in Faye's eyes. As an only child, she'd never experienced sibling rivalry, but it seemed that the Armstrongs treated everyone like family and Faye had assumed her role with gusto.

Faye shook her head slowly, as if the burden was heavy. "I sure am glad I'm getting some help lately. Sarah and Jordan have been valued reinforcements in my battle to keep the Armstrong boys in check. Thank you for sharing. I will make sure to needle Grant until he confesses his devotion. It's part of my job as honorary little sister, you understand."

Mia nodded. "But my guest tonight isn't Grant. It'll be Casey Donaldson, a photographer who works the rodeo circuit. He's hunting for a story, so…"

Faye pursed her lips. "And there is no story. At all. And that will last until Grant changes it."

Relieved that Faye had understood as easily as Lucky, Mia said, "Exactly."

"Fine. Come in for dinner. We'll take care of

you." Faye pointed over her shoulder toward the kitchen. "Gotta smooth some feathers."

Mia trotted across the street to the Mercantile, conscious of the time.

She hadn't checked on a reservation at Bell House yet, but there was no way she was installing Casey Donaldson in the lodge room next door to hers. There had to be a room available at the bed-and-breakfast in town on a Monday night in February.

She was in a hurry as she hustled into Handmade and slid to a stop at the sight of Prue and Walt Armstrong kissing.

There, in the middle of the afternoon.

Just kissing as if it was the thing to do.

Stammering and excusing herself was what she wanted to do most, but she froze.

"Hmm, looks like we got a crowd started," Walt murmured as he stepped back and tilted his hat back down. "Hello there, Mia. What's got your tail on fire?"

Prue half smiled, half scoffed. "He's not smooth, is he? But he will always offer to help. When you get an Armstrong man, they fall on a scale like that. Romance on one end, utility on the other. We can nudge them toward the middle."

"Um…" Mia cleared her throat. "Today I could use some assistance." She wasn't sure how much Walt knew about the dinner she and Grant had

had with Prue. Then she remembered the kiss and guessed there weren't many secrets between the couple. "There's a photographer headed to town—" she checked the time again "—and if he's early, he might be in front of Bell House any minute. I talked with Lucky and Faye, but if you could do your thing—" Mia waved her hand at Prue "—to let everyone know that this is the person hunting for a story, the one you originally were warning them about, it would be good. It's my fault he's here, so I have to do whatever I can to try to fix this."

She shoved her phone back in her pocket and shuffled her feet as she waited for Prue to agree.

"Your fault?" Prue asked, her intent to find out exactly how Mia had caused this evident on her face.

"I'll explain it all eventually, but I won't have another chance to get the word out before he's here." Mia clenched both hands. "Let's take care of this first."

"Why didn't you set him up at the lodge?" Walt asked. "All of us would be watching him then."

Her automatic grimace made him whistle loudly. "That was a thousand words right there. I'm guessing he's not your bestie?"

"Casey's fine, just not my cup of tea," Mia replied. "He can be pretty dogged about things when he wants to be."

Prue's narrowed eyes convinced Mia that she was reading between the lines. "Well, Rose will be glad to host. There isn't much she can't handle." She punched a button on her phone. "Rose, we've got an undesirable headed into town. Can you make sure he's comfortable but ready to leave tomorrow as the sun comes up?"

Mia crossed her arms over her chest, amused at the opportunity to watch an expert at work behind the curtain.

"Jordan still complains about the bells that kept her up all night when she stayed there. Was that Silver, or...?" Prue covered the phone to say, "All the rooms are themed and all the doors have wreaths to match the theme. There's one that jingles with teeny, tiny..." Prue nodded. "All right. That sounds perfect. And the Christmas decorations will add to the experience. Not a word about an Armstrong, okay?"

When the phone call was over, Prue put her phone on the counter next to the cash register. "Handled. Nobody on earth is better than Rose Bell at resolving a tricky problem. We've been friends for four decades. Never seen her rattled except when Patrick Hearst asked her to the Picture Show the first time." Prue shook her head.

"As if the whole town couldn't see they were meant to be together."

Mia bit her lip and decided not to mention how many different people had said the same to her about Walt and Prue...who had just been caught making out during work hours.

"You talk to Grant today?" Walt asked.

"Not yet, but I have a new strategy, the third option we needed. I hope Grant likes it. I'll show Casey around town for photos, escort him into the Ace High and run interference. Casey's a good photographer, so everyone should definitely be friendly. Just careful." Mia was hoping to avoid tipping off Casey the way she'd been alerted that there was a story under the surface. "And I'll leave town same time as Casey, bright and early, so as long as Rose's performance is successful, he'll be none the wiser. It would be best if Grant stays close to home. I guess I won't be able to say goodbye in person."

"Close to home puts him right next door," Walt drawled. "You could drop in anytime you wish."

Mia appreciated that open invitation. Leaving without a proper goodbye wouldn't be the end of the world. This wasn't her last visit to Prospect.

Seeing him again would make leaving that much more difficult and there was no other option right now. She was driving out of Prospect bright and early in the morning.

"Let me give you my number. If anything comes up tonight, call me." Mia took Prue's contact info and entered it into her phone. "You can also get in touch with me through the magazine and I have email there." Desperate was how she sounded. She didn't want to leave and she wanted to see Grant now and tomorrow and the day after.

"I'll be back for Western Days no matter what happens." She knew Prue thought it was a promise to get the town the coverage she wanted most, but Mia heard it as an attempt to comfort herself.

This visit wouldn't be her last chance to kiss Grant Armstrong.

CHAPTER FOURTEEN

GRANT PROPPED HIS boots up on the old coffee table in the center of the lodge's lobby. Jordan had uncovered the worn gem in the Majestic's magical storage room while she'd been applying every bit of elbow grease she had to clean up the lodge. The furniture in the lobby wasn't stylish, but it had obviously been built of real wood, hand tools and enough time to make it sturdy.

That was a good thing. He was frustrated that he hadn't had a chance to speak to Mia all day long. That made sitting still in one place difficult.

It had taken most of the day to get the skittish rescue horse loaded into the trailer and settled back at the Rocking A. The caution required to approach the old gelding had paid off as soon as he and Matt unloaded him in the barn. Grant would swear he'd seen relief replace flat distrust in the horse's eyes as soon as he'd stepped inside the empty stall.

Grant figured he'd had the same expression the same night he'd come back home. He'd been so hurt and angry that his best friends in the world had betrayed him but stepping into the comfort of the Rocking A and his family had been a relief. He'd had a long way to go then, and his future was still hazy, but having a safe place had convinced him recovery was possible.

Rodeo had been his first chapter; he'd find his way through the next one here in Prospect.

He and Matt were a good team, and it was eye-opening to see his brother at work like that. Together, they'd managed to get the horse fed and watered, and the last he'd seen Matt, his brother was carrying on a one-sided conversation as he brushed and examined his newest patient.

When Faye called to tell him that Mia had made it as far as the Ace High with *The Way West*'s photographer, he'd decided that missing Mia wouldn't do. He needed to see her, so camping out in the Majestic's lobby had been his only option.

Every Armstrong he talked to that day made it clear that he should avoid Prospect until Mia called the all-clear.

He was doing his best to trust that there was a logical reason for this photographer to appear now. Had she arranged the photographer to get shots for Western Days?

That didn't make any sense.

Had Mia called for help with her investigation?

The one she'd sworn was never a thing as recently as the night before.

Maybe.

He understood Mia was trying to contain the exposure for now. Why? If she wanted the story bad enough to call in the photographer and Grant was ready to talk, what was the plan here?

Then his mother had mentioned that Mia had confessed the photographer's arrival was her fault and she was trying to control the damage by any means necessary, including activating Rose Bell's unique people-handling skills.

It all added up to a confusing picture. He wanted to trust Mia, but he needed answers.

Unfortunately, the sturdy furniture was not conducive to waiting comfortably or quietly.

"I said you could wait in the lobby, even though those were not the instructions you received from Mia," Jordan said as she skidded to a stop in front of the check-in desk, "but I never once agreed to you putting those boots on the furniture or huffing your displeasure like the wolf trying to blow down a straw house." Then she smacked a hand to her forehead. "Have I been possessed by Sadie Hearst? I swear that was her voice, not mine." Then she pointed. "Boots on the floor."

Grant sighed *again* but it was clear this would be a losing battle so he straightened on the hard seat and saluted. "Yes, ma'am."

Jordan walked over to sit in one of the rocking chairs. "These aren't too bad. That couch? I think it was made before cushions were invented."

Grant grunted his agreement. "What project are you working on tonight?"

"My office. Would you like to see it as a distraction from impatiently waiting for Mia to come home?" Jordan said as she nodded wildly and held out her hand. She'd popped up out of the chair before he could convince her otherwise.

As she towed him into the restaurant, he said halfheartedly, "I don't want to miss Mia if she's leaving first thing in the morning."

Jordan froze in her tracks so suddenly that Grant stumbled while trying to keep from running over her.

"And why is that?" Jordan asked slyly.

Grant coughed into his hand. That was an excellent question. "I want to be clear on her plan. For the story."

Jordan narrowed her eyes and scanned his face. If she'd been shocked to hear Sadie's voice earlier, what would her reaction be if he told her he'd seen the same suspicious expression on her great-aunt's face many times?

Most often after he'd been caught doing something around the lodge that was off-limits, out-of-bounds, and that he'd definitely been ordered more than once to stop.

Having the lodge next door growing up hadn't meant a lot to him, but the ghost town that sat up in the hills above the lodge? He'd trespassed there plenty. He and his brothers had all spent more time climbing around those buildings than anyone should have. The weathered structures there drew him in.

When the weather was right and the walls of the house crowded in on him, he still took every opportunity he could to ride up there.

"Sadie will probably let us know when Mia comes in. If she doesn't, I bet it won't take Mia long to come looking for me." Jordan motioned him to follow. When he wasn't right on her heels, she said, "What? We're friends. People like me."

Grant chuckled as he obeyed her orders and trailed through the doorway of the restaurant and took a slight left to the corner behind the host station. "Did you find a completely new room hidden inside the storage room? This place keeps on giving," he drawled.

Jordan rolled her eyes and flipped on the light. "Turns out, when you remove all the carefully stored inventory and return it to where it belongs, there is actually a room inside the storage room." She held her arms out to show him…the empty storage room. The washer and dryer remained, but all the furniture pieces, bedding, and odd bits and pieces that had been neatly arranged inside had been removed to make way for a perfectly acceptable office.

"If and when we get the funds from Sadie's estate, and if and when there's any left after the repairs we have to make to get the lodge restored, and if and when we can make another door into the closet to join it to the back of the kitchen—" Jordan pointed vaguely at the wall that must separate them from that space "—I'm going to sweet talk Clay into moving these appliances out, but for now, I have a desk, electricity, soon there will be high-speed internet, and a laptop. Ta-da! The Majestic has a business office that is not the kitchen island in Sadie's apartment."

Grant spun in a slow circle. With the yellowed paint, dusty shelves and scratched wood floors, it wasn't an impressive space, but it made a lot of sense. He studied the washer and dryer. "Might be easier to put up a wall here—" he toed a line with his boot to show her where he meant "—to build a laundry room." He tapped the opposite wall. "Then cut a door right here. To the back hall. Laundry in and out without interrupting restaurant service. If you wanted, you could use that door for entry to your office, too."

Jordan shoved a paint brush at him as she paced off the space to envision it. "You could put up a wall, couldn't you, Grant? No need for Clay to leave his construction company in Colorado

Springs to come here for that." She clutched her hands in front of her face and gave him puppy dog eyes. "For your favorite sister-in-law." Then she held up both hands. "Someday."

"Someday you'll be my favorite?" His lips twitched as he pointed the paint brush at her.

"Someday I'll be your sister-in-law." Then she patted his shoulder. "You and I know that I will always be your favorite. Thank you for helping me paint this room." She tapped the paint can and scooted to sit on the desk. "I think Sadie would have loved this color." The lid came off, and Grant could see Jordan was going with a sunny pastel yellow for the Majestic's new business office. If Sadie Hearst had been a paint color, he figured it would look exactly like that.

"I will help you paint, not because you roped me into it, but because I find myself with too much time on my hands. I'll load up Damon and Micah this weekend and get it all knocked out." He handed her back the paint brush. "We might be able to do something about this floor, too." They'd refinished the floors in most of the lodge because both boys loved power tools and the floor sander had been popular.

"What about the wall? And the new door? And can you put a keyed lock on both entrances, one with a code that you enter?" Jordan asked as she imagined the possibilities. "Someday, there will be a night manager, maybe even an assistant manager, too, so we'll need access codes. Things like that."

Grant blinked as he tried to trace the winding journey from relaxing in the lobby to figuring out high-tech security systems for the Majestic's corporate offices, but it didn't make sense to waste a lot of energy asking himself how he'd gotten there. It happened so often around the Hearsts that he'd acclimated by now.

"Let's work on the construction piece. We may need expert advice for anything else." Grant picked up a binder from the solid desk. It reminded him of his mother's organization system for Western Days, the large black binder that she'd handed unceremoniously to Matt when she'd chosen him to lead it this year. "What's this?"

Jordan shrugged. "Right now, I have more ideas than time or money, but that doesn't mean they won't work someday, so I put notes or advertisements in there to jog my memory." She flipped through the pages and tapped one. "In the summer, we should have a band playing on Friday nights. Old country, the kind that will have people two-steppin' on the deck outside. We'll also need to expand the deck."

Grant knew his eyebrows shot up, but she wasn't paying any mind. Something had caught her attention and now she had a goal in mind. Jordan flipped steadily until she said, "Here it is. This is the business opportunity that I wanted to talk to you about." She held up the binder so he could see a hand-drawn flier for a trail ride. The artist rendering of a horse was memorable. There had to be a thousand glossier ads to choose from, ones with photos of real, beautiful horses, so he studied her choice to guess why this one made it into the binder. Then he saw the reference to a "special Halloween ghost ride."

He met her stare. "Jordan, please tell me you aren't planning to lead city slickers into the mountains on the hunt for Bigfoot or things that go bump in the night." Her fear of horses in general was well-known among all the Armstrongs, and that would seem confirmation that he was on the wrong track, but with Jordan and her inventive ideas, he wasn't sure.

"Not me. You." She gripped his arm as he straightened, prepared to march outside to wait for Mia in his cold truck. "Not ghosts or paranormal, but the ghost town. Trail rides to Sullivan's Post. Along with riding lessons. Kids. Adults. You know you enjoy working with horses and their riders." Jordan smiled encouragingly. "Imagine having a job where you ride up to the ghost town and help people learn to love horses."

Grant propped his hands on his hips as he considered that.

What did it mean that it was so easy to imagine?

"You could work as much or as little as you like, bring in money for the ranch, train the horses as needed." Jordan held her hands out as if it was so simple. "As long as you can pretend to be a people person for as long as the trail ride takes, I don't see how you can lose."

Grant grunted his amusement at that. "I'll have you know I was pretty popular on the circuit. Men, women and children loved me."

She patted his arm as if to say, "Of course you were, sweetie."

"Does anyone ever tell you no?" Grant asked, unwilling to jump on board immediately. He had a reputation to uphold as the troublemaker. Was her suggestion actually brilliant? Sure, in a world filled with only round holes, Jordan had managed to build her own spot, one perfect for a square peg. She and her sister kept generating these ideas that were so right for the town that it was tempting to wonder why they had taken so long to conjure.

Prospect had needed the Hearsts to roll into town with no other option except to make room for them. The town was going to be better for it, too.

Grant was the agitator. He kept people from getting too comfortable. In a battle of personalities, he wasn't sure he would win against Jordan Hearst.

"Sounds okay, but what if I had something else in mind for my golden years besides free labor spent on this lodge and escorting tourists on amusement park trail rides?"

"You like to argue. I also enjoy arguing, but it is late. If you had plans for your retirement, you'd be doing them already. No one makes it to the top of the standings in the rodeo circuit without putting in lots of hard work." She held up a hand. "Don't try to deflect this truth by trotting out the cheating thing. You've been the first one to volunteer for every job around this place, big or small. You might have fooled your family with skillful misdirection, but I have been playing that game for decades. Get real with me. You need something to do. You're amazed and impressed with my judgment and foresight. After Western Days, you'll be ready for something challenging. You can count on me and the Majestic for help."

Jordan held her hand out to shake.

"As long as it leaves plenty of time to rebuild the Prospect Rodeo Club, I'm in." Grant hadn't realized he'd made up his mind to give it a shot until that very second. But after working with Matt and getting his promise to help, and spending time thinking of Mia and his family and what life would look like after this cheating scandal was resolved... In his mind, it was easy to picture introducing kids to the rodeo he loved, teaching them to give it their all and win the right way.

He so needed Mia here, because he didn't want to wait any longer for the story to finish.

And selfishly, he'd missed her company all day.

"I don't know what a rodeo club does," Jordan said, "but I have no doubt the Armstrongs can build the best one in the West. We will all make time for that, Grant."

Grant had returned the handshake when Jordan added, "I know you're waiting here for Mia to show up because you need to see her before she leaves. Right?" She held on tightly when he tried to pull away. "You like her. Are you going to tell her?"

When he realized that Jordan might not be as strong but she was twice as determined to hold on, Grant stopped trying to free himself. "Is this grade school? Should I hand her a note and ask her to be my girlfriend? Do adults do that?"

"I had high hopes that you were the Armstrong brother with all the romantic grand gestures, but if a note's all you've got, do it. You'll be sorry if you let Mia go without telling her how you feel." She held her hands out to indicate the dingy storage room with a bright future. "While we wait, you can paint and rehearse everything you'd like to say. I can give you feedback."

"Or I can head home. Will you please ask your lodger to call me when she returns from Prospect?" Grant pointed over his shoulder. "Should I leave a note at the front desk?"

Jordan tapped her temple. "Nope. I have it committed to memory."

In the lobby, Grant inhaled slowly, determined to shed some of his restlessness before sliding behind the wheel. "That's a sign of new maturity, Armstrong," he muttered to himself. Almost every ridiculous stunt that caught up with him had been the result of shooting off half-cocked. The way sweet vanilla filled his nose surprised him. Should it? No. He'd heard plenty of people talking about the Majestic's delicious-smelling ghost but he'd yet to experience the phenomenon himself.

Until tonight.

"All right, Sadie, if you were here, you'd be filling my ear about something I'm doing wrong or about to mess up." Grant scrubbed his hands over his face, tired and confused about how his life had ended up with him talking to his imaginary neighbor. "She's leaving. And that's for the best. Once we have published this story..." Then what? That was the question. How did he want to complete that sentence?

He stared around the lobby. Some kind of visible manifestation might be nice. Then he remembered the way Sadie Hearst's eyes had gleamed with fire when she got angry.

The vanilla stayed with him as he moved through the lobby and arrived back at his truck. The urge to ignore his mother's delivered message about staying at the ranch was strong. If he went into town, he could track Mia down easily.

Then he could say his piece and get on with his life.

But it was hard to forget that everyone in Prospect, including Mia, had done their best to protect him from becoming the gossip of the rodeo circuit while he figured out how he wanted to proceed.

So he turned toward the Rocking A instead of storming into town. Light blazed from every window along the front of the ranch house, and trucks lined the yard. That meant most of the Armstrongs were inside. There were enough of them now to make a crowd wherever they went.

Instead of going inside to face the chaos and noise, the usual scene when the whole family was gathered, Grant decided to spend time in the barn. On a cold night like this, it was a good idea to check to make sure all the horses had feed and water.

Whenever he needed to get his head on straight, horses never let him down.

CHAPTER FIFTEEN

MIA WAS RELIEVED when Casey trotted up the steps to Bell House without giving her an argument. That meant her tightrope walk was coming to an end. Heading back to the inn was also the first suggestion she'd made since he'd slid out of his SUV earlier that afternoon that he agreed with. There was no "playing devil's advocate" or "it would be smarter to…" or even "let's try this instead." Every idea had to be Casey's, no matter whose thought it might have been originally. She hadn't forgotten that part of the challenge of working with him, but she'd either gotten softer from working with more reasonable photographers lately or he was determined to show off his skills.

She was exhausted by running interference and advocating for the shots she would definitely want for her piece on Western Days. They'd taken a few exterior shots before the sun set, and then moved inside to get some "local color." They had managed to get nice photos of the Mercantile and the pretty park behind it, Bell House, the Prospect Picture Show and Homestead Market. These were "the landmarks" as Casey called them.

Not because he thought they were particularly noteworthy, but because they were what Prospect had to offer.

The urge to snap at him about the beauty of the Majestic Prospect Lodge burned, but her careful plan to keep Casey separated from Grant was stronger. Instead, she took him on the side trip to see the future spot of Prospect's Cowboy Games across from the high school. He had brightened momentarily at the way golden light filtered through the breaks in the line of mountains to scatter across Sam's field as the sun set, so Mia was satisfied that he wasn't completely immune to the charms of the town.

Casey had also shown true excitement for the dishes coming out of the Ace High kitchen. And when Faye had deposited a slice of chocolate pie with a toasted meringue that rose all the way to heaven, she and Casey had both been speechless.

That might have been the straw that broke his bad mood because Casey was rubbing his stomach in an I'm-so-full-but-I-regret-nothing sort of way. In this, they were on the same side.

"You want to come in?" Casey asked. "We haven't had much of a chance to catch up. Seems like you had a story to tell about every single citizen of Prospect."

She had.

Except anyone named Armstrong. She'd stayed carefully away from the danger zone.

It had been an exhausting few hours. "It's been a long day. You did good work. I expect we'll have plenty of shots to use when it's time to cover Western Days."

Mia forced her feet to remain planted.

"See if you can get me assigned to that story when you come back for the festival. We work well together." Casey reached out to touch her arm. "Unless... Are you seeing someone, Mia?" He exhaled in a gust. "Of course you are. Why didn't you say so? Is it a secret?" His teasing grin flashed as he bent to stare into her eyes.

"It is. That's it, Casey. It's great that we've had this time to catch up, though." She cleared her throat nervously because he was too close to the truth...all of it.

"Are you involved with someone here in Prospect?" His eyebrows rose and he waggled them as if they were plotting something. "The only way I see you needing to keep that a secret is if it's an Armstrong."

Mia managed not to react as he tossed out the name between them, but it was likely he could add up the pieces now. She had to trust that Jesse

Martinez would make good use of his connections and that together they were up for the challenge of beating whoever Casey might call with the tip. He'd been working with the busiest freelance writers covering the circuit for a while now. Casey would know exactly who to contact to get the story out there.

"No answer to that," Casey murmured as he looked as if he had the answer anyway. "I guess we know where Grant Armstrong is hiding. Want to share why?" He shook his head. "I guess I'll have to be content with understanding why you reached out to me in the first place, huh, Mia? Trolling for information. Interesting. I didn't know you had the sneaky reporter's side to you."

Mia hated that he called her behavior out. She had used him for connections.

"Thanks for stopping by to grab these shots. I know my mother will love that sunset photo. Be sure you submit it to her." She had to get out of here before Casey started reading more secrets from her face. "This will probably be our last assignment together. I wouldn't want to drag you away from the action for craft shows and fried foods." Mia raised her hand to wave over her shoulder as she walked back down the sidewalk, willing him to get the hint to stop pushing for more info. "Safe travels on your way to Nevada."

She knew it was Utah.

Mia also heard him correct her, but she waved cheerfully in the dark night, got into her car and pulled away from the B-and-B after saying a quick prayer that Rose Bell was as good at quelling overly interested visitors as Prue promised.

Rose Bell was their only hope of sending Casey on his way, and Mia had stacked the deck against her. He knew there was something brewing here and he even had a good idea of what. Heading out of town in the morning might help lead him away, but the clock was ticking on Grant's story and the discovery of his whereabouts.

She jerked in her seat as the phone rang.

"Is that nerves or a guilty conscience, Mia?" she muttered as she punched the button to answer.

"Hey, Jordan, I'm leaving town now. I think we limited any potential exposure." She hoped. Now wasn't the time to launch into the evening's saga.

"Good, good, I'm calling to deliver a message." Jordan paused so Mia frowned at the display.

"Okay? What is it?" Mia asked, her patience running out.

"There's been a cowboy sprawled in my lobby tonight. Waiting."

Mia hadn't known Jordan all that long, but it was easy enough to imagine mischief on her face to match her tone. "Didn't he get the message that I had this situation under control?" Yes, her control was slipping, but no one needed to know that at this point.

"I believe he received multiple messages, but the caution is wearing thin. I've finally shooed him home, but Grant requests a conversation with you at your earliest convenience." Jordan cleared her throat. "Like now? I promised I'd pass along the message."

"Okay. I'll call him and explain...everything I've done this afternoon. If he's got concerns or wants to change direction on his story, I'll take care of it." Mia clenched the steering wheel. How would she stop what she'd set in motion? Jesse Martinez was good at his job and had been for a long time. There was no telling how far he'd made it with her tip without stepping foot in Utah.

And Casey had gotten a late start, but he'd make up for lost time.

"Hmm," Jordan said, "you should stop in at the Rocking A now. Face-to-face conversations are so much more pleasant." Then she ended the call.

Mia cursed under her breath. Jordan was up to something. Then she remembered Walt and his standing invitation for her to visit the Rocking A. Had they traded notes at some point in the afternoon to put Mia and Grant in the same physical location?

This whole town was always up to something.

How did people who lived here deal with the constant "something" going on?

Instead of calling her back, Mia slowed down as she neared the turn to the Rocking A. Then she realized this was an excellent excuse to satisfy her curiosity about the place Grant called home.

"Unless they're having a party because..." Mia slowed down to park next to a long line of trucks. She turned off the ignition as she asked herself if she was brave enough to crash a house full of Armstrongs and pulled out her key.

Then she noticed the shaft of light spilling from the partially open barn door.

Instinct whispered that if she had to track Grant, there was a good chance the trail started with a horse.

CHAPTER SIXTEEN

GRANT DUMPED THE last pitchfork of dirty hay on top of the pile in the wheelbarrow and brushed his shoulder across his jaw to scratch the itch that never failed to appear when he was mucking stalls. Travis would lecture him tomorrow for tackling Sonny's stall instead of leaving it for him, but it was always easier to brood when he had something to occupy his hands.

"Therapy by mucking out stalls, Jet. Can you imagine?" he asked and ran a hand over Jet's muzzle before he dumped the wheelbarrow outside the barn. If he didn't offer Jet and all his buddies a treat after all the hard work they had done, standing around and watching the silly cowboy shovel hay, they might cause a ruckus. He stopped by the office on the way back to grab the apples Travis kept on hand for special occasions. When his pockets were full, he guided the wheelbarrow back toward the empty stalls. When Sonny's stall passed inspection, he refilled Sonny's water bucket and then led Travis's horse back inside his usual spot for the night. "Please leave a tip if the service is satisfactory, sir."

Sonny butted his hand, asking for a scratch behind the ears, so Grant obliged.

"The service here is nice. If you want to apply for a housekeeping job at the Majestic, I'll happily give you a reference." Mia had climbed the bottom rung of the stall to hang her arms over the top. "I don't know how good the tips are, but I am sure you could learn to make a bed."

Grant pulled off his work gloves. "I had given up on hearing from you."

Mia said, "Jordan told me you wanted to talk, but then she suggested I come in person rather than use the phone."

Grant crossed his arms. "I hear you've been busy. Not working on our story with someone else, are you?" He wondered how hard he'd have to push to get Mia to explain how this whole thing with the photographer had happened. He studied her face. Mia was a beautiful woman, but he could tell the day had been long and exhausting. There were fine lines around her eyes and mouth, and more than anything, Mia looked like she needed rest.

"About that..." Mia motioned between them. "Can you come out of the stall or should I come in?"

Grant eased out of the stall and closed the gate.

"Sonny's a gentleman, so either would have been fine. You like horses, right?"

She nodded and reached inside his pocket to pull out an apple. "I do, but I learned to be careful until I know them. My grandfather came out one morning to find me all cuddled up with a foal and explained loudly that I had to be careful because even pets can be unpredictable sometimes."

Grant watched her twist the stem off the apple and grip it firmly. As she pushed and rolled her hands, the apple cracked into two perfect halves.

"Very handy trick for someone who spends a lot of time with horses."

"My grandfather taught me how to do that, too." She stepped over to their new rescue's stall. "Will I lose a finger if I offer it to this distinguished gent? My grandfather rode a chestnut American Paint like this one. What's his name?"

Concerned that the horse might require folks to be more cautious around him now that he'd been fed and had some rest, Grant stepped closer. "This guy might be as unpredictable as your grandfather warned. Matt and I went to pick him up today. Looks like he's been hungry and hobbled for way too long, but he's getting some high-quality care here." Grant took the half she offered and reached through the slats to give it to the horse. "Don't know whether Matt has thought of a name for him yet, but he's pretty sure this old guy will be our horse now. Not too many people looking to adopt geriatric riding horses."

Mia leaned in to stare into the horse's eyes. "All you need is a little love, right?" When she glanced up at Grant, he wasn't sure whether she was including him in that statement.

But he was ready to agree.

A little love was all he wanted, too.

"I think you should name him Stretch." Her lips curled as she waited for his answer.

Grant sighed loudly enough that the Paint's ears twitched. The fact that the horse didn't retreat gave Grant hope he was settling in. "Stretch Armstrong. Do you know how many times my brothers and I have been called that?"

"What's one more?" Mia asked as she spun away, the other half of the apple in her hand. Grant grinned as he followed behind her.

"I didn't know you were the kind of man who rescued animals. That's…cute."

Grant frowned. "Cute?"

"Who is this?" Mia asked as she held out the apple to Lady.

"This is Lady. My mother's horse. She's almost 100 percent human at this point. You only need to worry about losing a finger if you try to walk out of the barn without giving her a treat, too."

Mia chuckled. "Rude. I don't believe a word

he says, Lady. His mother mentioned Armstrong men struggle with romance and I'm starting to believe it. It's a good thing they're so cute."

After the horse delicately accepted both the treat and a rub on the nose, Mia turned to face him. "I'm glad you helped Matt today."

"I was happy to be there." Grant braced his hand on the stall next to Mia's shoulder. "I parlayed my assistance today into a promise from Matt that he'd help me with Prospect's new rodeo club."

She wrapped her hands around his biceps and squeezed. "I knew you couldn't say no!"

He wasn't certain what her faith in him was founded on because he hadn't been sure himself until he'd roped Matt into the task, but he liked it that Mia had believed it was inevitable.

"I wasn't sure what you would do when you heard about the magazine's photographer skulking around." Her smile grew wide. "Would an angry Bad Boy of Bronc Busting storm into town and demand answers about why I had invited him to Prospect before I had run it past him first?"

"Storming isn't my style," he said before he coughed into his hand.

She raised an eyebrow as if she was skeptical about his truthfulness.

"What was your other guess?" he asked because he was curious. "Mucking out stalls in the barn?"

"No, but now I can see that was shortsighted of me. I'm realizing that time with a horse is your answer to a lot of different emotions. Anger. Sadness. Happiness?"

Grant pursed his lips as he considered that. "You're reading me like an open book. One filled with mostly pictures."

Her smile eased something inside of him.

"The photographer is here because of me, but I didn't invite him and he didn't have any information to go on." Mia ran her hand over his sleeve, brushing off bits of hay. When she would have stepped back, he clasped her hand tightly. "Casey and I had worked together in the past. When I was using my best detective skills to find out what the good people of Prospect might be hiding, I saw a photo from Nationals that Casey had taken. I called to test the waters, to see if there were any hints about what might be going on in the rodeo world." She wrinkled her nose. "Gross, right? Trying to use my connection without explaining what was going on?"

Grant tangled their fingers together and led her over to the next stall. "This is Jet. He's mine."

She sighed. "Oh, he's so handsome." Jet had heard similar comments his whole life and knew how to work a crowd, so the horse hung his head over the top rung and stared into Mia's soul. If hearts made a sound when they tumbled into love, it would match Mia's murmur of pleasure.

His horse always was better at flirting than Grant, but it burned to see it in action with a woman he wanted to impress.

"And from that, he followed you here?" Grant said. "The photographer?" He wasn't sure she cared to continue her story, but eventually she blinked.

Grant hoped that some day, they'd have plenty of time to stand next to each other in the barn and stare into each other's eyes.

"Yeah, he called my mother to find out what kind of assignment I was on, and whether the magazine was looking for photos, because he had time before he needed to be in Utah on the weekend. She called me to give me orders to show him around and I...did a kind of Paul Revere move, running through town to warn the neighbors that the enemy was coming. I messed up. I'm sorry. I'm starting to realize that I don't have either the variable ethical standards or the sleight of hand needed to be a great reporter." Mia grimaced. "And now my mother understands the same thing."

Grant studied her eyes as he tried to decipher exactly what she was telling him. "So *The Way West* won't be able to publish the story about the cheating scandal, even if we can find proof to support my story."

Mia immediately shook her head. "Oh no. *The Way West* will print it. We just have to get it first."

Since that had been the plan all along, Grant wasn't understanding what had changed.

"And when my mother was asking me why I hadn't pitched a shady what-happened-to-Grant-Armstrong story when I headed for Prospect, I realized that my reputation isn't going to give your story the weight it needs."

Grant settled on the bag of feed and pulled her down next to him. It wasn't romantic, but it was warm and he was grateful to have Mia's hand in his. She settled into his side.

"What about your big break? The one that would change her mind and convince her to give you control of the magazine?" Grant asked.

Mia shrugged. "Your best bet to protect your name or your brand is to have a pro doing the reporting. I gave Jesse Martinez a couple of targeted hints. I'm meeting him in Ogden. Together we'll find the proof that we need to build this out without you or I'll pass him your name and number to get in touch." She straightened her shoulders. "When I get back to Billings, I will convince my mother to hold off on the original idea, because the scoop she's been dreaming of is coming in, one way or another. I'll get her to promise to run that story and the one on Western Days, and then we'll…" She stopped. "We'll figure out what to do about the magazine from there. She wants to step down, but the more time I spend in Prospect, the better I understand that I don't want to step up. I want to tell stories. I don't want to stare at spreadsheets all day and worry about the cost of office space. I keep hoping for a lightning bolt of an answer, but the universe is being very quiet so far."

Grant wrapped his arm around her shoulders to pull her closer. He hated how worried she was about her own future, something that she hadn't even considered before he and Matt had pulled over to change her tire. Surely she wasn't giving up on the universe?

When she eased back, he glanced down at her face. Her eyes were narrowed suspiciously. "You thought I had sold you out to Casey to get your story, didn't you? Like Red and Trey?"

Grant shook his head. "I can honestly say that… I was confused but I wasn't angry. I wanted to talk to you, not hear cryptic directions from various sources, but…" He paused as he tried to replay the long afternoon in his head. "I don't think I ever once believed you had turned on me, and I gotta say, that is something. Walking away from you never occurred to me."

Her slow smile filled him with warmth. "Really?"

"I'm as surprised as you are. I'm learning something in my old age," Grant drawled. "Or maybe it would take a lot to shake my faith in you."

She pressed her forehead against his. "We haven't known each other for long. My mother, who has known me my whole life, will give you a list of my faults. I'm flaky, Grant."

"Not sure that's true, but even if it is, what does that have to do with trusting your heart?" he asked.

When she leaned back to blink up at him, he couldn't read her face, but the kiss she pressed against his lips was much easier to understand. He wasn't sure exactly where he was headed with Mia, but as long as he considered each step instead of reacting immediately and regretting the fallout, he was making progress.

"But you're still leaving in the morning," he whispered against her ear after she wrapped her arms around his neck. "I want to take you out for a ride. I can show you the ghost town, one of my favorite places in the world, and we can discuss Jordan's wild plan to have me running trail rides up there for the lodge's valued guests." He pressed a kiss against her jaw. "And then you can help me recruit teams for these Cowboy Games and find cheap wigs to create beautiful manes for old wooden horses, and at least a thousand other things that my mother will cook up as we go."

"I can't believe how fun all of that sounds." Mia grinned at him as he chuckled.

"Fun? Okay, no, but wouldn't we be good at it together?" he asked.

"We would." She nodded. "We will. I have a plan."

He checked her expression. "A plan. You have a plan?" That didn't fit with the free spirit who counted on the universe to direct her steps.

"Yes, I am familiar with the word, Grant, even if I don't always carefully plot out each journey." She held out her hand to count off the points. The thumb went first. "Get Grant's story tied up and ready for print. That's number one. Then figure out what to do with the magazine." She unfolded the third finger. "Figure out how to write for a new editor, maybe even a book editor, but one who doesn't have the same last name or pay my credit card bill."

Grant unfolded her ring finger. "Make it back to town before Western Days weekend."

She nodded and then wiggled her pinky. "What's number five?"

Grant grew serious as he stared into her eyes. "Figure out what we do about us?"

Her eyebrows rose but she considered it and

smiled. "Reasonable. What are we if we aren't on opposing sides of your big secret?"

He leaned closer. "That's already been answered." He pressed a kiss to her lips. "What we need to know is what comes next."

"And when I leave, when there's distance between us, our heads could clear and we'll realize that what we had was some kind of weird chemistry caused by this one moment in time. Breathing room will fix that and then we can be good friends." She grimaced. "And don't worry if it happens. You won't be the first man to break my heart by realizing what a great friend I am."

Her eyes didn't match the sunny grin.

"You don't really believe that will happen, do you?" Grant asked.

"Are you certain you don't want to head back out on the circuit? No matter what, there will be some fallout from the story, but you could return to the competition, dispel any doubts by winning." She tipped his hat back. "You want to stay in Prospect. Whatever happens with the story, you want to stay on this path instead of going back." Mia brushed her hand over his shoulders.

"I do. It's weird. I get it. But since you got here, I feel more at home than I ever have anywhere else." Grant covered his face with his hands. "I can't believe you've got me emoting like this. If you were one of my brothers, I'd knock your hat in the dirt to get a fight started right about now."

"That must be a sign of growth." Mia's lips were twitching. "I don't know if you'll have other reporters hanging around town, but let your friends and neighbors tell other Armstrong stories to their hearts' content." Mia stood and frowned. "Even Faye was singing your praises this afternoon. I think her tough shell might be covering a gooey center."

Grant stood to follow her back to her car. "I'm going to be waiting for you to call me, Mia."

"I'll let you know how the story is going," she said with a smile.

"Tell me about the magazine and your mother and your travel and…whatever." Grant nodded. "I just want to hear your voice."

Her teasing grin faded. "Why am I nervous about leaving Prospect? I drove all over these United States on my own, with hardly a thought, before I had a flat tire outside of town and met this cowboy who wanted to keep me safe." She squeezed his hand. "I'm happier here than I ever have been. I can't explain it, but it's hard to give up."

"If you need me, I'll be there as fast as I can." Grant bent his head. "No matter what happens when you get to question number five."

Mia blinked rapidly and he was almost certain

it was because of tears, but she stood on her tip-toes and pressed a kiss to his lips before trotting out to her car and driving away.

He was still staring down the lane when Travis bumped his shoulder. "You coming inside? You're bound to freeze solid out here."

Grant turned to his brother. "You ever wonder why I needled you so much when we were growing up?"

Travis reared back. "No! Why? Why would I need to know that? That's entirely a you problem."

Grant chuckled, relieved that he could laugh even though he was already missing Mia fiercely. "Okay. I was going to apologize, but never mind."

Travis slung his arm over Grant's shoulders and urged him toward the house. "Quit being weird. You're creeping me out. I knew you were the closest thing I had to a friend then, even if you were ornery. You still are."

"Which one? Ornery or a friend?" Grant asked as they climbed the steps up to the porch.

"Oh, both." Travis rolled his eyes. "You are most definitely still both, but no one can argue what a good brother you are. Damon and Micah are waiting to spend some time with their favorite uncle."

"And you and Keena are ready to cuddle up on the couch, huh?" Grant asked, relieved that life went on inside the Rocking A, same as it ever had.

Mia had changed his world, but he still recognized the most important parts.

And when she came back, they'd figure out how to assemble all the new pieces.

CHAPTER SEVENTEEN

MIA FOLLOWED JESSE MARTINEZ into the lobby of the hotel outside of Ogden, Utah, after a long day of driving and then tagging along with the experienced reporter through the event center while he shook hands and made chitchat. They had met for lunch to discuss how they might pursue a story about cheating without pointing any fingers to their possible source. Mia's part of the investigation was to ask friendly questions about their hometowns that she could use to build into theoretical stories some day.

"I have no idea how you do this," she muttered to Jesse as he pointed to the quiet bar where they were supposed to find Annie Mercado. "I want a nap and different shoes. I don't even care which order they come in."

Jesse grunted. "Years of conditioning. There'll be time to rest after you file the story, Mia."

She nodded. If the man who had to be considering retirement could do this, she would force herself to keep up. "I'm just going to wash my face. Maybe that will kick-start my brain."

He hitched the strap of his laptop bag over his shoulder. "I'll make sure no one's waiting for us, grab a quiet table near the back."

"Order me something with caffeine in it?" Mia requested before trudging toward the restroom. The aggressive fluorescent lighting hit her first, but she realized she wasn't alone before she cursed out loud.

Annie Mercado was washing her hands at the sink. "This place oughta hand out sunglasses at the door, right?"

Mia inhaled slowly and sent a grateful thank you toward the universe. Her faith had been shaken lately, but she was almost certain that the lightning bolt was about to strike.

"Since I've been on the road half the day, I definitely needed a wake-up call." Mia set her bag and notebook down before running her hands under the cold water and pressing them to her face. "I'm Mia Romero. I came with Jesse Martinez. I'd shake your hand, but…" She waved her dripping hands ruefully before repeating the process. Her brain needed to be alert and ready right now.

"Yeah? Where are you coming from?" Annie fluffed the limp curl of her bangs as she stared into the mirror.

"Prospect. Colorado." Mia did her best to study Annie's face without letting her know she was under observation.

A slight frown wrinkled the young woman's forehead. "Why do I know that name?"

The sizzle of electricity didn't surprise Mia this time. She was in the right place at the right time.

"Could be the Western Days festival they have," Mia said as she yanked paper towels from the dispenser, "or it's the hometown of Grant Armstrong. Do you know him?"

Annie crossed her arms over her chest. The hem of her shirt rose enough to reveal a red and white gingham belt.

Mia instantly recognized Sadie Hearst's distinctive plaid. Annie Mercado was wearing part of Sadie Hearst's line of women's Western wear.

There was no hint of vanilla in the air, but it was impossible not to feel Sadie's presence.

"Sure. We've met. He's kind of a hero of mine, you know, because he's pretty fearless in the saddle." Annie's demeanor suddenly shifted. "Why do I get the feeling that you also know Grant Armstrong?"

Mia tried to control the grin on her face and play it cool. "Oh, I do. I was just talking with him about these Cowboy Games he's organizing for Prospect's upcoming Western Days and his plans to put together a new Prospect Rodeo Club for the kids in town." Digging in her purse for a brush seemed a casual way to divert some suspicion. How could she be digging for information while she was trying to fix her hair?

"I guess the story of his retirement is true? It doesn't make much sense. He was on top." Annie's eyes narrowed. "Did something run him off?" Her lips were a tight line. "Or someone?"

Mia desperately hoped the racing of her heart wasn't clearly audible in the restroom as she bit her lip. "If I said yes, would you have a guess what or who might be involved?"

She wanted to channel Jesse's cagey expression and ask the perfect leading questions, but the closer she got to what she wanted, the harder it was to be patient.

"Red Williams is a shady character if I ever saw one, so he'd be my first guess as to what might convince a man to take all his prizes and head home," Annie said with a sniff. "I tell every newcomer to the circuit not to give him the time of day."

Mia nodded. "Why is that?" Before Annie could answer, she held out her hand to stop her. "Before you go any further, you should consider what you tell me and whether you want to be named in a published news story or not." She desperately wanted this to be the break they needed, but not if it came at the expense of another innocent person's career.

"How about this? I'll tell you what I know. We can compare notes to see if we're on the same page." Annie picked up the white hat from the countertop and Mia saw the distinctive Cookie Queen gingham band. "About the fourth or fifth competition, the first time I placed in the winner's circle, Red approached me with an offer to be my manager. He had a tried-and-true method to get me to the top, he promised. I fell for that for a hot minute, but it quickly became evident that his plan didn't involve coaching, helping me improve, or anything other than helping himself to a piece of my winnings and making phone calls that he could never explain to me." She pursed her lips. "Where I'm from, we don't do business that way. I even reached out to the Association to make a complaint, something official that might cause them to look into his dealings with new riders, but I only had one tiny piece of evidence to go on."

Mia clenched her hands together. "What was that?"

"Red accidentally copied me on a text where he congratulated another rider on their winning time." Annie shook her head. "Before we rode."

Mia knew her mouth was hanging open but she was too excited to speak.

"Yeah, Red said it was a joke, something he

might say to psych out the competition." Annie rolled her eyes. "To me, that was more smoke, even if I wouldn't touch that fire."

Mia pressed her clenched hands to her mouth.

Annie patted her shoulder. "You okay, hon?"

After nodding wildly for a moment, Mia gathered herself. "I am. We are on the same page. If you trust me, trust Jesse, I want this story for *The Way West*. We will put so much smoke out there that the Association will have to take this seriously."

Annie moved over to open the door, and Mia met her own eyes in the mirror. "I did it. I got the story."

"Yes, you did," Annie said with a smile.

Before she could second-guess herself, Mia decided to press her luck. "And I'd love to tell you more about Prospect. It's the home of Sadie Hearst. The Colorado Cookie Queen."

Annie pointed excitedly. "That's where I recognize the name. I loved watching her on TV, and I always wear a little bit of her clothing line. I'm such a fan."

Mia's smile could not be contained. "You have to come to Prospect then. There's a lodge. The ghost of Sadie might even be hanging out there. A museum. Big, fun Cowboy Games coming up. Lots of kids there to get interested in rodeo." She squeezed Annie's arm. "If you decide to make a visit to Prospect, they will treat you like family. I promise."

Annie looked a little overwhelmed, so Mia decided to wait until after the story was finished to press her luck and ask for a special Western Days visit from rising star Annie Mercado.

But she wasn't going to waste a single minute of this opportunity the universe had given her.

ON FRIDAY, Mia opened the doors to *The Way West*'s corporate suite. She was tired but energized and ready to get on to the next battle: the conversation about what to do with the magazine. She'd driven all day to pull into her condominium's parking deck after sunset and then spent a long night tossing and turning as she tried to get comfortable in her own bed again. Instead of marching in bright and early, she was dodging lunchtime traffic in downtown Billings and already anticipating a difficult conversation.

Stepping inside the magazine's offices always boosted her confidence. She could remember coming down on the weekends to "help" her grandfather read the stories in each issue before he approved the magazine to be printed. Most of her help had consisted of stapling things, removing those staples, spinning in his office chair and asking for change for the vending machine on the bottom floor of the historic old Sunrise Building. It had been built in 1914, and for as long as Mia could remember, it had housed the magazine. During the magazine's heyday, employees had spread out across all three floors, but now the staff had been condensed to one suite with a few cubicles and a larger open area that held desks for anyone who might need a temporary work space.

As she wound between the desks, she saw that Jesse's cube was dark. The computer was showing the lock screen. He'd sent her the final version of Grant's story for approval that morning.

Her mother should have read it by now, complete with Mia's name following Jesse's on the byline.

The executive assistant was on the phone when Mia stepped up to the counter, but she waved Mia into her mother's office. It had been updated once or twice from when her grandfather's heavy desk had filled the room, but there was still a wall of windows that showed the sidewalk below and beautiful old trees that were ready for spring.

"Well, I guess it's technically still morning for a minute or two," her mother said as she stood to hug Mia. The scent of her expensive perfume was comforting, even as it illustrated the differences between them. She tugged the edge of Mia's oversize sweater down. "Jesse says he couldn't have gotten this story without you." She motioned at the cushy chair across the desk. "Tell me about Prospect and Grant Armstrong and why you forgot to mention you knew him better than you let on when we were discussing what kind of story would or would not be appropriate for me to run about him."

"Jesse is being too kind." Mia fiddled with the hangnail that had been bothering her since somewhere near Idaho Falls.

"Is he?" Her mother held out her hands. "It was a relief to find out what was behind his sudden jaunt to Salt Lake City. Especially after I got a phone call from Casey."

"I knew he was going to be hot on the trail of this story, too, after he showed up in Prospect like that." Mia shrugged. "Jesse and I had to beat him to it. If we get it in this month's edition, *The Way West* will have the first story and the best story out about Grant and a cheating scandal involving some of the biggest names in the sport right now."

"After all the story ideas you've pitched and all our arguments over giving you a chance to write something big, you passed it over to Jesse." Her mother's slow smile was beautiful. "A proud mother would view that as a sign of growth, and the first step to managing a magazine. This story is exactly what we needed, Mia."

"What did you tell Casey?" Mia asked to buy

time. The next part of their discussion was going to be hard, especially now that her mother was beaming with pride over Mia's work. She hated to see that fade too quickly.

"I told him the magazine was already put to bed, ready to print. That I couldn't possibly change that on the basis of such a vague inquiry. Then I distracted him by making an offer on a full dozen of the shots he took in Prospect." She sighed. "Are any of these pictures I bought from Casey going to work or have I wasted money the magazine desperately needs?"

Mia rubbed her forehead as she considered how much to tell her. "You are going to pull the magazine back and put this story in, aren't you?"

Her mother's inelegant snort surprised Mia. Carla Romero did not often do anything as normal as snort. "Of course I am. This is big. Huge. I've already got the art department laying out new pages. Jesse is hoping to get a quote from the Association before we print, but the clock is ticking. We'll go on without it and have a follow-up next month." Her mother smiled. "In the Prospect Western Days issue, for which I have a nice collection of photos already. Sure hope there's enough going on in Prospect to make all that space worthwhile."

"There is. So much." Mia thought about all the work Sarah and Jordan Hearst were doing.

There were going to be plenty of new stories about Prospect to come.

Her mother didn't say anything, and Mia wanted to squirm in her seat. She'd always been much better at the waiting than Mia was. Nine times out of ten, Mia would confess immediately to whatever it was she suspected her of when she did this patient, watchful routine.

Mia would confess things her parent hadn't even discovered yet.

It was a powerful tactic, but today her mother gave in before it worked. "You know, I've been going back and forth between being angry that you didn't bring this story to me immediately and hurt that you didn't trust me to discuss this idea at all." She shook her head. "But I understand that I bear some of the responsibility for both of those issues."

Mia knew her shock showed on her face but she immediately tried to cover it. She wanted to say the right words, but she had no idea what they might be.

"When I took over from my father, I was so concerned about doing things his way." Her mother held her arms out to indicate the office. "I mean, staying here, in this space, in this exact office, in this location, it's indulgent at this point because there are smaller spaces with lower rents that would have eased some of the burden over the years."

Mia crossed her hands over her stomach. "The memories of the time I spent here, trailing behind Grandad, are always close by when I'm working in the office."

Her mother smiled. "Me too. I have my memories of scribbling stories on one side of the desk while he worked on the other, and then I can see you banging on the stapler while he bit his tongue and tried to ignore the scratches on his expensive furniture. If I had done the same? He would have explained to me about the finishes of antique desks, but 'Mia-mine' could do whatever made her happy."

The message behind her words sank in. "Writing for the magazine makes me happy. It does. But managing this business won't."

She nodded. "I get that. So, even though I was extremely shocked and proud and excited that you took control of this Grant Armstrong story the way you did, I agree that it's time to figure out the next phase for *The Way West*."

Mia bit her lip. "I always want the best for the magazine. Being the kind of news reporter you wanted was my goal for a long time, but this story showed me that it's not what I was meant to do. I was lucky to meet Grant and Annie. I'm thankful that a conversation with you helped me see that Jesse was the reporter this story needed. And watching him work…" She put her hand over her heart. "I don't have the instincts he has as a reporter or the business savvy you have to run the magazine. And I know that I'll never be happy or really successful in either role. I like small towns and craft fairs and funny characters and telling those stories. I like following the universe's direction to the next interesting project. I think I need to be in Prospect to be happy."

Her mother's slow smile instantly relieved some of the emotional stress building in Mia's abdomen. "I can't say that I support your theory about the universe gifting you with these moments, but…" She held up her hand as if she thought Mia might argue. There was no reason to fight about that. Mia knew what she knew, and one of those things was that her mother would never trust someone or something else to make plans for her life.

And that was okay.

"But you're my daughter." Her mother reached across the desk to grasp Mia's hand. "If you aren't working for me, how are you going to pay the bills?"

"I guess I'll do whatever other writers do, the ones who were born to parents who didn't inherit a magazine." Mia realized she was going to have to get serious about quickly figuring out exactly what that might be.

"Struggle. That's what they do. I don't want that for you," her mother said softly. "I want you to be safe and happy. Always have and always will."

Mia rubbed the ache in her chest at her mother's words. She believed them. She and her mom might not agree on the plan for Mia's life, but there was no doubt that her mother wanted good things for her. "I can only do one of those things here. I can be safe, but to be happy, I need something more."

Her mother sighed. "Determination. I hear it in your voice."

"Yeah, that runs in the family, I guess." Mia smiled as her mother laughed.

"I have to admit that I definitely admire how well you know yourself, Mia. That is a gift that I want." Her mother stared out the window. In a month or so, the trees would leaf out and the view would transform from historic Billings architecture to a natural green screen. Both were beautiful. "The question that keeps popping up in my mind since I got serious about closing down the magazine is what in the world I would do with myself and my free time without this keeping me busy." She wrinkled her nose. "I hate to say it, but the fear of the unknown has been an incentive to keep grinding away here."

This was another place she and her mother were completely different. Mia never experienced this fear. The unknown might bring some jitters, a nervous energy, but she'd never been afraid.

"What if you hired a managing editor instead of closing the magazine?" Mia asked. As long as she was out of the equation, Mia would be happy to brainstorm solutions until the sun set. "You could take on a part-time role, oversee the finances and figure out what you wanted to do next?"

Her mother paused and gave the notion some thought before replying.

"Moving out of this space, switching to a fully remote working setup and running any required in-person work through a much smaller office would lower the overhead." Then Mia remembered her inspiration—the Cookie Queen Corporation possibly becoming their newest advertiser. "And I have a line on a new advertising partner. I plan to make a very personal pitch to the CEO of the Cookie Queen Corporation soon." Mia wanted to get on a plane bound for LA immediately, in fact, but she was going to make sure Grant's story got every bit of the magazine space it deserved first. She couldn't drop everything to run after her next exciting idea. Not when Grant's predicament and future was so important.

"You have a personal pitch to make to a corporate CEO?" Her mother's gaze drifted down Mia's outfit, but Mia decided to call it progress that none of her opinion was expressed verbally.

"I do. If I have the assistance of an experienced magazine executive to polish my proposals, I know we'll be bringing in new advertising dollars before next month to help cover an editor's salary." Mia was certain this pitch was going to work, no matter how she was dressed. Sometimes it was difficult to see how the universe could pull all the threads together, but this time, everything was clear to Mia.

"Would we only be prolonging the inevitable if we do that, bring on a managing editor and patch the leak in advertising? Is this magazine fading into history?" her mother asked. It was hard to decide whether it was sadness in her eyes at that idea or if it was resignation. "It might be unwise to believe it was meant to last forever. Rodeo has changed. The West has definitely changed since my father started the magazine."

This had been the heart of Mia's pitch to add the travel articles about interesting locations.

"Could you sell the magazine, Mom?" Mia inched forward to sit on the edge of her chair. "If you could do that, you could take whatever comes from selling the subscriber list and the advertisers and whatever photography and assets the magazine holds, and create something new. A digital property, one that leaves you all kinds of freedom to change as you wish. It could be a new you and a new focus on the West."

Her mother's grimace was an instant judgment and Mia respected that. "Online, Mia?" She blinked for a moment before she stood to stare out the window at the street below. "What would that even look like?"

Mia laughed. "That part is up to you. That's what I was getting at, see? There are no rules, but you have the opportunity to create something only you would make, not Grandad and certainly not your weird daughter. Lots of people try this, but they don't have your experience or your taste. I believe it could be great."

Her mother glanced over her shoulder. "And where would my 'weird daughter' fall in all of this?"

Mia followed her over to the window. "Not fully clear at this point, but I believe she's going to be in Prospect, Colorado, working on a project for the foreseeable future."

"So…" Her mother narrowed her eyes as she considered the possibilities. "For more than a sweet story about one hundred years of Western Days."

Mia nodded. That much she knew.

"And does the handsome cowboy who happens to be lying low there play a part in that foreseeable future?" her mother asked.

"I would definitely not be surprised if he becomes the only permanent piece of my future planning." That much was becoming clearer. The number of times she had almost called him on the way home was embarrassing and only the uncertainty between them had stopped her from phoning to discuss the story, her plans for the future, his trail ride business, the funny roadside signs and why there was always a line for the women's restroom no matter which gas station she chose.

Her mother blinked but seemed ready to accept that.

"If you were to decide that you needed a change of venue," Mia said as she slowly worked through the jumble of thoughts in her head, "there's this adorable place right outside the historic district of Prospect. The town newspaper used to be there, but it closed years ago. It might be a wonderful place to get a feel for small-town life in the modern West, where rodeo is a piece but not the heart of the story."

Her mother's slow smile convinced Mia to wrap her arm around her shoulder. "All you need is an internet connection, Mom."

"You've been saying that for years." She slipped her arms around Mia's waist and pulled her close.

"I've been right for years, too," Mia responded.

They were laughing when they stepped apart. "Let's see what the new pages for this month look like and make sure Jesse's story has all the room it needs. Will you help me with that? We can also hunt up some photos while you tell me about Grant Armstrong." Her mother pointed at the desk. "It's not Grandad's, but we can still both work there."

Mia nodded and pulled her chair around to watch as her mother paged through the magazine layout. The future was still unclear, but there was no doubt in her mind that she was in the right place at the right time.

CHAPTER EIGHTEEN

TWO WEEKS AFTER Mia left town, Grant had reached the end of his patience with staring at the same four walls of the ranch house's living room. His brothers were ready to lock him in the barn for everyone's safety. There had been zero reports of strangers around town asking probing questions about Grant, but he had done his best to lay low. The cabin fever was getting to him.

When the bitter cold receded and warm sunshine called him to come outside, he marched into the kitchen and said, "Who's up for a ride to the ghost town today? I gotta get Jet out of the barn, stretch his legs some." And clear my mind, Grant thought.

"I want to go!" Micah said immediately. He never missed an opportunity to ride out with Grant. The kid hadn't met a horse before he got to the Rocking A, but his enthusiasm was making up for lost time. "Can I go?" He turned to Travis immediately to wait for permission.

Grant knew how far Travis and the boys had

come from the early days when Micah had mistrusted almost everyone except Damon, the older boy who had become Micah's truest brother.

And he'd always been pretty comfortable with Funcle Grant, too. He took some pride in that.

"Still pretty cold. The ground's going to be slippery in places." Travis tipped his head back. "Damon, what do you think? Should we all go?"

Damon shoved a whole slice of bacon in his mouth as he nodded. As long as no one took the kid's plate away before he was ready, Damon was up for almost anything. Since he'd grown at least two inches since November, it was a constant struggle to keep the kid filled up. "I'll bring a biscuit or two. Just in case." He reached over to wrap two in a napkin and shoved a third in his mouth.

Travis turned to Grant with raised eyebrows but shook his head. "As long as you can guarantee that we will return before Damon gets hungry enough to pick one of us to eat, we're all in."

Grant chuckled. "Good. I gotta get some fresh air." Wes walked in. "You up for a ride?"

Wes immediately nodded. "Always."

After they had all the horses saddled, Grant lifted Micah up to sit in front of him after some brief negotiation. They were working on his riding skills and the kid was going to be an awesome cowboy, but with the higher degree of difficulty, thanks to the snowy patches and terrain, everyone felt better if he rode with Grant. Even Micah.

They were quiet as they rode across the pasture and through the gate onto the Majestic's land. Sadie Hearst had been the Rocking A's neighbor for a long time, and they'd always had permission to journey across and up to Sullivan's Post.

"As long as they can act right," Sadie would always tack on when they were kids.

It was as if she knew that, most of the time, they were ready to act all wrong when they were out of sight of Walt and the barn. Now that Jordan and Sarah had taken over the Majestic, the gate between the two properties got regular use and no one was surprised when Sarah stepped outside to wave at them.

Wes immediately peeled off from the group to go over for a hello kiss, but she sent him back with a wave, and they continued the steep climb up the hills.

"Think this is too challenging for beginners?" he asked Travis and Wes. The idea of running trail rides had grown on him. Jordan had been right, but he was delaying telling her that, because she didn't need any extra confidence in ordering people around. He smiled inwardly at the thought.

Travis motioned with his head toward Damon, who was in the lead. The older boy was guiding the horse, but most of the time, his head was swiveling left and right as he took in the landscape. "I'd say on the right horses, you should be fine. Damon's had you teaching him for a while, so he might be ahead of the casual visitor, but he's not worried at all. And with enough experience on the trail, the horses will do most of the heavy lifting all by themselves."

Wes joined them. "You may want to consider a minimum age for your riders, and be sure to put that in the advertising. Micah could do this, but it seems risky to let kids you don't know loose up here."

Grant frowned. "You mean I have to bring kids up here, too?"

"Hey," Micah said in outrage from his spot in front of Grant. "Kids love this stuff."

Grant chuckled. "You aren't a kid, Micah. You're middle management in a kid's body."

"Uncle Grant loves kids," Travis said and squeezed Grant's shoulder. "So much that he's going to run a club for them, teach them all about rodeo."

Micah craned his head back to stare up at Grant. "Can I join the club?"

Grant bent his head so they were staring at each other upside down. "You're number one on the list, but I need you to do me a favor."

Micah tried to nod enthusiastically and started

to tilt so Grant steadied him. "Talk Travis and Wes into helping out, would you?"

The kid's wicked grin convinced him he had his best man on the job.

Wes gave him a stern side-eye but Grant wasn't worried. His brothers would probably have agreed if he'd made a simple request, but Micah could be relentless when he had a mission.

His brother rubbed his forehead, looking slightly worried. Most likely with his usual consternation over Grant's impulses to shake things up. "With the age limit, a solid contract, and your stern lecture about safety for the horse and the rider, Grant, you could do trail rides up here. If you want. If not, there's work around the ranch that will keep us all busy."

"But you have to be the one to tell Jordan you aren't going to add this amenity to the Majestic's lineup." Travis's grimace matched the twist in Grant's gut at the thought of Jordan's disappointment.

They made it to the ghost town. Snow was still gathered in drifts in the shadows but the wide main street was clear. The old settlement was in rough shape, many of the roofs missing, but the history was there. It would make a great attraction for visitors to Prospect if they could ensure everyone's safety.

"You guys ever wish we had sisters?" Grant

asked out of curiosity. It was hard to imagine life without Sarah and Jordan keeping them busy, but they'd managed happily enough before the Hearsts had rolled into town.

"Faye was trouble enough." Travis shook his head firmly.

Wes laughed. "Me, neither, but it's hard to complain, now that we have them. They have made things exciting around here."

"Grant, let me down. I want to check on whatever it is that Damon's looking at." Micah slid out of the saddle as he hurried over to where Damon was kneeling on the ground. Travis followed and moved to stand by them.

"Looks like…a bear track?" he said uncertainly as he turned to look over his shoulder at Wes. "Come here."

They were both headed over when Grant's cell phone rang. He'd expected to be out of range, but the clear skies had improved reception.

Then he saw Jesse Martinez's name on the display. "Hey, Jesse," he said as he turned away from the group studying the print in the snow. "What's up?" They had spoken off and on in the rush to get the story in under the magazine's printer deadline, but that was done.

"If you somehow missed the disturbance in the force, March's issue is out today. Your face is front and center wherever *The Way West* is on newsstands and will be landing in mailboxes in the next day or two." Jesse cleared his throat. "I sent a copy to Annie Mercado and Red Williams. I heard back from Red before sunrise this morning. He's unhappy with his image in the article. The angle of the story was misrepresented to him by me in order to sell magazines and he's exploring his options with legal redress." Jesse hummed. "Yeah, that's what I wrote. 'Redress.' To me, that does sound like he's got a lawyer feeding him lines, so in case that blows up, I wanted you to have fair warning. I wouldn't be surprised if Red's worried about losing everything. The whispers I've heard include a lifetime ban from the sport as well as legal or civil penalties he might face."

"What about the Association? Any word on their investigation or outcome?" Grant kicked his boot against the icy edge of the closest snow drift as he waited to see if panic or fear surfaced.

"I've already talked with Carla Romero, and she had a legal review to make sure there's no case against us. That doesn't mean Red won't try it. As far as sanctions by the Association for not reporting the scheme when you first learned of it..." Jesse let the sentence trail off.

"Okay, we can weather some bad press if that's what it boils down to, but please let me know if you hear anything more from the Association or their lawyers." If there were penalties of some sort…

Then he noticed that Wes had turned back to listen to his side of the call. "My oldest brother is a lawyer. If it comes to a battle in court, we'll be ready." The idea of a drawn-out legal or financial fight involving his family made his head hurt but he knew they had his back. Together his family would figure it out.

At that moment, Grant realized he'd accepted that standing up to Red to defend himself was the right thing to do, no matter the consequences. He hadn't done anything wrong except trust the wrong person.

And the only way to make that right was to ensure no one else made the same mistake if he could help it.

"Good. My hope is Red's mainly rattling his cage at this point. We have the evidence, and I can't imagine Annie Mercado being afraid of anything."

Grant wished he'd had a chance to meet the young woman who had taken over all the space his disappearance had created. The few times he'd wandered into rodeo territory on the internet, she'd been front and center. And she was smart enough to do it without Red Williams.

"You still up for any interview requests that might come in? Wouldn't be surprised if there's a

TV appearance, and everyone would be relieved if I offered your pretty face instead of my mug." Grant heard a screech in the background. "Oh boy, he's up already. You have kids yet, Grant?"

He laughed as he watched Micah sneak up on Damon to slip snow down his collar. "Nope, just an uncle so far."

"You better get started. I wish I was a younger man, now that I know how challenging grand-kids are. If I hear anything else, I'll text or call."

"Okay, sounds good." Before Jesse could hang up, Grant asked, "Hey, how's Mia?"

The silence on the other end of the line was loud because all noise stopped around Grant. He turned to check on his family and saw that every single eye was locked on him.

Eventually Jesse said, "Well, now, I did not expect this." He chuckled. "She's a firecracker, but I believe you are fully aware of that. She has stirred up some conversation around the office. Appears there's a plan to shut down production of the magazine. Every time I've seen her in the past week, she has been moving at high speed."

Grant raised his eyebrows at Travis and Wes, but they shrugged in response.

"Oh," Grant said and wished he had something more interesting to add, but no, nothing was coming.

"Wonder where she might have got the idea to

move out of Billings and change her career path, cowboy," Jesse drawled. "It ain't like she's ever been one of those career-driven journalism types, like yours truly, but it did seem like my job would last as long as I wanted it to. Now Carla Romero's finally made some decisions about her future and the magazine's, and so I'm a man faced with retirement myself. You got any good tips for me?"

"Uh, no. For me, leaving rodeo just means a new job, new pursuits, not retirement." Grant was stuck on what it meant that Mia was moving out of Billings, away from her mother and career.

And he wished he'd heard the news from Mia herself.

Jesse laughed again and the tension seemed to evaporate. "Carla and I have worked well together for decades now, and I never saw such a smile on her face as I did when she made her announcement about stopping production."

Grant propped his hand on his hip, anxious to pace as a hundred different questions arose, but Jesse said, "Mia left town yesterday, so I'm not certain how she is at this moment, but it seems that things are moving at a fair pace here in the office. Most of the staff are planning a nice long vacation with a piece of the generous severance package Carla is offering."

Grant sighed. "To be honest, all I needed you to say was 'fine' or 'good,' something to convince me not to call Mia and ask her how soon she was coming back."

"It's like that, is it? You've got it bad." Jesse chuckled. "I bet you'll hear her coming from a mile away. She's got some plans. We talked 'em over a bit and I expect she's ready to shake things up."

Grant liked the sound of that. "I don't doubt it, Jesse. Thanks for the heads up about Red. We'll be ready and if you need to pass any phone calls along to me to field, I'll be happy to take them. Working with you has been a pleasure."

"Yeah, I'm thinking I might pack up the family and bring them down to see these Cowboy Games. Mia tells me there ain't another competition like it. Got a grandson that would sure like to have his picture taken with you. What would you say to that?"

Grant rolled his shoulders as more of the tension eased. Surely if his reputation was going to take a beating, Jesse would know and he'd keep his grandson far, far away. "We're going to have the perfect photo opportunity set up just for that. I'll be happy to meet you all there." The loud screech that interrupted him made him second-guess the "happy" part, but he wasn't going to take it back. Jesse's T-rex soundalike grandson was a problem for another day.

After he hung up, he saw that Travis and Wes

were both watching him, arms crossed across their chests, as if they were patiently waiting for him to come to his senses.

"What?" he asked.

Damon stepped between them. "You aren't trying to play it cool, are you, Uncle Grant? Girls hate that."

It was satisfying to watch Wes and Travis turn puzzled stares at the teenager, but it was impossible to argue with his certainty.

Still, Grant had a long history of arguing. "How would you know? Did your girlfriend tell you that?"

He tipped his head to the side, anxious to hear the answer.

Damon sniffed. "No, but Keena has been giving me hints on how to talk to girls that I like. Poking them is a bad idea, but asking them about their favorite song on the radio and then remembering some of the words is a good tip. I tried it and Trina Smith responded favorably."

All three of the adults exchanged a glance. The evidence was strong. It should work.

"What was her favorite song?" Travis asked.

"It changes, but she started singing 'Love Story.'" Damon shrugged. "That Taylor Swift song? I figured that was a good place to start, so the next day at lunch, I mentioned hearing the song, something about Romeo and Juliet."

Damon rocked back and forth in his boots. "She's been sitting at my lunch table ever since. Keena would probably help you if you asked her nicely, Uncle Grant."

His wicked grin as he watched Grant come to terms with his own need for dating help made Grant laugh. And it wasn't a chuckle, it was one of those laughs that he couldn't stop, not even if he was worried that the people watching would think he'd lost grip on reality. Luckily, Wes and Travis were laughing along. Micah had joined the conversation, but his confusion made it clear he wasn't quite ready for Keena's flirting advice.

Before Grant could second-guess himself, he pulled out his phone and dialed Mia's number. When she instantly answered, his worry melted away.

"Hey, I had my phone out, staring at the screen, wondering what you were up to and whether I would bother you if I called you," Mia said before asking, "Can we make this a video call? I've missed your face."

Grant mimed a celebratory high five to Damon, Travis and Wes before he switched the call. "You've missed my face. That might be the nicest thing anyone has ever said to me. I've missed your voice, your face and the weird way my heart stutters when you're around."

The low whistle Travis let out made Grant

scowl over his shoulder, but considering all the grief he'd given Travis over his courtship with Keena, he deserved it.

"Do we have an audience?" Mia asked as she moved closer to the screen, as if she could stick her head through to peer around.

"No one important, my brothers and my nephews." Grant waved a hand to shoo them away. They ignored him.

"And you're being sweet in front of them?" Mia silently said "wow," her eyes big in surprise. "Grant Armstrong is a romantic gentleman. I love to see that."

He shifted his shoulders, aware that he was losing this argument and then decided it didn't matter. "Jesse called to tell me the magazine's out. Are you happy with it?"

Her pleasure filled him with that fizzy, happy glow that he was still coming to terms with. "I am. It's good work and my name is on it, too. Now that my mother and I finally see eye to eye, it's not quite as important to me anymore. I still appreciate it, though." Then she rolled her eyes. "But if she tells me one more time how I'm using all the business and journalism classes I've taken, I'll have to run away from home forever. Do I have the degree? No, but I never once complained about taking the classes. I like the classes, I just didn't want to waste my life on things I didn't love." She inhaled slowly. "Sorry. She and I are coming around to understanding each other. Slowly."

Grant would have listened to her theories on education and the universe for as long as she wanted to share them. He was so happy to see her. Then he realized she was walking as she talked. He could hear garbled noises, too.

"Where are you?" he asked.

"Baggage claim at LAX. This place is a nightmare. A horror movie. A nightmare that takes place inside a horror movie." Mia disappeared for a second before her face popped back up on the screen. "Remind me to carry on the next time I need to fly to Los Angeles."

"What are you doing there?" Grant asked. Whatever he'd expected her to do next, this was not on the list.

"I want to explore this idea I had for what I'll do once the magazine is finished." She slung a bag over her shoulder. "I've got a meeting tomorrow with Michael Hearst at the Cookie Queen Corporation and then I'm back to Billings. After that, I'm going to drive back down to Prospect to stay until Western Days. I'm looking forward to being within kissing distance again."

Grant wanted more information on this trip to LA and the career she was planning there, but he forced a smile on his face. "Kissing distance is the right distance."

Her sweet smile reassured him. "Gotta find a rental car in this maze. I'll call you when I get back to Billings, okay? And be on the lookout for photographers and reporters who want to have their own follow-up to your story. I don't want you or your family caught off guard."

Grant nodded. "I hope your meeting goes well."

"Oh, it will. I have no doubt about that. I miss you, but I'll see you soon." She waited for him to say goodbye before ending the call, but before he hung up, he asked, "Hey, what's your favorite song?"

Her eyebrows shot up.

"You know, that they play on the radio?" Grant ignored the way Travis and Wes grinned.

Mia pursed her lips. "Interesting question. When I was driving back to Billings, I heard Miranda Lambert's 'If I Was a Cowboy.' Since I'm part tumbleweed myself, I've always liked that." Then she moved her face closer to the screen. "But if I was there with you and we didn't have such an audience watching us, I'd go with The Chicks and sing 'Cowboy, Take Me Away.'" When she leaned back, he could tell she was pleased with herself.

He had to admit that he liked her answers. A lot. But the reminder of their audience was helpful. "Good to know. I definitely want to discuss this again. Soon. Within kissing distance. Call me when you can."

After he hung up, Damon came over and patted his shoulder. "It wasn't smooth but it was effective. I could tell she liked the effort."

Grant wasn't sure why his teenage nephew's approval made him feel so much better, but at this point, he was prepared to count that as a win.

And when Mia returned to town, working her song into conversation would be his best idea yet.

CHAPTER NINETEEN

Mia was on the phone with her mother when she pulled into a visitor parking spot in front of the headquarters of the Cookie Queen Corporation.

"I told you the traffic in LA would be horrible. Why not take a taxi or a ride share?" her mother asked.

Mia didn't even consider answering the question, because she knew her mother would be on to something else in a matter of seconds. Even if they were getting along better, her mother might never be a calm voice of reason when Mia was traveling away from home. Is that how all mothers were?

"It was a wrong turn, Mom. Everyone makes a wrong turn now and then." Had she made a poor decision by turning the wrong way into a one-way entrance into the parking lot? Yes, but no one else knew that and she had done her best to calmly get the rental car headed in the correct direction to begin with. "I'm still early for this appointment, so there's no reason to be so anxious."

Her mother sighed. "You're right. I worry about you, but you've done much harder things on your own. This is a meeting. That's all, and we both know you're the right person for this project."

Mia studied her reflection in the mirror before giving herself a firm nod. "I absolutely am. Thank you for helping me get my presentation in order. We made a good team on this pitch."

"We did, and I'm glad." Her mother's voice had lost some of the boss tone.

"Are you thinking about what happens after the last issue?" They'd agreed that the last issue would be the one following the Western Days spread. Mia was certain that was the best decision. "I want you to consider a visit to Prospect. The pictures are beautiful, but there's something about the place that you have to experience to understand."

"It's not some magic destination where your future is revealed." Her mother laughed. "But I guess it did exactly that for you."

Mia studied the lipstick her mother had pressed in her hand at the airport before dropping it back into her purse. Today was not the day to take risks with new cosmetics. "Not my whole future, but important pieces of it. Even if it doesn't do the same for you, it's a pretty place where you could slow down and clear your mind. You could try painting. Jordan texted that the Wi-Fi speed is exceptional at the Majestic. What more could you ask for?" Her mother's chuckle helped Mia relax. "Think about it."

"You'd be okay if I followed you down there for a stay?" her mother asked.

Mia stared at the boxy office building that sat in front of a small water feature and a lot of neatly arranged landscaping. There were a couple of smaller buildings ranging out on either side, but Sadie's headquarters stood tall in the center.

"I really would. You could help me research." Mia checked her borrowed briefcase and wondered if she was going to look like a little girl in her mother's high heels when she walked into the lobby with the expensive briefcase…borrowed from her mother.

"Maybe I will. Call me when your meeting is over. I know how it will turn out, but I want to celebrate with you and listen nervously while you maneuver LA traffic back to your hotel by the airport."

Mia shook her head. "I will definitely call you as soon as I'm done."

They ended the call, and Mia considered sending Grant a text. Talking with him, seeing his face had boosted her certainty that she was on the right path. Every step felt more solid.

"But the sooner you get a contract, the sooner you'll be back in Billings." Mia opened the car door and slid out, being very careful not to ding the expensive SUV parked in the next spot. She had always been lucky enough to have nice things, but there was something about this vehicle that convinced her that the owner took serious pride in the ownership. That had something to do with the high gleam and crystal clear finish. The image of her dusty car, after less than a week in Prospect, flashed through her mind.

It had never occurred to her to be bothered by the dusty film.

"Another sign you'll fit right into small-town life, Mia." She gripped the briefcase handle firmly and strode toward the revolving door. It was whisper quiet as it moved, and Mia was standing in a tall, modern lobby in an instant. As she waited for the receptionist to end her call, Mia studied the furnishings. There was a photo of Sadie behind the reception desk, her warm smile inviting, as it was in every photo Mia had found. She was seated behind a desk and the large mountain vista currently hanging behind the Majestic's check-in desk was her backdrop. Below that were photos of the Cookie Queen Corporation's current board of directors and Michael Hearst, the CEO she was here to pitch to. She was happy to recognize Patrick Hearst, Sarah and Jordan's father, who she'd met in Prospect.

"Michael's in another meeting, but he said he'd

be down to meet you soon." The receptionist stood and pointed at the hallway. "If you'd like, he suggested you tour the displays of Sadie's memorabilia, which we've been in the process of adding under Sarah's direction. Would you like water?"

Mia nodded gratefully. "That would be wonderful. Nerves give me dry mouth, which makes it difficult to speak."

The receptionist's expression flashed confusion before she smiled and then produced a bottle of water from a small refrigerator behind her desk. She offered it to Mia.

"That was too much information, wasn't it?" Mia waved a hand between them. "Nerves."

The receptionist shrugged. "No one holds onto their reserved professional demeanor here for long. Some companies say their employees are family, but Sadie Hearst lived it."

Mia nodded. "Good to know. Did you work with Sadie long?"

The receptionist paused as she calculated. "I've been here nearly five years, so I was lucky enough to get to know Sadie well. She was exactly as you'd expect her to be from her shows. There was no acting. That lovely personality was real."

"I've gotten to know Sarah and Jordan. I believe you." Mia moved toward the display as the receptionist stepped away to answer the ringing phone. The first display case was filled with a couple of mannequins dressed in Sadie's line of Western wear and images of Sadie's life arranged in a timeline from when she launched her TV show until her death. It was an impressive visual of how quickly Sadie made each step. She didn't hesitate.

Before Mia could look at the other memorabilia, the elevator dinged and the doors opened. Michael Hearst stepped out. He was escorting another man who Mia would have bet her entire paycheck was the owner of the spotless SUV outside.

His suit was expensive. Mia didn't know much about men's suits or designer labels in general, but the fit was perfection.

When the two men shook hands, Mia noticed a tattoo across the top of one of the man's hands, which revised her assumption from international royalty to... Well, she had no idea, but he was a handsome one, whatever he was.

He was no Grant Armstrong, but there was only one of those.

"You must be Mia Romero." Michael Hearst held out his hand and shook hers before pointing at his associate. "This is Brian Caruso. He's the executive chef and owner of Rinnovato. Have you heard of it?"

Mia's eyebrows rose because the restaurant

was one of the most exclusive in LA, known for serving truly decadent Italian cuisine.

"I know you by reputation, of course, but I've not been lucky enough to eat in your restaurant." Mia smiled politely, curious about what was happening but always ready to pick up tiny bits of interesting news here and there.

"Mia's been in Prospect with Sarah and Jordan." Michael patted the chef on the back. "Brian is working with us to produce a web-streaming show coming from the lodge for the Cookie Queen website. This is something new. We're trying to keep traffic coming to the Cookie Queen website now that we won't have Sadie providing recipes there. Sadie kicked around the idea of producing her own series, but we could never agree on a budget or a concept. I'm sure you've heard Sarah and Jordan plotting their next phase of expansion at the Majestic Prospect Lodge." Michael shoved his hands in his pockets. "Brian's helping us identify two competitors for this web-streaming competition. The winner will get a nice prize and the chance to run the lodge's kitchen for a year. Brian is also going to lend some of his star power as a judge."

"If you're in town this weekend, drop by Rinnovato." Brian rubbed his hands together. "I'd love to pick your brain about what I'm getting myself into by agreeing to spend a couple of weeks in the mountains at a fishing lodge."

He said the last words slowly as if they were un-familiar. "I don't fish. I don't mountain much, either."

There was no need for him to confess that. She could have guessed from his shiny car and his equally shiny shoes, but she wasn't picking up a snobbish vibe. Uncertainty made sense. So did investigating to find out, before he rolled into town.

She might go with the flow and depend on the kindness of strangers when the only bed-and-breakfast in town was fully booked and she had no reservation, but it was more than fair that oth-ers preferred to plan their trips more thoroughly.

"One of the prettiest places I've ever seen, and I'm a travel writer. You'll be impressed," Mia said. "I guess you'll be leaving for Prospect soon if this is happening before Western Days. I'm on my way back, too."

"Yes, we're going to take advantage of a school break. My daughter is also coming. If Sadie loved the town, I expect I will, too. I owe her so much that I'm happy to expand my horizons."

Mia immediately wanted to ask twenty ques-tions, but Brian checked his expensive watch. "I better hit the road. I have to pick my daughter up from her mother's house soon."

Michael nodded and then motioned Mia toward the elevator. "I hear you have a business proposal for me. I am intrigued."

While he showed her to his office, Mia realized that she had been turning this way and that to see as much of the Cookie Queen offices as she could and immediately reminded herself that she should try to act like someone who had either a business degree or a journalism degree, at the very least.

Now, situated in Michael's cool office, she calmly opened the briefcase and pulled out two folders. "I have two pitches today. They are separate but related." She straightened her shoulders as she slid the first one across his polished desk. "Inside, you will find a proposal for a biography of Sadie Hearst. Written by me. For the Cookie Queen Corporation. Or not. You will have the right to approve the manuscript and ask for revisions. We will work together to locate the right publisher." Mia clasped her hands together tightly. "I have been lucky enough to spend time where Sadie grew up. I've read her cookbooks and even some of the recipe files Sarah and Jordan have on hand in Prospect. I've created a chapter-by-chapter outline. My initial concept is to use her most popular recipes as the introduction to each period of Sadie's life. You see the first chapter features her famous Cowboy Cookie."

"The one that started it all out at the lodge," Michael murmured as he scanned the first page.

She forced herself to pause to give him time to read the pages she'd roughed out as an example of her style. There was very little doubt in Mia's mind that she'd nailed the exact mix of information and comfortable tone that reflected Sadie perfectly.

"A biography. And you've listed how it would be marketed and sold along with Sadie's cookbooks. Did Sarah put you up to this?" Michael smiled slowly. "It's exactly the kind of thing she would do, eliminate any question I might ask in order to assure a victory."

Mia sat taller in her seat. "I will take that as a compliment. It's the first book proposal I've written, so I was following my gut." It was good to know her gut had good instincts, and that the time she'd spent suffering through college courses she did not enjoy could possibly return dividends at this late date. Who knew spreadsheets had so many good uses?

"It's a good idea." He leaned back in his cushy chair. "I need to do my own research, because we've been publishing Sadie's cookbooks for some time, but this would be a completely new direction. Figuring out the pay structure and the legalities of the contract won't be simple."

Mia still took that as a win. "I'm going to start

this project as soon as I get back to Prospect. I'm excited about it."

He frowned. "You aren't a great negotiator—are you aware of that?"

"I've had a strong suspicion that was true," Mia said slowly, "but I believe Sadie and I are connected somehow. You wouldn't want to disappoint her by offering a subpar contract."

He chuckled. "You never met Sadie, right?"

"Not in person." Mia had met so many people who knew Sadie, though. She'd walked in Sadie's footsteps here and in Prospect, and she wanted to be friends with Sarah and Jordan. Mia would say she knew enough about Sadie Hearst to trust that her memory would convince her great-nephew to deal fairly and honestly with her.

"Sadie was tough on me." Michael smoothed his tie. "We knew I was going to be sitting here someday, but I struggled to figure out how to be good at this job. Sadie? She didn't cut me any slack while she watched me like a hawk. This place, these people, they were her family, too, so she had high expectations for me." He shrugged. "And I'm glad, especially now that she's gone. I feel the weight of responsibility of keeping this business healthy. Sadie taught me how. I just have to follow her instructions." He tapped the proposals in front of him. "And lean heavily on Sarah."

Mia smiled. "I'm going home to Prospect. When you're ready to talk about what the contract looks like, we can iron it out, but…" She slid the second folder across the desk. "This is going to be important, too. Are you familiar with *The Way West*?"

He nodded and pulled out the advertising fee structure for the magazine. "I am. I don't know if we advertise in the magazine."

"You should. The next issue will feature Prospect, Western Days and the new Sadie Hearst museum, prominently." Mia grinned. "Advertising in the issue makes sense, but you should also consider coming in early on the digital platform my mother is planning to launch after the magazine's print version folds. With a long-term agreement, I can see plenty of opportunity for hosting Cookie Queen Corporation content and providing fresh material for your websites, possibly produced in Prospect." If Mia got her way.

Her mother would surely see the benefits of moving her work to Prospect once Mia got through listing all the reasons to do so. "I expect that will be a late summer or fall project, but you could discuss advertising terms for the magazine and any savings that might come from signing before the website launches." Mia licked her lips nervously, relieved to have gotten every single bit of that out without stumbling or blacking out from nerves.

Michael propped his elbow on the desk and

rested his chin on his hand. "This might be the most interesting sales pitch I've ever experienced. Gutsy. Bold."

Mia gripped the armrests of the chair. She would have chosen those adjectives for Sadie. He would appreciate them, right?

"More interesting than the biography you're going to buy that you didn't know you needed?" Mia asked.

"Yeah. Even more than that." He closed the folder. "I'll give your mother a call to see what terms we can agree to. Since you seem certain this is in everyone's best interests."

Mia was learning that the gifts of the universe sometimes depended on knowing when to make graceful exits, so she stood and offered Michael her hand. "My phone number is listed on both proposals, but if you need an alternate method to track me down, I'll be staying at the Majestic."

Michael stood as she walked toward the door. "Hey, Mia…"

She opened it and paused.

"Remind Sarah that she promised to reserve a room for me. I'm thinking I might need to see what Western Days is all about." He waved her folders. "I'll be in touch about Sadie's biography."

She nodded, exited his glass office and stepped onto the waiting elevator, poised and serene.

Her neutral expression held all the way through the lobby and out into the parking lot.

The spotless SUV was gone, confirming Mia's hunch about the driver.

But as soon as she was behind the wheel of her rental and the car door was shut, she did a celebratory dance to end all celebratory dances. Her faith in the universe was holding strong, and her confidence in her own abilities was growing every day.

Now all she had to do was enjoy it...within kissing distance of Grant Armstrong.

CHAPTER TWENTY

ON FRIDAY NIGHT, Grant was breaking down a cardboard box, and wondering how much longer his unpaid shift at the new Sadie Hearst museum was going to last, when his father inched up beside him.

"Don't let Sarah see us conversatin'," Walt said in a low voice through stiff lips. "I don't want to get my pay docked, but you doin' okay? How you're looking over your shoulder has me worried we're gonna be ambushed by that ol' scalawag Red Williams again. I'll create a diversion to distract Sarah if you need to escape out the back."

Grant grunted his amusement before shooting a careful glance over his shoulder. "She is determined to get this place set up tonight, isn't she?" He tossed the flattened cardboard on top of the stack next to his foot and picked up another box. "If Red shows up here, he'll regret it. Catching me out on the sidewalk in front of the Ace was one thing. No way would he wade into this herd of family and friends to try to take me on."

His father narrowed his eyes. "Shoot. I been working on my resting mean face."

Grant studied his father's expression. To him, it read more "the print's too small and I can't find my glasses" than a real threat, but he appreciated the effort.

He squeezed his father's shoulder. "Mia texted she was on the road early this morning. I expected her to be here by now, that's all. If Red's still around, we'll handle him."

Walt carefully stacked the cookbooks he'd been told to remove from boxes and place on shelves. "That Red Williams fella is a bushwhacker, riding into town with his own reporter. That's some grade A nerve right there. I'm glad you didn't mince words, son."

If he hadn't been surprised by running into Red on the street in front of the Ace High after an excellent dinner, he might have been more careful in how he'd handled the encounter. Shock and the immediate anger that welled up when he'd seen the man who had betrayed his trust had burned right through the polite restraint Prue had tried to teach him.

Grant didn't regret a single loud, honest word.

After that exchange, where Red promised he'd find a way to get even, Faye refused to serve him in the restaurant and Rose Bell had no room in the bed-and-breakfast. Red was either too smart or hadn't learned about the Majestic, because he had loaded back up into his truck and driven out of town instead of hanging around any longer with no place to sleep.

Prospect had rallied around Grant.

Even if he had gotten into more trouble than he should have growing up, his neighbors had stood with him.

That felt good.

For the first time in months, Grant was nearly relaxed. He didn't know what the final fallout would be from the Association's investigation yet, but his family and friends were nearby.

There was only one piece missing tonight: Mia.

Grant tossed the flattened cardboard down and took the box his father handed him. "How much trouble will I be in if I sneak away to call Mia?" No one was quite sure what the punishment might be for lollygagging, but the intense expression on Sarah's face had quelled even Jordan's usual complaints. She had settled into a spot on the floor, next to the large display of Sadie Hearst merchandise, where she was grimly arranging DVD collections into her best artistic vision, which Sarah would undoubtedly rearrange while muttering under her breath. But the firm management style was getting results.

A couple of hours ago, when they'd walked into what was once the tailor's shop, the place had been full of neatly organized stacks of unopened boxes. But now…so much progress had been made. This would be an amazing museum. Even he could see it. The mannequins were arranged here and there throughout the space to showcase Sadie's glittery style. All of the memorabilia Sarah had chosen for the museum's opening collection was carefully lit in glass cases. Informational placards were attached. All in all, they were still looking at cleanup but the space had been transformed.

"I'm not sure I'd want to work for her long-term, but you cannot argue with the results," Wes said from Grant's other side.

Walt raised his eyebrows.

Wes chuckled.

"I love all of you," Sarah said as she stuck her head into the mix, "but if you have time to talk, you need more to do."

Wes pressed a kiss to her lips. "You're doing a great job, babe."

Sarah's expression softened immediately. "Thank you, babe. You are, too." Then she marched off in another direction.

Grant could see that his mother had been volunteered to work on the display at the reception desk. "This place is terrific. I hope Sarah can take a minute to enjoy what she's done."

Wes nodded. "Yeah, me too. She's concerned

about Michael's opinion on whether she's spent the corporation's funds well, but most of all, I know she wants to make Sadie proud."

"Can't imagine anyone finding fault with this place," Walt said. "Not sure what counts as state-of-the-art in terms of museums, but the group Sarah's been working with has included some high-tech features, all controlled by an app. Can you believe that?"

It wasn't surprising that Sarah and Jordan would want the best for their great-aunt.

When Grant had pictured a Sadie Hearst museum, he'd expected the photos and pieces from Sadie's life that were on display, but the modern touches that Sarah had incorporated were a nice surprise. The rough walls behind the facades on Fashion Row had been covered in a large sepia-toned photograph that spanned three walls and depicted Prospect's Old Town. The cases blended in and every piece Sarah had chosen stood out, but also seemed to belong to the setting. It was jaw-dropping.

He pulled his phone out to check for a text but noticed that Sarah, Jordan and Prue had formed a committee in front of the large display of Sadie-inspired merchandise. Their heads were together. He couldn't make out the words, but they would converse, scatter to make minute adjustments and return to the center to repeat.

Eventually Sarah spoke up. "Okay, everyone. I can't tell you how much I've appreciated what you have helped me out with tonight. This place is…" She covered her face with her hands, overcome with emotion. "It's my dream and it's coming true and I miss Sadie desperately, but I love it and I love you and I…"

Jordan wrapped her arm around Sarah's shoulders and hugged her tightly.

Grant could hear boots shuffling nervously and wondered if Sarah was about to be mobbed by a group hug, but she waved her hands in front of her face and sniffed loudly. "I want you to be the first ones in town to see this."

Grant crossed his arms and leaned carefully against the counter as Sarah turned down the lights, using the tablet in her hand. Whatever came next, it was going to be special.

MIA PULLED THE door closed quietly so she didn't interrupt Sarah, who was speaking in the middle of the room. She moved in between Amanda and Lucky, who were at the back of the group facing the large screen on the longest wall of the museum space. There were shelves of Colorado Cookie Queen cookbooks and DVDs on one side and small housewares arranged on the other.

"We want this place to celebrate Sadie, but we know she would say she was nothing without Prospect. Amanda gave us permission to use a recorded greeting that Sadie did years ago for the Picture Show. Rose Bell and Prue Armstrong added local town color in the way of old photos and oral history, and the rest of this… Well, I hope you like it." Sarah tapped the tablet in her hand and then she moved to the back of the group. When she saw Mia, she immediately towed her closer to the screen.

She and Jordan stood on either side of Mia as the presentation started to play. A smooth narrator spoke over a changing slideshow of old photos, covering the foundation of the town, first as Sullivan's Post in the hills above the Majestic Prospect Lodge, and then after it moved and spread in its current location as Prospect.

Mia was entranced as antique stills of rough silver miners and finely dressed town politicians blended into color photos of the 1960s and 1970s.

"Cowboys in bell bottoms. I never would have guessed," Jordan murmured as she bumped Mia's shoulder. When they snickered, Sarah hushed them.

"We're getting to the best part," Sarah said sternly.

It was something to watch the transition go so smoothly, and when Sadie Hearst burst on the scene, the background music changed. The tone lifted, and the warm, happy buzz Mia experienced anytime she saw Sadie Hearst's smile returned instantly.

Sarah and the museum consultants had included publicity shots of Sadie on a TV set, but most of the photos were lovely candid shots. There was one of Sadie in a hammock with three little girls crowded in beside her and a sweet-looking woman making rabbit ears behind Sadie's head.

"We had to get our mom in there, too." Jordan blinked rapidly. "Brooke is going to kill us when she finds out we put that one in." Since the youngest girl's smile was ragged, thanks to a missing front tooth, Mia thought she understood why Brooke might not be pleased.

Then the video introduction started. Sadie was standing on the wood sidewalk in front of the Prospect Picture Show. She was wearing dark jeans, a red-and-white gingham button-down shirt, with white fringe forming a V on the front, and a bright white Stetson.

"Well, now, I was hoping we'd meet right here. You found me in one of my favorite spots, the Prospect Picture Show in my hometown, the prettiest place you ever saw. Do you like cowboys?" Sadie's sly grin flashed. "Don't we all? Whether it's a silver-screen hero or one a little more down-to-earth, betcha find that cowboy here because you are lookin' in the right place. Come inside, grab a treat and find your seat. Welcome to Prospect. We sure are glad to see you." The last frame was of Sadie standing, hands propped on her hips. When the presentation was over, the lights came up slowly.

Everyone was quiet until Prue said, "Hard to believe, but I miss Sadie more than I realized. Seeing her face like that, hearing her voice, is a gift. This is perfect."

Sarah sniffed and nodded. "Yeah, it's pretty great, and this is only the beginning. We have so many plans, things that needed more time to work through, but the future is exciting."

Mia spotted Grant's curls above the crowd and waited until he met her gaze to inch closer to him. Sarah exclaimed and grabbed her hand before she made it far. "Oh wait, the book. We're going to have a biography. Maybe even by next year's Western Days. Mia sold Michael on a book all about Sadie!"

A flush of embarrassment filled Mia's cheeks. It was tempting to downplay the whole thing, but she knew it was going to be fun to work on and wonderful when it was finally done, so she matched Sarah's enthusiasm instead. "I did! There's still so much to figure out, but this book is going to be awesome, I promise."

"A book! And I don't have to write it!" Jordan shouted as she hopped next to Mia.

When they were all laughing and out of breath,

Mia shot past the congratulatory crowd to launch herself into Grant's arms. "Finally. I've missed you!"

He pulled her tight to his chest. "Not as much as I've missed you. It's as bad as losing my cell phone when you aren't here."

She pulled back. "Work on your romantic metaphors, please."

"It's like I was missing my favorite pair of boots?" He motioned toward the door and they stepped out onto the quiet sidewalk. "I will definitely need coaching on metaphors in general, but I promise to get better."

Mia pulled him away from the window and pressed her lips to his. "Lucky for you, I intend to stick around Prospect. I can coach you every day if you need it."

"I am a lucky, lucky man." His sweet smile filled her with a wild fluttering in her chest, the butterflies she'd heard of so often. "Not sure who is happier to hear your long-term plans, me or Jordan."

Mia rested her forehead against his chest. "Wait until I propose working part-time at the Majestic in exchange for a place to stay for a bit."

He laughed. "They need lots of help, inexpensive help. Jordan may get down on one knee and propose marriage."

Mia stared at him. "You think? I wouldn't mind a proposal."

He dropped a kiss on her nose. "Way ahead of you. I was considering the when and where of it just now."

"Oh, I can wait for the right time." Mia smiled. "The universe hasn't disappointed me yet."

EPILOGUE

Western Days Weekend—
Cowboy Games Winners' Ceremony

GRANT SMILED AS Mia hugged Annie Mercado and accepted the third-place trophy for the overall score of the coed teams in the Cowboy Games. The award—a bronze-colored bucking bronco with a plaque on a wood base—would be a great reminder of a great day, and he was gratified to see both of their names listed.

"Not too shabby a finish. You and Grant make a good team. Mia, you looked like a champ in the saddle during that relay race. Prue just edged you out by a nose, dropping her last boot in the bucket seconds before yours."

Annie was right. Mia had ridden almost as well as his mother through the relay that had all the women racing to drop a total of ten old boots painted in their team colors in a bucket in the fastest time.

As soon as he got Mia alone, he'd tell her she'd

managed that perfectly to earn his mother's undying love. Although Grant was certain Prue Armstrong and Mia Romero were family already.

Annie shook his hand with enthusiasm. "Next year, work on your coffee-brewing skills and I bet you move into second." Her lips were twitching as she added. "At least."

He deserved the ribbing. He and Mia had been neck-and-neck with his mother and father in the standings until the cooking competition. Their teamwork through the timed mucking out of the stalls, washing laundry by hand and hanging it to dry, and the three-legged hay bale race had been impeccable. His steak seared over the campfire had been fine, but the coffee unfortunately was as strong as battery acid and the judges had given him zero points for that round.

"Come back next year. These games will be bigger and better," Grant told her. "My coffee may be the same."

"Wouldn't miss it. Call me when you want to schedule some time for me to work with your club." Annie moved on through the crowd to where a group of young women were waiting for her to sign autographs.

Mia's arm slipped around his waist and she stood on her tiptoes to press a kiss to his lips. "Sad you didn't crush the competition? We'll demand a rematch."

He turned to stare into her eyes. "How could I be sad when you're here? Our team… I never knew to wish for someone like you."

Mia blinked before she touched his chin. "All I did was play a few silly games with you and laugh my fool head off while I did it. I can be so much more for you than that."

And she already was.

Grant shook his head. It was important that she understood how much bigger today was. "First, you gave me peace. You tackled my enemies head-on when you didn't have to. Because it was the right thing to do for all of us." He smiled down at her. "That was huge. For a lifetime, I struggled to find that peace, and then there you were."

Her forehead wrinkled as if she wanted to argue.

"But today…" Grant's voice dropped to a whisper. "There's no other word. I'm happy. You're amazing, Mia. One of a kind and so much fun. That laugh of yours was better than a first-place finish. I can't imagine ever feeling more love and more happiness than I do right now."

Her eyes teared up, which wasn't his intent at all, so he immediately added, "Unless we win the whole thing together next year, of course. That might top this."

Her snort of laughter sent a fizz of joy through

his veins and he held her tightly to his chest. "I love you, Mia Romero."

Her adorable grin as she stared at him from under her Cookie Queen Western Wear hat would stay with him forever.

"I love you, too, Bad Boy of Bronc Busting." She traced her fingers over his jaw. "When we met on the side of the road that day, I was pretty sure you were too handsome for my own good, as well as kind and loyal and… You just get better looking, better everything, unfortunately. You're stuck with me now. There's no running away."

As Grant watched Damon and Micah make kissy faces behind Mia's back, his mother and father smiling and looking on, he realized coming home to Prospect had been the best decision he could have ever made. The universe had been drawing them both here.

Grant grinned. "With you by my side, there's no other place I'd rather be."

* * * * *

For more fun romances from acclaimed author Cheryl Harper, visit www.Harlequin.com today!